Tate's thoughts drifted to Detective Nick Bennett.

She could tell he wanted her to open up to him, but how would a man like him ever be able to understand her problems? If she revealed too much, somehow her son could be in danger. And what could she do then to stop it?

Closing her eyes, she tried to concentrate on something pleasant. Unbidden, her mind conjured up a pair of steady gray eyes in a tanned face, and a mouth that looked hard and a little grim, yet that she imagined could be soft and warm.

Now she knew that Nick Bennett wasn't the man for her. No man was.

But she could dream....

Dear Reader,

What is there to say besides, "The wait is over!" Yes, it's true. Chance Mackenzie's story is here at last. *A Game of Chance,* by inimitable *New York Times* bestselling author Linda Howard, is everything you've ever dreamed it could be: exciting, suspenseful, and so darn sexy you're going to need to turn the air-conditioning down a few more notches! In Sunny Miller, Chance meets his match—in every way. Don't miss a single fabulous page.

The twentieth-anniversary thrills don't end there, though. A YEAR OF LOVING DANGEROUSLY continues with *Undercover Bride,* by Kylie Brant. This book is proof that things aren't always what they seem, because Rachel's groom, Caleb Carpenter, has secrets…secrets that could break—or win—her heart. *Blade's Lady,* by Fiona Brand, features another of her to-die-for heroes, and a heroine who's known him—in her dreams—for years. Linda Howard calls this author "a keeper," and she's right. Barbara McCauley's SECRETS! miniseries has been incredibly popular in Silhouette Desire, and now it moves over to Intimate Moments with *Gabriel's Honor*, about a heroine on the run with her son and the irresistible man who becomes her protector. Pat Warren is back with *The Lawman and the Lady,* full of suspense and emotion in just the right proportions. Finally, Leann Harris returns with *Shotgun Bride,* about a pregnant heroine forced to seek safety—and marriage—with the father of her unborn child.

And as if all that isn't enough, come back next month for more excitement—including the next installment of A YEAR OF LOVING DANGEROUSLY and the in-line return of our wonderful continuity, 36 HOURS.

Leslie J. Wainger
Executive Senior Editor

Please address questions and book requests to:
Silhouette Reader Service
U.S.: 3010 Walden Ave., P.O. Box 1325, Buffalo, NY 14269
Canadian: P.O. Box 609, Fort Erie, Ont. L2A 5X3

THE LAWMAN AND THE LADY
PAT WARREN

Silhouette®

INTIMATE™ MOMENTS®

Published by Silhouette Books

America's Publisher of Contemporary Romance

This book is dedicated to my cousin, Vi Brown, with love and affection.

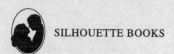 SILHOUETTE BOOKS

ISBN 0-373-27095-X

THE LAWMAN AND THE LADY

This edition published by arrangement with Harlequin Books S.A.

® and TM are trademarks of Harlequin Books S.A., used under license. Trademarks indicated with ® are registered in the United States Patent and Trademark Office, the Canadian Trade Marks Office and in other countries.

Visit Silhouette at www.eHarlequin.com

Printed in U.S.A.

PAT WARREN,

mother of four, lives in Arizona with her travel agent husband and a lazy white cat. She's a former newspaper columnist whose lifetime dream was to become a novelist. A strong romantic streak, a sense of humor and a keen interest in developing relationships led her to try romance novels, with which she feels very much at home.

Chapter 1

She was drop-dead gorgeous! Detective Nick Bennett couldn't help thinking as he stood in the shadowy doorway of the private hospital room staring at the woman talking softly to the patient in the bed. Small-boned yet with a lush figure that her white silk blouse and slim charcoal slacks couldn't disguise, she had a wild fall of auburn hair resisting all attempts at taming by the gold clip at her nape.

He was here to do a job, not gawk at a beautiful woman. But, at thirty-three and having been around the block a few times, Nick wasn't often stopped in his tracks by a woman who could cause his mouth to go dry. She didn't have the freckled skin usual for a near redhead, but rather her coloring resembled that of a fresh peach. Stunning, Nick thought. Absolutely stunning.

His gaze shifted to the reason he was here, the woman lying in the hospital bed looking as pale as the starched white sheets. A sixty-five-year-old widow, Maggie Davis had arrived home and interrupted an intruder who'd proceeded to attack her. Her doctor had told Nick just now that she had a broken arm most likely due to its being severely twisted behind her back, two cracked ribs, several bruises and a swollen cheek from a nasty punch to her face.

What could this small, elderly woman have done to warrant such a beating? Nick wondered. According to the notes taken by the first officer on the scene, the downstairs of her two-story house had been thoroughly ransacked. Had the thug been looking for valuables to steal or searching for something in particular?

The officer's notes indicated that Tate Monroe, twenty-nine years old, lived with Ms. Davis, along with her seven-year-old son, Josh. Tate had been at work at Brennan's Book Emporium in downtown Tucson where she was the manager. The report didn't indicate where the boy had been, but he hadn't been with Maggie Davis at the time of the assault. Fortunately.

Sensing his presence, Tate Monroe straightened. Eyes the color of the green Caribbean Sea, where he'd once vacationed, met Nick's assessing gaze. A frown creased her forehead and a look of wariness had her taking a step back. She glanced quickly to the corner chair where a young boy was asleep. Probably her son, Josh.

Although the male in Nick would like to question Tate Monroe, preferably alone in a quiet place, the detective in him was more interested in the now sleeping boy. The officer's report indicated that, though hurting badly, Maggie had mumbled that the man beating on her kept asking where Josh Monroe was. However, no matter how hard he hit her, she wouldn't tell him anything. Why would the trespasser be interested in the schoolboy son of a single mother? Nick asked himself.

He stepped inside the hospital room and watched the wariness in Tate Monroe's eyes deepen. Deliberately he moved close to the bed and gave Maggie Davis a reassuring smile.

"I'm Detective Nick Bennett from the Tucson Police Department, Ms. Davis," he said, his voice gentle as he made note of several purpling bruises on her neck. He flashed his badge, then put it in his pocket. "I wonder if you feel up to answering a couple of questions."

Tate moved closer to Maggie's other side, wishing the police had sent a Columbo-type older, rumpled detective instead of this tall, attractive cop with his short black hair and gray eyes that seemed to look right through her. She dealt much better with silver-haired fatherly types. "She already told the officer at the house everything she knows," Tate told him protectively. "The man had his hands on her throat, bruising her. It hurts her to speak."

"It's all right, Tate," Maggie managed to say in a croaking voice, reaching toward the younger woman.

Mrs. Davis was a small woman with sharp blue eyes and snow-white hair worn short and curly. Rimless glasses sat low on her nose. Despite her many bruises, she squared her shoulders against the mound of pillows and seemed unafraid, as if to say she's no one's victim. This time Nick's smile was one of admiration.

"I don't want to cause you more discomfort," he told her. "Why don't you just shake or nod your head by way of an answer?"

Maggie nodded, but Tate again protested.

"You don't have to do this *now,* Maggie. I'm sure the detective can wait until you're feeling better." She spoke to Maggie but her narrowed gaze was on Nick.

"No, no," Maggie whispered. "I want to help catch the man."

Nick found himself liking the spunky senior citizen. "Did you recognize him?"

Maggie shook her head. "Wore a ski mask," she rasped out followed by a short cough. She grimaced at the pain in her throat, but gamely continued. "He had black hair in a long ponytail and wore black pants and shirt.'' She began coughing more strenuously.

Tate decided she'd had enough. ''No more questions for Maggie today,'' she told Nick. ''Let's go out in the hallway and I'll fill you in.'' She again glanced at the boy sleeping soundly in the corner chair before turning to Maggie. ''I'll be right back. Try to rest.''

Leaving the room with the detective close behind her, Tate felt uneasy. She knew he was trying to help find the creep who'd done this terrible thing to Maggie and that persisting with questions was part of that objective. Nonetheless, she wouldn't allow Maggie to be upset further. Despite her show of bravado, the older woman was more fragile than she seemed. Tate had been terribly shaken up since she'd received the phone call at work about Maggie's ordeal. Her hands were still trembling as she led the way to a small alcove off the hallway.

Swinging around to face Nick Bennett, she crossed her arms over her chest and took a moment to study him. He didn't look like her mental image of a detective. He was quite tall, several inches above six feet, causing most people to have to look up at him. That probably came in handy if he used it to intimidate suspects.

His face was tan, angular, square-jawed, his eyes a pewter-gray and somewhat hooded. His shoulders under a blue shirt open at the throat and a tan lightweight sport coat seemed wide as a fullback's. His hands were big and looked callused, as if he worked outdoors. The clean, pressed jeans he wore hugged powerful thighs and long, long legs. He noticed her taking inventory, yet didn't seem impatient. He appeared relaxed but there was a hint of intensity in his steady gaze. Right now, he looked slightly amused as he waited for her to speak.

''What is it you need to know?'' Tate finally asked him.

''Good-looking boy,'' Nick began, waving a hand toward

the room where the child slept. "Lucky he wasn't with Maggie today. Where was he?" Maggie had told the officer that she often baby-sat Josh Monroe.

"On a field trip to the zoo with his second-grade class on the last day of school."

"Does he still take naps?" How was it that at two in the afternoon, a second-grader was fast asleep?

"No, it's just that he has asthma and the vegetation at the zoo spiked his allergies. I picked him up after I got the call about Maggie and gave him his medication before he could work up to a full-blown attack. It makes him sleepy."

"I see. Do you know anyone who'd do this to Ms. Davis and why?"

Tate drew in a deep breath. "Maggie's a wonderful woman, but she's a tad eccentric. It's been rumored for years that her late husband brought back some valuable artifacts from World War II and a large sum of money, then hid them all over the house. Would-be thieves broke in a while back when no one was home and thoroughly searched the place then, too, leaving a godawful mess."

Nick found himself fascinated with her expressive face, the way emotions came and went, her full lips bearing just a trace of pink lip gloss. He took out a small notebook and pen, thinking he'd better make a few notes since he was having trouble concentrating standing so close to her. "Any truth to the rumors?" he asked, jotting down a few key words.

"None at all. Contrary to the stories of hidden riches, after her husband, Elroy, died, Maggie had to turn her large home into a boardinghouse for college girls since it's near the University of Arizona. The income supplemented her social security checks. She has no living relatives. Their only child, Peggy, died in a boating accident at the age of twelve. Maggie gets by on very little and still owes on back taxes. Thank goodness Elroy worked for the city so she has good health insurance."

He was staring at her, Tate noted. She'd been stared at since her early teens and was quite used to it, but she felt oddly disappointed that this calm, confident man was like all the rest. Why that was so, she couldn't have said.

"And you think the rumors of hidden wealth caused someone to break in and search the place?" Apparently Tate didn't know that the intruder kept asking about her son.

"Well, sure." She dropped her gaze and studied her black leather flats. "What else could it be? I'm certain we'll find that nothing's missing because Maggie doesn't have anything of value. Perhaps that's why he beat her up, because he was frustrated to realize the rumors were wrong."

Funny how she averted her eyes just then and her husky voice sounded nervous. Now she shifted her feet, tightened her arms and gazed longingly toward Maggie's room. In the course of his career, Nick had studied body language, something that helped him determine a person's unspoken thoughts. And veracity. He was certain that Tate Monroe wasn't telling him everything and that she badly wanted to get away from him.

"That's one theory, I suppose," he said. "How long ago did the other break-in occur?" He'd check it out when he got back to the precinct, but he wanted her version.

On safer ground, she looked up. "Two years ago, I believe. We weren't living with Maggie at the time."

"Mmm-hmm. I would've thought that word would have spread that there was nothing of value in Maggie's house. Random thieves seem to pick up on that kind of information."

Tate shrugged, trying for nonchalance. "Maybe this thief is new in town, or maybe he's cocky enough to believe he could find buried treasure that someone else missed. I really don't know."

He shifted gears somewhat, hoping to keep her a little off balance. "Is that how you met Maggie, staying at her boardinghouse when you were in college?'' That had to be some time ago, Nick thought, since she was twenty-nine with a seven-year-old.

"Yes. There are three bedrooms and two baths upstairs. My two roommates and I were the first to live in Maggie's house. She has a first-floor bedroom off the kitchen. We stayed until graduation.''

"Maggie was like a house mother, then?''

"More than that.'' Tate's expression softened as she thought back. "For one reason or another, none of the three of us had had a strong maternal influence before meeting Maggie. She not only filled in the gaps, but she became something of a surrogate mother to all of us. And many of those who followed, I'm sure.'' A bit embarrassed at having revealed so much, Tate assured herself she'd only done it because she felt that the more the police knew, the quicker they could find the man in the ski mask.

And she prayed he'd turn out to be a random thief and not the man she feared it might be.

"Tell me about your roommates,'' he said, watching her carefully. "Do you stay in touch with them?'' Tate Monroe was without a doubt one of the most beautiful women he'd ever met, yet there was something about her that bothered Nick. Not just because she was holding something back, not an uncommon happening in any investigation. But rather there was a deliberate distancing, a warning not to get too close. Was it because he was with the police or was it something about him personally that caused this edginess in her?

"I honestly don't see what they would have to do with this break-in. They're both married and haven't lived in Tucson since graduation. They...''

"Humor me.'' He'd noticed the absence of a wedding ring on her finger and wondered where Josh's father was and if he had anything to do with Maggie's invasion.

Resigned to his insistent probing, she began. "Molly Ship-

man was the first to move in at Maggie's. She had a full
scholarship and is positively brilliant. She dropped out in her
senior year to get married. The marriage broke up after four
or five years and she was taking accounting courses to become a C.P.A. when she met Devin Gray, the author. They
got married about a year and a half ago and built a house in
north Scottsdale.''

"Do they ever visit Maggie?''

"Whenever their busy lives permit. We all try to get together on Maggie's birthday every year.''

"I see. Go on.''

She watched him taking notes, thinking he was way off
base if he thought her friends would ever harm one hair on
Maggie's head. "Laura Marshall comes from money, a lot
of money. Her father owns a large real estate company with
several branches in Scottsdale. I think she attended U of A
partly because she wanted to get away from his smothering
control. She had a bad first marriage to a real jerk who just
wanted her father's money, but just recently she married a
really nice guy. Sean Reagan's an obstetrician and Laura
sounds very happy.''

"You haven't met him? You didn't attend the wedding?''

He was probing an area she didn't want to get into. Tate
glanced out the window across the hall and watched fronds
from a tall royal palm shifting in a gentle May breeze. She
wished she were out there, away from the sickly smell of a
hospital and the scrutinizing gaze of this man. "No, I
couldn't make the wedding.''

Nick noticed her faraway look and wondered why she
didn't make it a point to attend a close friend's wedding. She
seemed genuinely pleased at both friends' good fortune in
finding happiness the second time around, yet there was an
underlying sadness in her voice. "Since they're both well-
off, have either of these women offered to help Maggie with
her financial difficulties?'' He was wandering off the subject,

but she'd aroused his curiosity. He wanted to know what kind of people her best friends were.

"They sure did. After Molly married Devin, they offered to pay Maggie's overdue taxes, calling it a loan to salvage her pride. But Maggie refused. Laura has access to a large trust fund and she offered as well, but again Maggie wouldn't go for it."

"What about you?" Nick asked, wondering if it was the cop or the man wanting to know.

Tate squared her slender shoulders and her green eyes turned frosty. "I'm not rich nor do I have a wealthy husband, but I help Maggie all I can. I pay rent, pay her for watching my son when I'm at work, buy groceries and I help out around the house. Is that what you wanted to know?"

Nick drew in a deep breath and wished he hadn't as the lightly floral scent of her wrapped around him. He managed to hold his ground, but not easily. "What about the boy's father?"

Tate's expression tightened. "He's been out of the picture for years." She narrowed her eyes, not bothering to hide her annoyance. "Anything else?"

Nick pocketed his notepad and pen. "I'll need to go through the house and check the inventory as soon as possible. I'd like you to be there to let me know what if anything is missing."

Shoving her hands into her slacks pockets, Tate looked up at the ceiling, praying for patience. Why had she been naive enough to think this conversation would end her involvement? "I want to stay with Maggie for a while yet. I can meet you at the house about four." She turned, anxious to walk away from his scrutinizing gaze.

"That's fine." He knew his next statement would probably rock her, but she had to be told sooner or later. "And I'll want to talk with your son."

Frowning, she swung back. "Why?"

"The first officer to arrive on the scene wrote in his report that Maggie told him that the man in the ski mask kept asking where Josh was. Would you happen to know why that would be?"

The blood drained from Tate's face as she reached a hand to the arched wall to steady herself. *No, please, no. It couldn't be starting all over again, just when things had settled down. How long must she keep running?*

Her protective instincts on red alert, Tate straightened and licked her dry lips, trying belatedly to conceal her reaction from this observant detective. "No, I don't. Josh has known Maggie all his life. Seeing her hurt like this is very hard on him. I won't have him interrogated."

Nick almost smiled, but knew that wouldn't win him any points with this mama bear protecting her cub. "I seldom grill little boys. I'd simply like to talk with Josh. With you present, of course. There has to be a reason the intruder asked about Josh, and perhaps whatever that is will be the key to his identity. You do want us to catch the man who did this to Maggie, don't you?"

"Of course I do." Her words were clipped, angry. Guilt and fear mingled with her need to safeguard her son. Tate felt torn and very tired. "Please understand, I need to shield my son. He's been through a great deal in his short life." With that, she turned and left the alcove, walking quickly back to Maggie's room.

Watching her go, Nick wondered what exactly Josh had been through to make his mother so protective, and where his absentee father was. He'd have to be careful, to go slowly in questioning both the boy and his mother. Someone had hurt Tate Monroe, hurt her badly. He hoped he could convince her that he was one of the good guys.

After stopping at the precinct to make a few calls, Nick Bennett drove his Taurus out of the parking lot heading for

Maggie's house on Mesquite Drive. He was in one of his infrequent reflective moods.

For as long as he could remember, Nick had wanted to be a cop like his uncle Paul, a homicide detective up in Phoenix, much to the dismay of his parents. His father, Anthony, who'd been a building contractor until his recent retirement, had wanted Nick to go into business with his two older brothers, Tony and Sam, who now owned and operated their lucrative construction firm. But, although Nick had spent his high school and college summers working for Bennett Construction, he knew he wasn't cut out for that kind of work.

It hadn't been easy disappointing his family, especially his mother, who wasn't happy about the dangerous side of his chosen profession. Ten years later, since he'd never had to fire his weapon in the line of duty and never been injured, Roseanne Bennett was relaxing. A little.

The thing was, when a man came from a big, loving Italian background where family was the most important thing, going against their wishes made him feel like a rat abandoning ship. Fortunately they'd set aside their disappointment and these days, his dangerous work was rarely mentioned. Now, all he heard was their nagging about when was he going to get married and give them grandchildren like his two brothers and two sisters had. Always something, Nick thought, but with a smile.

All this introspection had been brought about by his conversation with Tate Monroe. She was a woman alone raising a son and living with a widow who had no family left. Nick thought about the weekly dinners and holiday get-togethers at his parents' big cluttered house, everyone talking at once, laughter and lots of good food, and he felt sorry for those who didn't have that kind of camaraderie and unqualified acceptance.

Which brought him back to wondering just exactly what it was that Josh Monroe had been through in his short life.

Nick couldn't imagine having children without his family's moral support. Where was Tate's family?

Nick pulled up in front of Maggie's sprawling white house at exactly four, but the only vehicle nearby was the police car belonging to the officer guarding the house since the front door lock had been broken. Mesquite Drive was a narrow street in an older neighborhood of mostly two-story frame homes painted a variety of colors and sporting wide front porches. A teenage boy rode by on a bicycle, balancing a friend on his handlebars, both staring at him. Across the street, an older woman pulling a grocery cart stopped to talk with a middle-aged man trimming his shrubs, their eyes on him. Next door, a man with white hair put down the newspaper he was reading and eyed him, openly curious. Crime scenes always interested people.

Getting out, he wondered if Tate had calmed down or if she'd stand him up.

The yellow crime scene tape was still in place. Nick stepped around it and greeted the officer sitting on a rocking chair on the wood porch painted a deep gray. "Hey, Bobby. How's it going?"

The young officer scrambled to his feet. "Pretty quiet, Nick. A few nosy neighbors gawking is all."

"I'm expecting one of the occupants soon. I'll wait for her inside. Has a locksmith been called?"

"On his way."

Nick checked out the jimmied lock and wondered where all Maggie's neighbors had been that one hadn't noticed this guy messing with her door, then going in. And why had Maggie marched right in when she'd returned home and found the lock broken? The woman was too gutsy for her own good.

Inside, he stopped, hands on hips, looking around. What a mess! Cushions yanked off the couch and tossed on the floor, books and curios from the bookcase flung aside, the desk drawers methodically upended and emptied. The man left no space untouched.

Then the fingerprint guys had come through dusting every surface with fine black powder. When Tate saw this, she'd be horrified. No sooner had the thought formed than he heard a car with a wheezing engine pull into the driveway. Glancing out the window, he saw Tate and her son climb out of an older yellow Buick LeBaron convertible. A '92 or '93 he'd guess and probably had the mileage to prove it.

Her arm protectively around the boy's shoulders, Tate guided Josh onto the porch and nodded to the officer who greeted them both.

"Is that yellow tape necessary now?" she asked the police officer. "People are driving by and staring."

Nick answered for him. "Officer, you can take the tape down now." He held the door open for them, aware this would be her first glimpse of the wreckage.

"Thanks," Tate said, stepping inside. She looked around, her lips thinning, the hand on her son's shoulder tightening. Otherwise, she gave no sign of how upset she must be inside. Nick had seen worse, but she probably hadn't.

"Listen," he began, "I can call this cleaning crew that we recommend. They're honest, reasonable and work fast. Why don't I help you look through things to see if anything's missing, then I'll call them to do the heavy stuff?"

She'd wandered to the large kitchen where canisters of coffee and sugar and flour had been emptied onto the floor, some dishes smashed as if in an angry frenzy, doors to the cupboards hanging open, spice containers helter-skelter on the counter. Tate felt her shoulders sag at the enormity of the cleanup task. But she couldn't afford to pay a crew no matter how reasonable they were. And this was her obligation, not Maggie's.

Since her frightening conversation with the detective at the hospital, all she'd been able to think of was that her worst nightmare was beginning all over again. He'd tracked her down and found her again, just when she'd begun to think he'd forgotten all about her. And now Maggie was hurt and Josh was in danger. Where could she go? Where could they hide? Would this ordeal ever end, and end happily?

Nick couldn't tell if the weary look on Tate's face had to do with the mess she was facing or something else. When she turned, he caught a hint of fear in her eyes. Anyone who's experienced a home invasion would have lingering fear, but he had a feeling she was afraid of something else. "Tate, did you hear me?" he asked gently.

"I heard you. We can't afford a cleanup crew. I'll manage." She placed her shoulder bag on the kitchen table, just about the only clean spot in the room as Josh spotted something and rushed over to a box upended near the back door. "What is it, sweetie?"

Kneeling, the boy choked back a sob. "My…my Pokémon cards. They're all over and some of them got wet." Obviously upset, he tried to pick up the scattered cards.

Moving to his side, Tate felt her heart twist. The new craze of collecting Pokémon cards and playing games with them had been the first thing Josh had shown real interest in in ages. She'd bought him as many as she could afford and Maggie had found a tin box to store his collection. "Don't worry, honey. You pick up the dry ones and I'll clean off the others. They'll be okay."

Having watched the scene, Nick wandered over. "I have two nephews who collect these, too." He stooped down and began to help the boy. "Which are your favorites?"

Josh looked at him suspiciously, moving closer to his mother. Tate had explained to him on the way over that Maggie's place had been trashed by bad guys and that the police were going to catch them. He'd been okay with that, but it was hard to tell the bad guys from the good ones sometimes, especially if you were seven, she thought.

She brushed a lock of her son's blond hair off his forehead. "Josh, Mr. Bennett's a detective. He's going to find out who hurt Maggie and made this mess. It's okay. He's here to help us." Tate prayed she was right, that Nick could find the person responsible and put him away for good. But if her worst fears were realized, she doubted that, even if identified, any investigation would get to the arrest stage. Unfortunately some people were above the law.

It was hard to tell if Josh believed his mother since he didn't answer Nick, but he did accept his help. Tate watched for a few minutes, then straightened. "I have to change clothes before I can start here. I'll check to see if I find anything missing as soon as I return. Josh, come upstairs with me, please."

Left alone, Nick decided this was way too large a job for one small woman. He found a utility closet next to the back door and pulled out a broom and dustpan. Then he went to work sweeping up the kitchen floor.

Changed into a navy T-shirt and jeans, Tate brushed her hair back, trying to tame the unruly waves, then quickly formed a ponytail. Her mind, however, was downstairs focusing on the mess someone had made of dear Maggie's home. And it was most likely her fault, all her fault. That sharp-eyed detective was already suspicious of her answers to his many questions. She'd have to watch that.

Sitting down, Tate pulled on her white canvas shoes and stooped to tie them. She hadn't known many cops, except the ones who'd come to her apartment a while back when someone she'd once trusted had sent a man to try to persuade her to give up her son. The police had taken lots of notes of her vague answers to their questions and then advised her to get a restraining order. How could she file charges against one of the most powerful men in the state, someone respected

and admired by nearly everyone? She knew no one would
believe her.

Familiar guilt washed over Tate as she sat still for a moment. One mistake and look at the ramifications, all these
years later and all the years in between. That mistake had
cost her dearly and now was probably the cause of Maggie's
beating. Fortunately the older woman would recover. But if
Maggie had died…

No, she wouldn't allow herself to go there. Rising, Tate
took a deep breath and swallowed the old guilt as she'd done
many times before. They'd get through this somehow.

She passed by Josh's room and saw that he was busily
playing with his Pokémon cards, talking to himself, involved.
Relieved that he was handling the break-in and that the intruder hadn't made it to the second floor, she started downstairs. Probably Maggie arriving home had interrupted his
search.

At the archway into the kitchen, Tate stopped, staring.
Nick had taken off his jacket and draped it over the back of
a chair. His shoulder holster, the gun barely visible, was a
stark reminder of his profession. But that wasn't the astonishing part. The floor had been swept clean, the broken dishes
piled into the trash bin and Nick was busily wiping off the
counter. "Hey, what are you doing?" she asked, surprised
enough to blurt out her first thought.

He glanced over as he turned on the faucet to rinse some
lingering sugar down the drain. "Just giving you a hand."
He saw the play of emotions on her face—surprise, annoyance, relief.

Hands on her hips, she walked over. "Do you pitch right
in like this for every case you handle? Must keep you pretty
busy."

Nick shrugged. "I've got the time. If you won't let me
call out a crew, then I'm volunteering."

She was clearly taken aback. "But I..." The doorbell ringing startled her. She swung around, a question in her eyes.

"Easy," Nick said, wiping his hands on a towel. "It's just the locksmith. Come tell him what kind you want installed. You really should have a dead bolt." He urged her toward the living room.

Silly to just about jump out of her skin at the sound of the doorbell, Tate told herself. The last thing an intruder would do would be to ring the bell. Besides, the young police officer was still outside. It was just her nerves, that was all.

While she talked with the locksmith, Nick watched her. In that casual outfit, her hair in a youthful ponytail, she looked younger. But there was no disguising that lush body, even though her clothes were anything but tight. She must have guys lined up at both doors.

When she finished, Tate turned and saw that Nick was picking up books and making piles by the bookcase. "Honestly, you don't have to do this."

Nick set down a small stack, then faced her. "Can you just say *thank you* and let it go at that?"

Her eyes narrowing, she couldn't help wondering what he'd want in payment. "I'm not used to accepting help without...without..."

"Without someone wanting something in return?" He shoved a pile of paperbacks onto a high shelf. "Well, that isn't the case here. Why don't you check out the desk? If something's missing, it's probably from there."

Okay, she'd take him at face value, Tate decided. At least until he showed his true colors. Which he probably would sooner or later.

It took Tate quite a while to sort out the piles of scattered papers and repack the desk drawers and the big file drawer. By the time she'd finished, Nick had completed the bookcase, straightened all the lamp shades, put the pillows back on the couch and had just dragged out the vacuum.

"As far as I can see, nothing's missing," Tate told him as she rose from the desk chair. "Of course, it's Maggie's desk and I don't know what all she had in it. We'll know more when she takes a look."

"Were there any valuable papers in there and are they still there?"

"Yes, a few. Maggie doesn't have a safe-deposit box. The deed to her house, an insurance policy, her will, even her bankbook are in those files, neatly labeled." She shook her head. "I can't imagine what he was looking for." Even if it was the man she suspected, she could think of only one thing he'd want and that couldn't be hidden on a shelf or in a cupboard.

Nick seemed lost in thought, Tate noticed. Funny how he managed to look even more masculine with one hand leaning on the handle of a vacuum. One of the few men who could carry that off.

"Apparently he didn't find what he was looking for," Nick mused aloud. Or was it *who?* Like maybe her son? He swung his gaze to Tate and saw her watching him. Though her expression was cautious, it wasn't devious. Since he'd told her the man had pressed Maggie for Josh's whereabouts, hadn't she figured out what he was searching for? "What about an address book? Does Maggie have one and is it still there?"

Tate moved back, opened the middle drawer and held out an aged leather address book. When he walked over, she handed it to him without a word.

Nick flipped through it, seemingly casual, but when he got to the *M*'s, he stopped. Tate Monroe's name was written in a shaky script like all the other entries, but there was no address or phone number next to it.

He looked into her eyes. "How long have you and Josh lived here with Maggie?"

"On and off, we've lived here several different times."

Evasive. "When did you return this time?"

"A couple of months ago."

He held out the page with her name on it. "And she had no address or phone number for you when you weren't living here?"

She was determined not to look away from those searing gray eyes. "We moved around a lot. I checked in with Maggie by phone."

Why did they move around a lot? Why wasn't she telling him everything? No matter, Nick thought, closing the book and handing it back. She would in time. He was a patient man.

"All right," he said, checking his watch. "It's time to go. Call Josh."

Tate stood, her eyes wide and suddenly suspicious. "Go? Where? Are you...arresting us?"

Nick raised a puzzled brow. "Arresting you? For what? No, I'm taking you to dinner."

She felt like flopping back in the chair as relief flooded her, but she tried to make light of it, as if she'd been kidding. "Oh, right. Thanks, but I think you've done enough for us already."

"Look, you've got to eat and I've got to eat. It's nearly six and Josh is probably hungry. Why don't we eat together?" Which would give him an opportunity to talk with the boy if only the mother would drop her guard a fraction.

Tate was sure Josh was getting hungry since his bag lunch at the zoo had been eaten around eleven. And, truth to tell, she didn't feel like cooking tonight or even like hanging around this house with all its mysterious shadows. "All right, but we pay our own way."

"Let's fight about that later. Go get your son and I'll make sure the locksmith's finished." Nick went to the kitchen and shrugged into his jacket before walking out onto the porch, thinking that Tate Monroe had to be the most distrustful woman he'd met in a very long time.

And the most desirable.

Chapter 2

They were both too subdued, Nick thought as he drove along. Buckled into the passenger seat of his Taurus, Tate stared out the window, her body language revealing an almost palpable tension. What was she so nervous about? he wondered. The possibility of another break-in, Maggie's condition or something more disturbing?

Glancing over his shoulder, he saw that Josh was gazing out the side window while his hands restlessly stroked the seat belt. He had to get them to relax, Nick decided, or he'd never find out a thing.

"Do you like pizza, Josh?" he asked the boy.

"Uh-huh."

Great start. Nick turned onto Broadway heading toward central Tucson, shifting his thoughts back to Tate. She'd wanted to change clothes, but he'd assured her that she was dressed just right for where they were going. Oddly, she'd not asked where it was he was taking them. "I'll bet you've never tasted pizza as good as Giovanni serves."

"Probably not." Tate kept her eyes on the road, wishing she hadn't agreed to go. She could have opened a can of soup for the two of them. She hadn't been out with a man in so long she scarcely remembered how to behave. Not that this outing could be considered a date. Yet she was as uneasy as if it were.

First, there was his maleness and his size coupled with a gentleness that didn't seem to go with the package. Then there were those searching gray eyes. Cop's eyes, to be sure, missing nothing, questioning everything. And last, but certainly not least, there were those probing inquiries. Tate was certain he'd asked them out so he could quiz Josh. She'd have to be on guard and she hated that. If only she could relax and put this whole nasty business out of her mind. But when would she be allowed the luxury of that?

"Giovanni, the guy who owns the restaurant, is a friend of the family," Nick began, hoping if he revealed some personal things, she'd be inclined to follow his lead. "We call him Johnny but his Italian name is Giovanni. See, I have two older brothers, Tony and Sam, and Johnny has two older brothers, Vic and Paul. We all grew up in this wonderful ethnic neighborhood over that way." He pointed west in the general direction of his old stomping grounds. "My folks still live there in this great two-story house. They raised five kids in that house."

Despite a case of nerves, Tate found herself interested. "Ethnic as in Italian? Bennett doesn't sound Italian."

"My father was born Anthony Bennedetto, but somewhere along the line, the name got changed to Bennett. Both my parents are first-generation Americans. But we had other nationalities around us—German, Hungarian, Russian. And more recently, Mexican. It was a great place to raise children. My mother used to say that if a kid fell down on Palmetto Drive, three mothers rushed out before he had a chance to get up." He smiled at her and noticed that at least she was looking at him and not the passing scenery.

"That must have been nice. I always wanted that for Josh, but…well, our plans don't always work out." Tate looked down at her hands, noticing they were in a near-death grip, and forced her fingers to relax.

His casual chatter was loosening her, so Nick hurried on. "No, they sure don't. My dad wanted me to work in construction like him and my brothers, but doing the same thing over and over day after day bored me. When I got accepted at the Police Academy, I think my mother spent all her free time on her knees saying the rosary that I'd flunk out. She hates that I'm a cop, even now."

"As a mother, I can understand that. It's a dangerous job." His gun was hidden by his jacket now, but she was acutely aware of its presence and what it represented.

"I suppose. But Tony broke both shoulders once falling off a roof he was prepping. Took him six months to recover. Sam got cut by a piece of rusty tin and ignored it until it got infected. He nearly wound up with blood poisoning. On any given day, any one of us can get run over by a bus, too. Danger is relative."

"You're talking accidents, which can happen to anyone. But your brothers aren't dealing with criminals who have guns and other weapons and might somehow wind up cornered and decide to use them on a cop. You go looking for trouble every day." And she wondered how he stood it. She'd had a small taste of danger and hated it.

"Not really, but trouble seems to find me anyhow." Nick pulled into a crowded parking lot adjacent to a stucco building painted bright green and sporting a big red-and-white neon sign that flashed on and off, reading *Giovanni's*. Strings of blinking red, white and green lights outlined the roof, the door and windows. Outside the main door was a huge fountain with cement cherubs pouring recirculated water. He saw that both of them were staring openmouthed. He was used to the place, as most everyone in the neighborhood was, but he knew it looked garish to a newcomer.

"The Italian flag colors, you know—red, white and green. It's not as gaudy inside, the pasta's to die for and the pizza can't be beat." Turning off the engine, he got out from behind the wheel and was about to go around to assist them, but Tate was already out and helping Josh unbuckle his seat belt. Okay, so chivalry was out.

Nick waited until they joined him before leading the way through the heavy wood door. Inside, he paused to let his guests absorb the atmosphere.

Dean Martin was crooning *That's Amore* through the piped-in music system, adults and kids alike were chattering and several waiters wrapped in big white aprons were serving large trays of food and pitchers of cold drinks. A table of four joined Dean, singing loudly and off-key. They competed with a round table consisting of six kids and two adults who were singing birthday greetings to a boy of about eight.

"It's never boring in here," Nick said, leaning close to Tate in order to be heard. He caught the very feminine scent of her hair and quickly straightened.

A big man with wavy black hair and a full mustache spotted them and came rushing over. "Nickie, how you been?" He grasped Nick into a huge bear hug.

"Fine, Johnny." Nick urged her forward with a hand to the small of her back. "I'd like you to meet Tate Monroe and her son, Josh."

"Glad you're here," Johnny said, his dark eyes smiling. "Any friend of Nickie's is a friend of mine." He turned, looking around, then swung back. "Two minutes and I'll have a booth for you, okay?"

"That'd be great." Nick kept his hand at her back, wondering if she'd leave it there after Johnny walked away.

In a smooth move, Tate shifted fractionally and slipped

her arm around Josh's shoulders, aligning the two of them slightly apart from Nick. "What do you think, Josh?" she asked the boy.

"It smells good in here," he answered shyly.

"And it tastes just as good," Nick told them as he caught Johnny's wave and led them to a booth where the table was draped with a red-and-white checkered cloth topped with bright green plastic place mats. He thanked his friend and accepted two huge menus, passing one to Tate who let Josh slide in, then followed him. Nick sat down opposite them.

"You can tell me what kind of pizza you like or I can let Johnny build us a special one," he told Tate. "Your choice."

Feeling a bit weary suddenly, Tate was glad to let him take over. "Why don't you order for us?"

"No green peppers, though, okay?" Josh added.

"I'll take the green peppers off yours, honey," Tate told him.

Nick signaled Johnny over. "Not to worry. Hey, Big John, we want one of your specials, an extra large, hold the green peppers. And to drink?" He looked inquiringly at Tate. "Root beer or..." He saw them both nod. "A large pitcher of root beer."

"Sure thing, my man. Be right back." An Italian opera was now playing and Johnny took up the aria with the tenor, singing loud and boisterously as he made his way to the kitchen.

"He's a bit of a character, but he has a heart of gold." Nick studied the boy who was watching the kids at the next table with the birthday celebration. There was such longing in those green eyes that were so much like his mother's. "Parties like that are great, aren't they?" he asked Josh.

The boy didn't answer, just kept staring. "When's your birthday, Josh?"

"In March," he answered, his eyes on the boy wearing the cone-shaped hat proclaiming him the birthday boy.

They'd finished eating and the table was piled high with gifts. Wearing a gap-toothed grin, the boy began ripping open the nearest package while the others cheered him on.

Nick remembered that Tate had said they'd moved around a lot. That probably meant that Josh had few friends, too shy to make new ones in each new place that he'd soon have to leave. But why had they moved around so much? He shifted his gaze to Tate who was toying with her spoon thoughtfully.

"Maybe next March, we can arrange a party for you and your friends here," Nick offered, hoping to lighten the mood.

"Don't," Tate said, her husky voice low but firm. "Please don't make promises that you might not be able to keep. False hope is a terrible thing to live with." She'd blurted it out before she thought how she'd sound, but this man they'd only just met had to know that she didn't want Josh counting on things that may never happen. And who knew where they'd be by next March.

Nick saw that Josh was still occupied in watching the kids, pretending he hadn't heard. "I didn't mean any harm," he said to Tate.

"I'm sure you didn't." She raised a hand to smooth back a curling lock of hair that was trying to escape the ponytail and sighed wearily. "People often make those kinds of statements and have no intention of following through. I'm not saying you're like that, but…"

"I'm *not* like that, Tate. I realize you don't know me, but I follow through."

The arrival of a short, dark-haired young woman carrying a huge pizza and a frosty pitcher cut short their conversation. "Nickie!" she said, greeting him. Quickly she put everything on the table, then leaned over to hug him. "Long time, no see."

"Hi, Gina. Yeah, I've been kind of busy." He angled his head toward the room. "You've got a big crowd tonight."

Gina nodded, smiling broadly at him. "Every night. You

know Johnny. He's not happy unless it's standing-room only. Did you see Joey and Fran across the way?''

Nick looked over and caught his friends' attention, smiled and waved. ''Your sister's expecting again, I see.''

''Oh, sure. Gotta keep Papa happy. He wants more grand-kids to spoil. He's after me all the time to get married, get married. Drives me nuts.''

''I know the feeling. Gina, this is Tate and her son, Josh. Gina's Johnny's sister.''

Tate acknowledged the introduction with a smile while Josh was busily eyeing the huge pizza. ''You enjoy,'' Gina said, leaving.

Nick picked up a plate and began dishing out the pizza slices.

Tate scanned the room, listening to an old Perry Como recording playing. The place, at least the music, was caught in a time warp. She had no idea neighborhood places like this still existed, ones where friends met regularly. ''The Italians have a way of turning a meal into a celebration,'' she commented, accepting her plate with a piece so large it hung over the edges.

''You've got that right,'' Nick said as he handed Josh his piece.

''Do you need help cutting that?'' Tate asked her son.

''Mom, you don't cut pizza. You pick it up and bite it.'' Wrapping both hands around it, curling the piece, he took a huge bite, demonstrating.

''Yeah, Mom,'' Nick echoed. ''Where you been?''

She smiled as she picked up her fork. ''Some of us are more civilized.''

''Fingers were made before forks,'' Nick added before tasting his piece. ''Mmm,'' he purred. ''This is better than…better than most pizzas.'' He'd been about to say better than sex, but stopped himself just in time.

Meeting his eyes, Tate guessed exactly what he'd been

thinking. For the first time, she gave him a genuine smile, one that reached those incredible eyes. "I agree, to your first thought, that is." When he laughed out loud, she joined in.

The atmosphere, the good food, the noise insulating them in their own little pocket of privacy—all seemed to relax them and they ate in comfortable companionship. When Josh asked for a second piece, Tate was truly shocked. She dished it out, pleased her picky eater had an appetite on this disturbing day. She was glad she'd accepted Nick's invitation after all, if the visit here made Josh put Maggie's ordeal out of his mind even temporarily.

Intent on keeping things pleasant, Nick searched his mind for a neutral subject. "You never came here when you were going to U of A? It's a big college hangout on weekends."

Tate dabbed at her lips with the paper napkin. "No. I didn't have a car so we stuck kind of close to the campus."

Nick finished his second piece, debated about a third, then decided to go for it. "I'd have thought some of your dates might have brought you here. It's been open about ten years."

Tate shook her head. "I didn't date much."

He had trouble believing that. A woman as gorgeous as she was had to have had her pick of men. "From where I sit, I find that impossible to imagine."

"I had to spend more time studying than either of my roommates. Molly was the smart one. She helped me a lot on subjects we took together." Remembering those happier times, Tate felt a rush of nostalgia. "We had these nicknames for each other. Molly was the brain and Laura was the big bucks."

"And you?" he asked, thinking that he knew.

Tate shrugged. "Seems silly now."

"You were the beauty, right?"

Her green eyes raised to his, studying him, not answering. She was trying to figure him out, Nick decided. He liked keeping her off balance. "Want to know what they labeled me in college?"

The spell broken, Tate nodded.

"Bookworm. I'm the first, the only one in my family to go to college, much less graduate. Now you'd think that would fill my parents with pride. Nope. As I said earlier, they wanted me in the family business, and you don't need a degree to build houses, or so my father said. I'd get tired of books and come back to them, he predicted. So I studied and studied so I could prove him wrong. I was dull, a regular nerd."

It was Tate's turn to register disbelief. "Come on. With your build, you must have gone out for football or maybe basketball. I can't believe you sat in your room studying instead of dating a whole flock of coeds." Even if she shaved off ten years, he was more than average attractive. Was he fishing?

"Not so. You can ask my family. Girls scared me so I hid behind books."

Still smiling, Tate shook her head in amazement. "Methinks you doth protest too much."

Josh drained his root beer mug and, having made it halfway through his second piece, sat back looking stuffed.

"You really like this pizza, eh?" Tate asked, handing him his napkin.

"It was great." Josh swiped at his mouth halfheartedly.

Now that they were well fed and smiling, Nick decided they were relaxed enough to give him some answers. "Josh, Maggie watches you after school and sometimes on weekends when your mom has to work, right?"

The boy shot a look to his mother.

"It's all right, sweetie. Remember, Nick's a detective and he wants to find the man who hurt Maggie. You can answer him." But she intended to guide this question session.

"Yes," Josh said.

"Do the two of you usually stay in the house or does Maggie take you places?"

"Sometimes we go to the park. I like the jungle gym."

"Have you ever noticed any strangers, someone you might have seen more than once, hanging around the park or near your house?" Nick watched Josh again glance at his mother before answering.

"There was this one guy. I saw him one day at the park, then later he was in a big black car across the street from Maggie's."

Now they were getting somewhere. "What did he look like?"

Josh screwed up his face, thinking. "Just a guy. He had black hair in a ponytail, not as long as Mom's. And both times, he wore black pants and a black shirt. He had on sunglasses."

Tate's gaze swung to Nick's face, recalling that Maggie had told them the intruder who beat her had a black ponytail and wore black clothes. She saw that he remembered, too.

"You're very observant, Josh," Nick praised. "You're doing great." Even though there was a look of anxiety on Tate's face. It seemed that the boy hadn't told his mother about the man in black. Did she recognize that description?

"Did the man come up to you, try to talk to you?"

Josh shook his head.

"About that car, can you tell me what it looked like?"

"It was black and really long. And the windows were dark."

"You mean like tinted windows?"

"Yes. The man got out of the car and stared at our house. I was watching from mom's bedroom window."

"He just stared, didn't do anything else?"

"He talked with someone in the back seat."

"Did that person get out, too?"

"No. The window was open halfway, but I couldn't see

him. He was smoking a cigarette and he tossed it out. Then the other guy got back in and they drove away."

Nick looked at Tate. "Your son has the makings of a first-rate detective. He seems to take in every detail."

"That's not the life I want for him, thank you." Tate stroked her son's blond hair. "Is that all?"

"Just one last question. Josh, if I showed you a bunch of pictures, do you think you could pick out the man with the ponytail?"

Suddenly frightened, the boy moved closer to his mother. "No. He had sunglasses on. I don't want to look at any pictures."

"Okay," Nick hastened to reassure him, as well as his mother. "No pictures." What had spooked the kid? he wondered. Realizing the tension was back, Nick signaled for the check.

There was a short discussion about paying, but Nick won. "You can pay next time," he told her.

Out in the parking lot, he held the door for Tate while she made sure Josh was buckled into the back seat. But before she stepped in, he leaned close to her, resolutely ignoring her scent that had been playing havoc with his concentration all day, and told her that if she could convince Josh to look at some photos or even give a more detailed description to their police artist, they'd have a better chance of finding this guy.

Tate's reluctance was evident as she quickly sat down. "I don't want him to be put through that if he doesn't want to do it," she said, and reached to close her door, effectively ending the conversation.

The ride home was even more quiet than the ride over. Nick hated putting that fearful look into her beautiful green eyes, but he felt sure that Tate Monroe knew more than she was revealing. However, he reminded himself, he'd have to move slowly if he wanted her to open up to him.

And meanwhile, he'd do a little investigating on his own.

When he pulled up in front of Maggie's, Tate had the door open before he'd shifted into Park. "Thank you for dinner. We both really enjoyed it, but it's been a long day and I've got to get Josh to bed." Moving quickly to forestall any resistance from Nick, she got out and helped her son.

Nick got out anyway. "Would you like me to go in and check out the house, just to make sure it's okay?"

"No, thanks. We'll be fine." With cops crawling all over the house most of the day, she doubted the intruder would return.

"Okay, then. I'll be in touch," Nick said, wondering if she heard. Or if she even cared.

"Good night, sweetie," Tate said as she pulled Josh's bedroom door halfway closed. "Sleep tight."

"Leave the hall light on, please, Mom."

"Okay." Even though he had a night-light on in his room, Josh liked the hallway lit in case he had to get up. Drawing in a deep breath as she made her way to her own room, Tate didn't mind. If a hall light meant her son would rest more easily, it was a small thing. If only her own sleep would be less fitful by the simple addition of a light on.

Checking her watch, she wondered if it was too late to call her district manager and arrange for a couple of days off until Maggie was home and settled. She'd also have to find a day-care center or summer children's program for Josh until Maggie was once more able to take care of him while she was at work. Picking up her bedside phone, Tate decided she'd best call now.

Ten minutes later, she hung up, ever so grateful that Judith Dunn was so understanding. How many times had she had to call her boss and explain yet another reason she couldn't be in? Too many to count. And all the times she'd taken a leave of absence, moved away for several months, only to return and have Judith pleased she was back and ready to go to work again. Of course, when she was there, she worked hard, but she still felt lucky to have Judith on her side.

Tate slipped off her shoes and began undressing. Lucky. It wasn't a word she associated with herself ever really. Luck wasn't something a person could rely on anyhow. *We make our own luck, good or bad,* her father used to say. How true those words were, she thought as she stepped into the adjoining bathroom and turned on the water. A hot soak would feel good.

Pinning her hair up onto her head, Tate gazed dispassionately at her image in the mirror. Most of her life, she'd had people tell her how lucky she was to have such lovely skin, such beautiful hair, such a lovely figure. She supposed that was luck of a sort, being born to good-looking parents from a great gene pool. But it was nothing she'd personally done. Her looks were just there, no big deal.

Others often made it a big deal, Tate acknowledged, testing the water with her fingers, then adding fragrant bubble bath. Men fell over backward over a beautiful woman until the woman no longer heard the compliments and wound up wondering if only her looks were of importance to them and not who she truly was. Women often became jealous even if she did nothing more than walk into a room. Tate knew she'd never deliberately done anything to earn that reputation, but there it was. Which was probably why she trusted only Molly and Laura.

And men not at all.

Shutting off the water, Tate climbed into the bubbly, steaming water gingerly, then lay back, closing her eyes. Her mother, from the little she could remember, had also been beautiful. Only she'd gloried in it, flirting outrageously, breaking hearts along the way. Especially her father's when she'd walked away from her family the year Tate turned eight and her brother, Steve, was only six. Later Tate had learned that she'd left a note saying she simply couldn't stay the wife of a small-town tailor. She needed to be free.

Dad had handled her departure better than Tate or Steve, who'd both blamed themselves way into their teens. Her father never spoke of their mother with bitterness, saying that she was like a beautiful butterfly who'd stayed with them a while, then had flown off to share her beauty with the world. However, he'd warned Tate that beauty was a gift and that she mustn't take unreasonable pride in it. She'd heeded his advice.

Tate inhaled the warm aroma, letting the soothing water heal her tired body and mind. Where, exactly, had being beautiful gotten her? Because she'd instinctively known early on that men wanted her mostly for one thing only, she'd been reluctant to date. Then one had come along who'd seemed way above the crowd, a handsome, charismatic man who'd looked into her eyes and actually listened to what she said as if her words mattered, as if she were important, special.

He hadn't rushed her into bed, but rather they'd talked for hours—about books and music and horseback riding and hiking—all manner of things. They'd taken long, leisurely walks in the woods together, cooked dinner at his place, camped by the river and slept under the stars. Gradually she'd allowed herself to trust him. Loving had followed as surely as night follows day. The morning she realized she'd been thinking of love and he'd been thinking of an interlude was one of the worst times in her life.

Tate trailed damp fingers through the floating bubbles, her mind floating, too, back in the past. Everything had fallen apart then and nothing had been the same since. Her warm and tender love had turned to bitter ashes. At first, she'd wanted to die—of heartache, of shame. But Maggie had pulled her through, talking softly, encouraging, some nights just holding her while she wept. And there'd been Molly and

Laura, more like blood sisters than friends, always there for her in those days when she'd been so needy.

The only good thing that had come out of that terrible time was Josh, her beautiful boy. He was the only male she could trust without question, the only one she'd ever allow to get close to her. And yet, because of her mistake, her error in judgment, both Josh and Maggie were in danger. Last year, when they'd been on the run, she'd known that Molly had been threatened, too. Then Laura had been stalked and even forced off the road, landing in the hospital. That had somehow frightened even the madman hounding all three of them, for there'd been no sign of him for many months. Tate had prayed he'd abandoned his sick plans.

How could she have been so naive?

No, she might as well admit her suspicions. The invasion at Maggie's wasn't caused by some intruder looking for valuables rumored to be hidden in her home. Tate could think of only one person who might have ordered the break-in and she could guess what his hired thug had been searching for. What she didn't know was how to handle him.

Sitting up, she soaped her washcloth and swished it around her shoulders and arms. Her thoughts drifted to Detective Nick Bennett. She could tell he wanted her to open up to him, but how could a man who'd come from the warm and loving family he'd described ever be able to relate to her problems? Get a restraining order, he'd suggest probably. But if she named names, he'd realize she couldn't do that. If she revealed too much and if somehow the news got out, the stalker would turn up the heat and somehow manage to take Josh. She couldn't be with her son every minute. And what could she do to stop such a man? Move again? The very thought started her trembling.

The bathwater had cooled. Tate pulled the plug, rinsed off and wrapped herself in a large white terry-cloth towel. As she walked into her bedroom, she thought she heard a car engine start up right outside. Cautiously, she moved to the window and peeked out between the soft folds of the sheer curtains. Just then, a sleek black car with tinted windows flashed on its lights and slowly pulled away from the curb.

Damn him!

With shaky hands, she drew the drapes closed over the windows, then did the same across the room before hurrying to Josh's room, his windows facing only the rear of the house. He was sleeping soundly, thank heaven. The new dead bolt had been installed and before she'd come upstairs, she'd checked the back door as well as made certain the window locks were all secure. Yet she knew that if someone really wanted to get in, they would. Not overtly though, for the man in question had too much to lose if an illegal move could be proven and traced to him.

Just because she felt better doing it, she went around and pulled drapes closed over all the windows. Both she and Maggie hated the closed in feeling, but Tate felt she had no choice if she wanted to get even a small measure of sleep tonight. Gazing around the living room, she felt such a wave of repulsion, of violation, that someone would come in here and touch their things. Would she ever truly feel safe here again? Was there even a secure place for her somewhere?

Climbing the stairs, Tate forced herself to square her shoulders. Damn it, she was *not* going to let him win. She would find a way to fight him. He was trying to spook her, to intimidate her into giving up. Apparently, he didn't know her as well as he thought he did, for she wasn't a quitter. Maybe Nick was right and she should persuade Josh to look at pictures of known area criminals. If the stalker was among them, if the henchman of the man she feared most landed in jail, perhaps he'd back off. She held little hope for this scenario, but it was worth a try.

Tate hung up the towel and slipped on an old University of Arizona football jersey that she liked to sleep in. Slipping under the covers, she prayed sleep would come and without the accompanying nightmares that so often interrupted her nights.

Closing her eyes, she tried to concentrate on something pleasant. Unbidden, her mind conjured up a pair of steady gray eyes in a tan face and a mouth that looked hard and a little grim, but that she imagined could be soft and warm. Nick Bennett wasn't the man for her. No man was. But she could dream...

Nick stepped closer to the open window in the living room of the small third-floor apartment and cautiously stuck his head out. The nervous Hispanic man, about thirty-five, was sitting on a narrow ledge holding his infant daughter in his arms while sweat poured down his face. "Mr. Espinoza, my name's Nick. Why don't you hand the baby to me, then we can talk better? I want to help you."

"Go away," the man sobbed. "No one can help."

The domestic violence call had come in just as Nick and his partner, Detective Lou Patrick, were heading back to the precinct from a routine check on a probation violator. It was the worst kind of call, the one where a woman and two children were in grave danger from an angry husband, the call police officers dreaded most. In many cases, the man was a loose cannon, totally unpredictable and usually dangerous. Lou had radioed back that they'd take it since their car was close to the address. Nick had done a quick U-turn and turned up the speed, but he hadn't turned on the siren, thinking the arrival of the police might push the guy over the edge.

As they'd entered the apartment, Nick saw a small, dark-haired Hispanic woman sitting on the couch cradling a boy of about six and moaning softly. She'd managed to tell them that she and her husband had been quarreling because she wanted to go back to work now that the baby was no longer nursing because they needed the money. But Jorge didn't

want her working. One thing led to another and when his
son had tried to protect his mother, Jorge had slapped the
boy so hard that he'd fallen, hitting his head on the end table.
Shortly before they arrived, Jorge had climbed out the window with the baby. Rocio Espinoza wailed out her fears.

While Lou called for medical assistance for the boy, Nick
decided to try to talk the distraught man back inside. Once
before, he'd managed to talk a jumper off a rooftop ledge,
but he was well aware how the slightest wrong move could
end in disaster.

Now, as he studied Jorge Espinoza hugging his baby and
rocking as tears coursed down his cheeks, Nick prayed he
wouldn't make a mistake. Peripherally he saw a fire truck
arrive down below, the men hurrying to get a net in place in
the event that Jorge either jumped or fell. Or, even worse,
tossed the baby down. He also noticed a TV truck pull up
and swore under his breath. Just what they needed, media
attention during a volatile situation.

Nick removed his jacket and took off his gun holster, leaving them with Lou. Taking a deep breath, he climbed out the
window and managed to sit down on the ledge several feet
from where Jorge watched him with sullen, unfriendly eyes.

"Don't come no closer or I throw her down," Espinoza
warned.

"Okay. But I don't think you really want to do that, Jorge.
I can tell by the way you're holding your baby that you love
her. Am I right?"

Jorge paused to gaze at his baby's face. "She'll grow up
to be just like her mother. Rocio was a good woman, but not
no more. She don't want to stay home and take care of the
kids. She wants to work in that bar every night where men
can stare at her and grab at her. I make good money. Why
does she want to work? Only for the men, for the attention."
He hugged the baby closer. "It's better my little girl dies
now than she grows up like her mother."

At least he now knew the problem, Nick thought as he searched for the right words. "It's hard, isn't it, working long hours and then having to stop to pick up the kids at day care, dinner not ready when you get home."

Jorge nodded as he swiped tears from his face with his shirt sleeve. "Yeah. She don't think about that. Already my son talks back to me. Where'd he learn all that? At that day care where the older boys teach him. He's got no respect."

Which was undoubtedly why he'd hit the boy. Was it the first time he'd hit his son? "I understand but, Jorge, there's a way to work this out." Moving ever so slowly, Nick scooted nearer, his eyes on Jorge's face. "I'll help you talk to Rocio. I know a nice family restaurant not far from here where she could work the day shift. The owner's a friend of mine and he's a good man. Like you, a hard worker. I could make sure your wife's home by the time you get here. What do you say?"

"The baby's too young to leave with strangers. They mess up your kids." Jorge met Nick's eyes for the first time. "You have kids?"

"No, but I have six nieces and nephews, so I know how you feel. Suppose we talk Rocio into waiting until the baby's six months old, or even a year? How about that?"

"She don't listen to no one. She disrespects me, you know." Jorge shifted his little bundle and the baby woke up and started crying, undoubtedly picking up on the tension. Inside the apartment, Rocio could be heard wailing and moaning.

Nick saw the TV cameras, two by now, trained on them, and wished the news hadn't gotten out. The EMS truck pulled up and two men jumped out, running into the building with their medical equipment. He swung his gaze back to Jorge and saw that the man was fidgeting on the narrow ledge, trying to quiet the baby.

He had to do something and fast.

"Look, Jorge, let me have the baby. You're a proud man, a good man. You don't want to hurt your daughter. Let's put her inside and then you and I will talk to Rocio."

Jorge shook his head, pushing to his feet unsteadily. "No, you're lying. You'll just lock me up and Rocio will be free to mess up my kids and shake her butt around at that bar."

Nick pressed his back to the building and managed to stand, but his heart was in his throat. He saw the net below, but would it catch them? "I promise you, Jorge, I will sit down with you and Rocio and work this out. Just hand over the baby."

Jorge shook his head vigorously. "You don't care about me. No one cares about me." Then suddenly, he lost his footing, his arms flailing out, trying to regain his balance.

In the split second before he went over, Nick grabbed the baby from Jorge's outstretched arm. The small blanket fluttered down after the man who screamed as he fell. Nick plastered himself to the building and drew in a shaky breath. Slowly he inched his way back to the window where Lou waited. Nick handed over the baby and crawled back inside, realizing his shirt was soaked through with nervous sweat.

"Did he make it?" Nick asked his partner.

"Yeah, he landed in the net, the idiot." Lou handed the little girl to her mother who was weeping unashamedly. The paramedics were working on the boy still on the couch.

Nick pulled his handkerchief out and mopped his damp face. "Man, I don't want to do that again anytime soon."

"I don't imagine you do" came a deep reply from the doorway. Lieutenant Ed Harris stood there scowling. "Didn't exactly follow procedure, Bennett. You're not the one who's supposed to go out there and talk a man in. We have a team of experts who specialize in that, or weren't you aware?"

"Yes, sir. But there wasn't time." Nick wasn't worried. He knew the lieutenant had to chew him out a little. But since it had worked out okay, he wouldn't come down too hard. However, if the fireman's net hadn't been there...

"I'll verify that, Lieutenant," Lou spoke up on behalf of his partner. "The guy was a ticking time bomb, ready to buy the farm he was so upset."

"I promised Jorge I'd sit down with him and his wife and try to solve this work situation," Nick mentioned.

"Yeah, well, that'll have to wait," Harris said. "He's got to have psychiatric counseling, anger control management and probably face child abuse charges as well as reckless endangerment of an infant." A tall, silver-haired man with deceptively lazy brown eyes, the lieutenant had seen a lot in his twenty-two years on the force. He walked over to Rocio Espinoza as the medics placed her son on a stretcher.

"What's going to happen to Jorge now?" Rocio asked, looking at all three officers.

"You can ride with the boy to the hospital if you like," Harris told her. "We'll have someone talk with you there."

Resigned, she gathered her baby close, then went over to Nick. "You saved my baby. Thank you."

"You're welcome." Nick put on his shoulder holster and jacket. "Let's get out of here before the media sticks a mike in our face," he told Lou.

The rescue of a baby from the third-floor ledge was all over the television news by noon. Tate had just settled Maggie on the couch, having gotten her released from the hospital, when Josh turned on the TV. He was about to channel-surf when the twelve o'clock news led off with the story of the daring save.

"Hey, it's Nick," Josh said as they played the tape showing the distraught father holding a blanket-wrapped infant and the courageous officer who'd climbed out on the ledge.

Maggie and Tate watched as the little scene unfolded, unable to hear what was being said between the two men up three stories from the ground, yet mesmerized by the drama. The camera's zoom lens captured the troubled expression of the father and the calm demeanor of the officer. Then suddenly they both stood and the man almost stumbled, losing his balance. At what had to be the very last second, Nick caught the baby. The camera backed up and the father could be seen landing in the fire department's safety net as the child's blanket floated down. Then they zoomed in for a close-up of Nick handing the baby inside before climbing through the window.

"Wow," Josh said as the voice of the newscaster went on excitedly explaining the events that led up to the daring rescue.

"I'd say that young man's a hero," Maggie said, relaxing back among the pillows.

Tate sat down at the far end of the couch and watched as a file photo of Nick Bennett in full uniform filled the screen and the voice-over told about another incident several years ago when the detective had kept a man from committing suicide atop a high-rise, then went on to talk about his career record, years of service and his three bravery citations.

Tate hadn't heard from Nick in several days, not since the night of their pizza dinner. Not that she'd expected to, really. She stared at his picture now, thinking there was something about a man in uniform. But he'd worn plain clothes that day and he'd looked vastly appealing then, too. As he probably would wearing only a smile. She felt color move into her face and wondered where that thought had come from.

"I wonder why they sent such a special officer for my little problem," Maggie said, wrinkling her brow.

Tate patted the older woman's outstretched legs. "Only the best, Maggie, because you're worth it," she told her with a smile.

"Thank you, dear."

"Are you sure you don't want to be in your own bed? Or

take a nap here? Josh can watch TV upstairs if you'd like to rest.''

''No, I want to be here and I like having Josh near.'' She smiled as the boy came over to her. ''It's all right if you want to hug me,'' she told him.

''I won't hurt you?'' he asked.

''No, sweetheart. Hug away.'' She shifted her right arm in its cast out of the way and reached out to the boy with her left. ''I missed you.''

''I missed you, too,'' Josh said, straightening, staring at Maggie's discolored cheek. ''I'm sorry you got beat up.'' He turned to his mother. ''Mom, I changed my mind. I'll look at the pictures Nick talked about. I want to help catch that man.''

Her little guy came through and she didn't even have to ask him, Tate thought with no small measure of pride. Apparently he'd inherited her soft heart. And that heroic rescue had convinced Josh that Nick was one of the good guys. ''I'll call Nick,'' she said, rising. ''Of course, with all this publicity, he may be too busy for us.''

Maggie's sharp blue eyes looked Tate up and down, seeing a lovely woman badly in need of a caring man. ''I doubt that, honey. If you call, he'll come.''

Chapter 3

Seated at Maggie's dining-room table, Josh turned another page of the big book in front of him, carefully studying each face before going on to the next as Nick and Tate watched. "These guys look really mean," he said. "Did they all do bad things like the man who beat up Maggie?"

"Pretty much," Nick answered, not wanting to frighten the boy, but also not wanting to lie. "Most of them weren't happy to have their picture taken so they look kind of angry."

"It's important that you pick the right one, if he's in there, Josh, so look really hard," Tate instructed.

"I know, Mom." He turned the next page.

"I sure appreciate you doing this for us, Josh," Nick told the boy, knowing that praise went a long way toward gaining cooperation, though he was curious as to why Josh had suddenly had a change of heart.

The boy looked up, in his eyes a question, uncertain whether he should ask. But Nick was a cool guy so he decided to chance it. "Were you just a tiny bit scared yesterday when you were up on that window ledge with that guy?"

He was a serious boy, Nick thought, comparing Josh to his far more carefree nephews. The kid didn't laugh much or even smile often. What had made him like that? he wondered. "Not a tiny bit, Josh. I was scared a lot. But everyone has to do scary things sometimes in order to help someone. I'll bet you've done a few yourself."

"Once I climbed Mrs. Stone's tree next door to get her kitten down when he got himself stuck up there, but it was only two branches up."

"Even two branches up would have meant quite a fall, for you and the kitten. But you did it even though you were scared. And I'll bet you felt good afterward."

"Did you feel good afterward yesterday?"

Nick drew in a breath, remembering that kids never let up. "Yeah, I was glad the baby was safe and relieved that we didn't fall. But I felt bad for that whole family. They've got a lot of problems to work out." More than he could explain to a seven-year-old.

He chanced a quick look at Tate and saw a look of approval on her face. And something else. A contemplative look, as if she were trying to figure him out. Well, Nick thought, at least he had her thinking. Progress. Maybe.

"Sweetie, you'd better get back to the pictures. You've got one more whole book to go." He'd already looked through two large mug shot books and not spotted the man. Tate was proud of her son's desire to help, but she wondered how a fleeting glance at a park and another from a two-story window of a man wearing sunglasses would stay in Josh's memory bank. She hated to disappoint both of them, Josh who was trying so hard and Nick who'd lugged the heavy books over in the hope they'd get a break.

"What happens if he doesn't pick him out?" she asked Nick.

He shrugged. "Back to square one. This is just one avenue for us to try. It could be the guy's never been arrested so we wouldn't have his picture on file. He could even be from out of state." Nick's steady gaze trapped her eyes. "Or maybe someone else hired him." He let the thought hang there between them.

Tate averted her eyes. "I suppose anything's possible." She rose and walked through the arch into the living room where Maggie was lightly dozing on the couch to check on her. Actually she'd left the table more to get away from Nick's intense look than because she felt Maggie needed her.

The older woman's eyes opened slowly and focused on Tate. "Did Josh find the man?"

"Not yet," Tate answered, straightening her pillows a fraction.

"I only wish he'd have pointed him out to me that day in the park. Maybe I'd remember his features. Four eyes are better than two, you know." Wincing, she shifted the cast on her right arm to a more comfortable position.

"Not to worry. Nick will locate him sooner or later. Want some more tea?"

"Yes, dear, that would be nice."

Tate went to the kitchen, passing through the dining room as Nick closed the third book and opened the final one in front of Josh. Turning slightly, Nick studied Tate.

She'd changed clothes after picking up Maggie from the hospital since the temperature was already in the nineties, not unusual for late May in Tucson. She wore a loose mannish shirt with sleeves rolled up over a white knit top and denim shorts that showed off her shapely legs. She wasn't very tall, five-five or six, which at his height of six-three made him over a head taller. Yet she held herself so erect that she appeared taller. He noticed that she'd gathered her wild reddish hair at her neck and reined it in with a gold clip. Nick's hands itched to run his fingers through the thick waves and watch it fall to her shoulders.

Knowing full well that she didn't need him to make a pot of tea, he meandered into the kitchen anyhow. "Need some help?"

Lost in thought, Tate was momentarily startled to find him at her elbow. "Oh. Thanks, but I can manage." Turning the kettle on, she saw he wasn't going to leave, so she waved a hand toward Josh. "No luck yet and that's the last book. I feel badly that we dragged you over here, wasting your time."

"You're not wasting my time. Police work is a slow process, not like in the movies or on TV where a witness sits down and spots the suspect on page two. I've learned to be a patient man."

Tate rinsed the pot and selected two tea bags. Maggie liked hot tea even in the summer. "I think I'll make some iced tea as well." She reached for the tall pitcher on the top shelf, but even on her tiptoes, couldn't quite make it.

"Here, let me." Nick moved closer to the cupboard and reached up, effectively hemming Tate in between himself and the counter. As he handed her the pitcher, their gazes locked. Just that quickly, he saw that unmistakable male-female awareness leap into her dark green eyes. He didn't move, scarcely breathed as both their hands encircled the pitcher. He wasn't even touching her, yet his senses were acutely tuned to her. Fleetingly, her face registered confusion and an almost heartbreaking need before she deliberately stepped back and looked away.

"Tate, I..." Nick wanted to say something, to acknowledge the moment, the connection, if only in some small way.

Her back to him, she shook her head. "Please, don't."

"Why not?" he asked, genuinely curious. He'd known a lot of women and was well aware that that indefinable connection didn't happen often. Hell, it scarcely happened at all. He also knew she'd felt it, too.

But just then, his beeper went off and Tate was saved from answering, from being confronted. Shaken yet relieved, she pointed to the desk through the arch. "Phone's over there."

Frowning as he recognized the number of the precinct dispatcher, he left the room. In moments, he hung up and turned back to Tate who was just closing the last mug shot book. "Not there, either?" he asked Josh. The boy shook his head.

Nick gathered up the books. "Thanks for trying." He looked into the boy's eyes, again thinking how much Josh reminded him of his mother, although he must have gotten his blond hair from his father. "If you ever see that man again, don't go up to him or talk with him, but study his face very closely. And let me know right away if he shows up here, okay?" He watched the boy solemnly nod, then turned to Tate. "That goes for you and Maggie, too."

Tate remembered the black car parked outside the other night and wanted in the worst way to tell Nick about it. But what good would that do? It would only open a can of worms she was unwilling to face. Even when she'd been confronted by the man Nick was looking for years ago, she hadn't seen his features, either, for he'd worn a ski mask then, too.

The woman should never play poker, Nick thought as he caught her evasive look. Why wouldn't she trust him? "I've got to go out on a call."

"Another rescue?" Josh wanted to know.

Nick smiled at the boy and ruffled his hair. "Nothing so dramatic. At least, I hope not." The call, unfortunately, was about a woman who'd been raped in the rest room of a supermarket. He was to meet his partner at the scene.

Hurriedly he said goodbye to Maggie and Josh as Tate followed him out onto the porch. "Are you going back to work tomorrow?" he asked her, wondering who would care for an incapacitated older woman and a young boy. Still, she had a job to protect.

"I've asked for a few days off, till Maggie's better. And I've got to find some kind of summer program to enroll Josh in." One that had iron-clad security.

Nick hadn't forgotten that the creep who'd invaded Maggie's house had been asking about the boy's whereabouts. This whole incident somehow involved Josh, which led him inevitably to consider the father as a suspect. "Tate, I have to ask you. Is it possible that the break-in has something to do with Josh's father?"

Tate stiffened, her features tightening. "I haven't seen him in years. He didn't even know I was pregnant." Which was the truth, as far as it went. "I...I've got to go in."

He knew he should have left by now, that he was needed at another crime scene, but he had one more point to make. He switched the heavy books under one arm and gently touched her hand. "Tate, I'm not the enemy. I want to help you."

She felt the heat, from his touch, from his words. Tears leaped to her eyes, wanting badly to fall. But she couldn't afford the luxury, nor could she let this kind man know her feelings. "I know," she whispered, then quickly went inside.

All the way to his car, Nick swore inventively. Around the precinct, he was known as the great communicator. More often than not, he could get suspects to open up to him, to instinctively trust him. Yet here, with this woman who'd somehow gotten under his skin, he couldn't get her to drop her guard, one he was certain she'd had in place for years.

Tossing the mug books on the back seat, Nick got behind the wheel. Where there's a will, there's a way, he reminded himself. He'd get Tate Monroe to trust him if it was the last thing he ever did, he vowed as he pulled away from the curb.

Nick left the interrogation room and stepped into the viewing room where the two-way mirror allowed others to ob-

serve and listen to a suspect or witness being questioned. He
and Lou had just done their good-cop-bad-cop routine with
Ronda Philips, the woman claiming she'd been raped in an
eastside supermarket rest room by a burly man with long hair
and a chipped front tooth wearing an oil-stained T-shirt and
carrying a big knife. Nick let out a ragged breath as he
watched the woman he'd just left rummaging through her
purse. "What do you think, Lieutenant?"

"I want to hear what you guys think," Harris told his two
detectives.

Lou Patrick shrugged. "I think she's on the up-and-up.
Nurse at the hospital said she had knife cuts along her inner
thighs, both shoulders and two nicks on her breasts. The
bruise on her cheek could have come from a punch to the
face when she resisted him. Only thing is, the rape counselor
said she had one major concern, that Mrs. Philips kept asking
for her husband throughout the exam whereas most rape victims are frightened and ashamed at first and want nothing to
do with their husbands for a while. But that's not a hard and
fast rule."

The lieutenant toyed with his paisley suspenders and nodded. "What about you, Nick?"

"I think she made the whole thing up. The doctor who
examined her said there was no bruising. And, like Lou said,
she keeps asking where her husband is, how's he taking all
this, when can she go home with him. Not the usual reaction."

"Lou, you were first on the scene. Did anyone in the store
mention seeing a guy like she described?"

Lou shook his head. "Nada. That supermarket's in an af-
fluent neighborhood. You'd think a grease monkey like she
described would stand out, that someone else would have
spotted him and wondered what he was up to."

"How about the husband?" Harris asked.

"We talked with him while she was being examined at the hospital," Nick answered. "He seemed more angry than upset. Blames himself for leaving her alone so much because he works long hours as a new attorney at a big firm. Just last week, they'd planned to take a trip, but a case he was on caused them to have to cancel. Ronda didn't take it well, crying a lot, brooding."

"Yeah, he swore to us he was going to cut back, to spend more time with her," Lou interjected. "I just can't figure what she's got to gain by faking a rape."

"How about sympathy and more attention from the husband?" Nick volunteered.

"We've got to follow through even if her story's suspicious," Harris told them. "Send her home with her husband and put out a description of the rapist." He walked out of the viewing room ahead of his detectives. "But don't let's drop this. Wait a few days, then call her in again, just to clear up some points. Put on a little pressure. If she's faking, maybe she'll break down."

"Right." Nick strolled back to his desk, his mind already back on what he'd been doing when they'd brought the rape victim in. Sitting down at his desk, he booted up his computer.

"Hey, Nick, you mind if I take off a coupla hours?" Lou asked. "We're not up for a while, fourth in line actually, and our shift's over in an hour. I'll have my cell with me. My son's first Little League game's today."

"No problem. Have fun." Nick went to work on a fishing expedition, keying in various lead words, hoping to learn a thing or two. More than one way to get information if the lady refuses to confide in him, he'd decided. Tate Monroe was a mystery he was determined to solve.

He wasn't an expert on the computer, nor could he surf the Internet or the police information network as expertly as some, but he usually could find what he needed. Strictly

speaking, the data he was seeking had little to do with the
home invasion of Maggie Davis and a great deal to do with
his curiosity and interest in Tate Monroe. Okay, so there was
no use hiding the truth from himself. He was intrigued by
the woman and wanted to know everything he could about
her.

As he scrolled through choices, highlighting a few, he began to make headway. Tate had been born twenty-nine years
ago to Dennis and Rita Monroe in Tucson. The father, who'd
died last year at sixty-nine, had been a tailor at an upscale
men's store, yet he'd earned only about thirty thousand in
his best year. That meant her father had been about forty
when she'd been born, nearly twenty years older than his
wife, Rita, who seemed to have vanished off the data base.
Nothing on her since way back when Tate was quite young.
She also had a brother, Steve, two years younger, a career
navy man, currently an instructor at the navy base in San
Diego.

So much for family. He punched in more facts he knew
in order to get facts he didn't know. Tate had entered the
University of Arizona at eighteen and graduated at twenty-
two with a Fine Arts degree in Literature. The bookcase at
Maggie's had been stuffed to overflowing and he had a feeling most of the books were Tate's. Her social security number, from the information sheet she'd filled out for the officer
on the scene, revealed that she'd never made much money,
mostly due to a sporadic work schedule. Not one year since
graduation had she worked the full twelve months. Why?
Nick wondered. Because of her son? *He's been through a
great deal in his short life,* Tate had said about Josh at the
hospital. What had she meant?

He tapped into Brennan's Book Emporium site, employee
information, and found Tate had been working there, on and
off, since a part-time job during high school. Currently she
was listed as manager of their eastside store; district manager

was Judith Dunn, and Tate's assistant was Dave Anderson. She'd lived for a while in an apartment on State Street. There was a gap five years ago where she'd taken a leave for nearly two full years, returned to live at Maggie's address, then left again, returning only four months ago. That was about the time her father had died.

Nick glanced around the bull pen and saw he was almost alone, so he continued his clandestine search. Strictly speaking, he'd wandered off Maggie's case and moved into personal information on Tate Monroe. Checking records on births and deaths again, he found that Josh had been born on March 1 seven years ago. A home birth, taking Tate's last name, father listed as unknown. That he seriously doubted.

Just for the hell of it, he checked her status with the police department and found a record of an assault two years ago, a man who'd invaded her apartment and attacked her. The police report said she'd had numerous bruises and contusions, a black eye and a cracked rib. The assailant, described as "tall, husky, with a long, black ponytail" had never been apprehended.

There was that description again.

Nick sat back in his chair, his mind busily considering possibilities. A coincidence that recently both Maggie and Josh and a while back Tate had encountered the big guy with the ponytail? Highly doubtful. If the man was one and the same, why wasn't Tate able to give them a description, if he'd been in her apartment? Tate had endured a beating similar to Maggie's and mostly likely dished out by the same thug. Why wouldn't she have mentioned this to Nick since it could hardly be labeled irrelevant? Did she know the man and was, for reasons unknown, trying to protect him? Josh was blond so it seemed unlikely his father would have black hair. Who was this ponytailed character?

Hands behind his head, Nick narrowed his eyes. Tate didn't strike him as the type who'd stand still for a beating.

Unless she had a very good reason. And where had her son been that night? Not a mention of a child in the report. The officer in charge had written that he'd advised Tate to get an order of protection, but there was no record of one being issued. Yet shortly after that, she'd taken a leave of absence from Brennan's and disappeared with her son. Curiouser and curiouser.

Where had she gone for nearly two years? An intensified search could find no trace of her. No job record, no medical reports, no address nor phone numbers available. Had she stayed with one of those roommates she put such store in? Something to check out since both were well off financially. Or did she have relatives somewhere who'd put her up along with Josh? No mention of any other Monroes related to her father. Could she have looked up her mother and gone to her?

Nick straightened, realizing that in getting some answers, he'd also brought up more questions. He checked his watch and saw that he was off the clock in twenty minutes. Maybe he'd run over to Brennan's and see if Tate's co-workers were inclined to discuss their manager with him. He'd have to be careful, though. If Tate found out, she wouldn't be pleased.

Dave Anderson, assistant manager at Brennan's, was about five-eight with a wiry build, thinning sandy hair and brown eyes behind horn-rimmed glasses. In the absence of his boss, he was in charge and took the job seriously. After checking his credentials, he ushered Nick to a quiet corner where two easy chairs faced a low table.

Brennan's encouraged their customers to linger, to browse through aisle after aisle of their thousands of books on every topic imaginable, to stop at their coffee bar at the far end of the huge room and have a latte while perusing a book. The homey atmosphere must work for Nick noticed at least two dozen people strolling around, sitting at the coffee bar or in comfortable chair groupings.

"What is it you want to know about Tate?" Dave asked, getting right to the point.

"First, I need to tell you that this interview is confidential, Mr. Anderson. Ms. Monroe is not in any trouble nor is she a suspect in any way. But the rooming house where she lives was invaded several days ago and her landlady badly beaten. I just want to ask a few questions, such as, have you seen anyone hanging around the store, someone who might have a particular interest in Ms. Monroe?"

Dave chuckled behind his fist as he crossed his legs. "Have you met Tate, Detective? She's a knockout. We have lots of guys come in here who notice her, some who practically drool over her."

Nick had suspected as much. "I'm sure you're right. But I mean someone who looks just a little different, who sits staring at her from one of these little seating areas you have, who stays longer than is usual. Maybe a tough-looking guy."

The man looked thoughtful for a moment, then shook his head. "I honestly can't remember anyone like that. This is a fairly upscale neighborhood. We don't get many tough-looking guys in here."

"That's why someone like that would stand out, eh?"

"I suppose. But I don't believe anyone like that's been in here. If I had a good description, perhaps I could watch out for him, maybe call you if I spot him?"

A junior detective, but he couldn't risk civilian involvement. "I can't give you a good description. Tell me, does Ms. Monroe ever respond to these...admirers of hers?" It was the man wanting to know, not the detective.

Quickly and emphatically, Dave shook his head. "No, never. She's nice, always polite, but she discourages every one of them. Listen, I've tried for years to get her to notice me. I've asked her out, done her favors, tried to win her over.

She just smiles and thanks me, but she won't date. Not any-one.''

Why that made Nick feel good he wasn't willing to think about right now. Rising, he stuck out his hand. "Thanks for your help. And please remember, this visit is between the two of us."

Dave pursed his lips together and nodded conspiratorially. "I'll remember."

"Here's my card if you can think of anything that could help our investigation." Nick left the man studying his card as he turned and walked through the big double doors. Keys in hand, he decided he'd drop in on Maggie to see how she was doing after being home from the hospital for two days now. If Tate was there, well, so much the better.

"The problem with growing old, Nick, is that it sneaks up on you and you're never ready," Maggie Davis said, then chuckled at her own observation. They were seated on her long corduroy couch across from the fireplace, Maggie stretched out at one end, Nick in the opposite corner, his body angled toward the small widow with the gentle smile. He could easily believe Maggie had been far more than a housemother to Tate, for she just looked maternal and loving. Much like his own mother.

"My mom says the same thing. She just turned sixty and although I don't think she looks it, she often tells me she feels it."

Maggie pushed her gold-rimmed glasses higher on her nose, thinking she liked this young man. Liked him a lot. His smile was warm and sincere. "Do you have any brothers or sisters?"

"Oh, yeah. Two older brothers, two younger sisters. I'm the middle one. They're all married. I've got seven nieces and nephews and another on the way. A big, noisy family."

"And you love it," Maggie said, and it wasn't a question.

"Yeah, I guess I do." But he wanted to talk about her and her roomers, not himself. "How are you feeling, really?"

"My throat's better, as you can tell from my voice. The ribs hurt, especially at night, and this cast is uncomfortable. But I'm doing okay. It could have been worse, I suppose."

Much worse, Nick knew. He glanced around the neatly kept room. "I guess Tate and Josh are out?"

Maggie sighed. "Yes, and I feel so bad that she has to scramble around to find someplace to leave the boy so she can get back to work. I can manage alone here if I move slowly, but I can't take care of Josh yet. Poor Tate. She always has so much to cope with."

She'd given him an opening and he grabbed it. "You mean because she's a single mother raising her son alone?"

"I know that lots of women do that these days, but it's never easy."

"What about Josh's father? Does he help, at least financially?"

"No, he's not even in the picture." Maggie picked up her ever-present cup of lukewarm tea and took a sip.

Exactly what Tate had told him. "Do you know his name?"

She shook her head. "Tate never said and I didn't ask."

Nick was puzzled. "But, according to my calculations, she was living in your house, still going to college, when she got pregnant. You must have seen the man, or did she date a lot of guys?"

"Oh, she had boys hanging around by the carload, but she was intent on studying. Then she met this man, not a boy from the university, an older man. That much she did tell me. Tate was young and naive. He filled her head full of promises, from what her roommates and I gathered, and she fell for him really hard. But he never came to the house. Tate always met him elsewhere. She was radiant, so very happy.

Then suddenly, something must have happened because she stopped going out and she cried a lot, wouldn't eat.''

Had the guy been married? Or maybe transferred out of the city? "He walked away from her and she found out she was pregnant?" Nick ventured since Tate had told him that Josh's father hadn't known about her condition.

"Yes. I told her that it takes two to make a baby, that she needed to tell him, but she refused. She said she wanted nothing more to do with him, not ever. So Molly and Laura and I helped her all we could, even delivered the baby right here in this house. And we didn't ask any more questions. It was none of our business, really." Implying it was none of his, either.

Maybe he needed to explain himself. "Maggie, I'm not asking out of simple curiosity." Although that was a part of it. "The officer you talked to the day you were hurt said that you mentioned that the man in the mask kept asking you where Josh was. Who would want to know the boy's whereabouts so badly that he'd try to beat the information out of you?"

Sighing, she lay back against the pillows. "I don't know. I really don't. I asked Tate and she simply said she'd take care of it and not to worry. But, of course, I worry. That girl's like my daughter, Josh like the grandson I never had.''

Nick leaned closer, needing to convince her. "Then help me, Maggie." He felt she knew more than she was telling, maybe small facts she wouldn't think important. "Tell me what or who she's running from. I want to help, but I can't if I don't know who's behind this. From what I gather, she's been on the run from the time Josh was about two years old, living with you, then leaving, returning, but never staying long. Why would a mother who loves her son the way I know Tate does do that to him, disrupting him regularly?"

Maggie's sharp blue gaze dropped to study her hands restlessly fidgeting in her lap. "I believe you do want to help her, but I don't feel comfortable telling you any more about Tate's past. She'll have to be the one to explain. And good luck on that. She rarely confides in anyone nor does she trust easily. She doesn't want to burden anyone with her problems.''

''But we can't help her if she doesn't let us know what's going on.'' Frustration had sharpened his voice.

''I know that.'' Her eyes had filled with tears and she dabbed at them with a tissue. ''She's going to need help, I can tell you that.'' She slipped her hand into the pocket of her robe and pulled out an envelope, holding it out to him. ''Maybe we'll all need help.''

Nick took the white envelope with Maggie Davis written on the front in black block letters. He withdrew the single sheet of paper and read the short message written the same way.

You'd better not talk to the cops or next time, I'll finish the job.

His mouth a grim line, Nick looked up. ''May I keep this? Maybe we'll get lucky and pick up a fingerprint.''

''Sure, take it.'' She drained her tea, looking drained as well.

''Have you shown this to Tate?'' he asked.

''No. I found it between the door and the screen this morning. It upset me terribly, but I didn't want to get Tate worked up as well.''

Maybe if Tate knew, she'd be more forthcoming, give him enough information to get this guy. It had to have something to do with Josh's father, but, if that was so, why was he trying to get his son in such a bizarre and unlawful manner? Why not go through legal channels, demand a DNA test, visitation rights, etc? Of course, he obviously hadn't paid child support, but some agreement could be reached on that with Tate. Or was she simply refusing to negotiate anything? Still, in recent years courts have recognized fathers' rights and would force the mother to comply, provided the man was legit. But was he?

More unanswered questions.

He had to try harder with this little widow. "Maggie, were you aware that a couple of years ago, the man with the ponytail forced his way into Tate's apartment and beat her up almost as badly as you?"

Maggie closed her eyes as she nodded. "Yes, of course. That's why Josh is so protective of his mother and so very fearful of men."

"He was there and saw the attack?"

"No, but he saw the results. Both her eyes were black-and-blue, she had a rib that was broken, not just cracked, and could hardly get around for weeks. The way she looked frightened Josh. The two of them moved away for a long while after that."

"Where did she go?"

"I wouldn't tell you that, even if I knew. It might jeopardize Tate and Josh's safety."

Nick drew in a deep breath, trying to be patient. "All right, we've got this guy in black who beat on Tate, who beat on you, who's hanging around the park and outside your home, who's sending threatening letters—and still Tate won't help me put him away? I don't understand."

Maggie didn't respond, just toyed with the hem of her robe, folding and unfolding it. Finally, she raised her eyes to study the detective's face for long minutes, as if trying to see into his heart, to determine if she could truly trust him.

"Talk to me, Maggie, please."

"She's afraid, Nick. Afraid for Josh and now me. Probably for herself, too." She waved a dismissive hand. "Oh, she hasn't said so in so many words, but that's what I think. Yes, I think Josh's father is behind all this. I can only imagine that he has something on Tate, or that he's a dangerous man and she's afraid to expose him. Maybe...maybe you can per-suade her to tell you more.''

"I don't know,'' Nick stated honestly. "She doesn't trust me.''

"She doesn't trust men, period. Ever since she was a young girl, men have been after her, but for all the wrong reasons. Then, when she thought she'd found someone who truly loved her, he betrayed her, too. Do you blame her for not trusting men?''

"I see what you mean. But it's hard to believe that, as attractive as Tate is, there's been no other man in her life since Josh's father.''

"But it's true. She never goes out, spends all her time working or with Josh and me. Period.''

"That's no life for a young woman, but I do see where she's coming from.'' And he wondered if he, with the best of intentions, could persuade her to trust him after all she'd been through.

He stuck the letter into his jacket pocket. "Maybe I can get some protection for the three of you in the meantime. I'll talk to my captain.'' Nick didn't hold out much hope for that, even with the threatening letter. The precinct was always shorthanded.

"We appreciate everything you're doing. You're a good man, Nick Bennett. You know, one of the few advantages of growing older is that you can speak your mind more freely. You're not married, are you?''

"No, ma'am. Never have been.''

"Why is that, a handsome fella like you?'' Now she smiled, but her eyes were serious.

Nick shrugged. "Never found that special lady who could make me believe in happily ever after. In my line of work, I see a lot of miserable marriages, and the results of those mistakes.''

"Ah, but look at your parents, and all your siblings?''

He smiled, conceding. "You have a point there."

"I know you're attracted to Tate, so I'm asking you to be careful. She seems able to handle everything that comes her way, but inside, she's battered and bruised, and very fragile. She's also very special and it'll take a special man to win her over."

"Thanks for the advice." Nick heard Tate's Buick chug into the driveway and stop. Maybe he could start by tuning up her car, he thought as he got up and went to the door. He saw the wariness on her face as she and Josh came onto the porch. "Hello there."

She was surprised to see him, and even more surprised at the way her heart stumbled at the sight of him in a pair of hip-hugging jeans and a denim jacket that was necessary, she supposed, to hide his gun. He looked so good, so solid. For a brief moment, when she'd seen him come out on the porch, she'd wished she could move into those strong arms and be held, to feel safe. To cover her momentary lapse of good sense, she made her voice sound cooler than it should. "Detective Bennett. To what do we owe the pleasure of your company?"

So she was back to being formal. She certainly wasn't going to make this easy for him. "I just came to see how Maggie's doing."

"You didn't catch the bad guy yet?" Josh wanted to know.

"Not yet." Nick held the door open for Josh as he went directly to Maggie for a hug, reassuring himself that she was all right.

Tate followed her son in, anxious to shed her business suit and heels on this warm day. But first, she checked on Maggie. "Are you okay?" she asked, rolling her eyes toward Nick with a question in them, her back to him.

Maggie took Tate's hand and smiled. "I'm just fine,

honey. Nick's been telling me all about his family. They sound wonderful.''

"Good. Are you in pain? I could get you a pill.''

"No, not yet, but thanks, dear.'' Maggie heard Josh race up the stairs to his room. "Did you find a summer program for him?''

"I think so.'' They'd checked out four and the last one seemed to fit the bill perfectly, though it was a bit more money than she'd planned on. But she'd find the cash somehow. "It's run by two no-nonsense women, one a former child psychologist and the other an educational counselor.''

Tate didn't add that the building and playground were both fenced and gated and security was top-notch. "They have all sorts of activities all day long, some educational and others just plain fun. The two women are very personable and kind, and all their personnel are bonded and screened. Josh seemed comfortable with them.'' And no men in charge, which her son couldn't seem to handle just now.

"I'm so glad. It won't be for long, Tate. I'll be up and around in no time.''

Tate leaned down and hugged the older woman, struggling with a rush of emotion. "I know you will, but healing can't be rushed.''

"You look warm. Go get changed.''

"Be back in a minute, then I'll start dinner.'' It was nearing six and she was hot and tired, but at least she'd accomplished what she'd set out to do today. She turned toward the stairs and saw Nick standing there watching her in that quiet, intense way he had. She'd forgotten for a moment that he was still here. "Did you want me for anything?''

A loaded question if ever he'd heard one, but he kept his face expressionless. "I'd like to talk with you, if you have the time. I'll wait until you finish dinner.''

A flicker of annoyance danced through her eyes for a moment, but she nodded. "Okay.''

Nick watched her hurry upstairs, unaware his face gave him away until he sat down alongside Maggie again.

"She is lovely, isn't she?" Maggie asked softly.

"Yes, she is that."

"And just as lovely inside as out. I hope you can see that."

"I think I can. I know that beautiful women scare some men. But I learned at an early age not to be put off by them." Nick stretched one arm along the couch back. He liked Maggie, admired her spunk, and decided to confide in her since she'd spoken so honestly with him. "You see, when I was in high school, I was kind of a nerd, a bookworm, and to make matters worse, I was shy. But a guy can dream and my dreams revolved around Lisa Hemmings. She had shiny blond hair that fell halfway down her back and these huge blue eyes. She was a cheerleader and very popular. Every time I saw her, my heart pounded so hard I was sure she could hear it. I was equally sure she didn't know I was on the planet."

"I doubt that." Maggie settled back, enjoying his story, enjoying him.

"Well, this big dance came up and, of course, I couldn't dredge up the nerve to ask her and if I couldn't have her, I didn't want anyone else. So the evening of the dance, I went to the movies—alone, wallowing in my self-pity. After the movie, I was walking out when who did I see strolling up the aisle but none other than Lisa, and she was alone, too.

"I was too stunned to remember to be nervous, so I went over and asked her how she'd liked the movie. We talked for a few minutes and I asked if she'd like to go get a soda at the ice-cream shop around the corner. She was easy to talk to and I finally got up the nerve to ask why she wasn't at the dance, a beautiful and popular girl like her. She told me something I've never forgotten."

"And that would be?"

"She told me that she had a lot of friends, but the boys

always assumed someone else had asked her out. They were afraid of being rejected by the prettiest girl in school, so they simply didn't ask. She said she'd spent many a school dance night alone at the movies. After that, we became good friends. Not dating friends, really, but buddies more like. I even stood up in her wedding a couple of years ago."

"I think your friend was right. As lovely as Tate is, I know she's lonely. Men admire her, and some even ask her out, but mostly because they want to prove to everyone they can attract a beautiful woman or because they want to sleep with her. That's a lesson she learned early in life." Maggie smiled into his eyes. "I'm glad you're different, that you see past the wrapping and want to see what's inside the package."

"I try to."

Maggie cocked her head at him. "I'm having trouble picturing you as a bookworm type. You look like one of those men in that cigarette ad. All you need is a cowboy hat and a horse."

Nick laughed out loud. "If you say so."

Tate carried two chilled glasses of iced tea out onto the front porch where Nick was examining the dead bolt that had been installed. He looked up as she handed him his. "Thanks, but aren't you going to eat? I don't want to interrupt your dinner."

"I'm not hungry. Josh and I stopped at the golden arches for lunch. I've had all the calories I can handle for one day." She sat down on one of two rattan chairs and sipped her tea, finding it refreshing. "I'd have asked you to join them for dinner, but it's only leftover meat loaf."

"I wasn't trying to wangle an invitation." He sat down alongside her in the second chair and nodded toward the door. "That lock's a start, but steel security doors back and front would be better. Or perhaps a burglar alarm system, one that's connected to the police department."

Tate set her glass down on the small table between them. "I'll be sure and do that with my first lottery check."

Chagrined, he backed down. He should have known money was in short supply since Maggie's house was quite obviously in need of paint and a bit of sprucing up. Best to change the subject. "So you've found a good place for Josh until Maggie's fully recovered?"

"Yes. It's called Little Miss and Mister. Ever hear of them?"

He nodded. "My sister Julia had her two kids in there last summer, mostly because she wanted to work in her husband's office and the kids were bored at home. She's a nurse and he's a doctor. She had only good things to say about the place."

"I'm glad to hear that."

"Josh has a little trouble with men, doesn't he?"

Tate stiffened slightly and hoped he didn't notice. "I suppose so, probably because he's not been around men much." She turned to meet his eyes. "But he's taken to you."

Nick frowned. "Yeah, why do you suppose that is?"

She smiled. "Because of that rescue. Up to then, he was nervous around you, too. We watched the whole thing on TV. He thought you were awesome. One of the guys in white hats."

So that was why Josh had agreed to look at the mug shots. "Nice to know. How about you? Do you think I'm one of the good guys?"

She kept her emotions in check and answered quickly. "Of course. You're with the police. We have to trust the police."

"You're evading again. You're good at that."

Why was he here? Tate asked herself. To confuse her or was there a real purpose? "You could have checked on Maggie with a phone call. Why did you come?"

"Follow-through. The department's big on follow-through."

He reached in his pocket for the envelope and handed it to her. "And because of this."

The moment she saw Maggie's name on the envelope, Tate blanched. When she read the short message, she turned even paler. "Oh, Lord," she whispered.

He took it back from her, pocketing it. "Now, let me ask you again, is there anything else I should know that might help me find this guy?"

With trembling hands, Tate picked up her glass and took a long swallow of tea. Finally she came to a decision, even though it wasn't the one she knew he wanted. Turning, she looked into his eyes. "If I honestly believed anything I know would bring that man to justice, I'd answer any and all of your questions. But, for now at least, I can't say any more."

Quickly she stood up, knowing she had to leave him before she gave in to the urge to confide everything, to let someone in, someone who might help her with this mess she'd made of her life. But she had to think of Josh. "I have to go in now. Thanks for coming by." Moving decisively, she closed the door behind her.

Nick heard the dead bolt slide home. Sighing, he rose, wondering what in hell he could do to get her to trust him. Because the man who wrote that note wasn't going to simply go away.

And he probably already knew Maggie had talked to the police.

Chapter 4

Nick studied the woman seated across the table from him as she dabbed at her eyes with a soggy tissue. It had been a week since Ronda Philips had reported being raped in the supermarket rest room. She wasn't a beauty, but she made the most of what she had to work with. Her sandy hair was cut short and sort of layered, her expressive brown eyes were her best feature and, although she was about twenty pounds overweight, her expensive black slacks outfit had probably been chosen to disguise that fact.

He'd asked her to come in to clear up a few questions and they'd been talking for about twenty minutes now. Nick's gut instinct told him Ronda was lying, but as yet, he hadn't been able to bring about a confession. He decided to try another tactic.

"You love your husband very much, don't you, Ronda?" he asked softly.

She looked up, thrown off balance. "Well, sure I do. What's that got to do with my...my being raped?"

"I understand he works long hours and that you're left alone a lot. Since your...incident, has he spent more time with you, making sure you're all right?"

Ronda brightened and even smiled. "Yes. It's wonderful, almost like when we were first married. Yesterday he even came home early and made dinner. Later, when I got upset remembering that awful man, Mark just held me in his arms for hours."

He kept his voice even, nonthreatening, not accusatory. "So then, you could say that your experience put your husband's attention back on you, where it belongs, right?"

She blinked several times, obviously uncertain how to answer. "I guess you could say that. I mean, it was awful and everything, but now, Mark scarcely wants me out of his sight." Almost as an afterthought, she added, "But I still hope you catch the man."

Nick decided to take a chance. "Actually we do have a suspect in custody who matches your description."

Startled, her eyes went wide. "You do? I can't believe...I mean, why would he hang around there? Surely he had to know I'd report him."

"We got lucky. Naturally, he says he didn't do it. He works at a gas station, a family man with two small children and a wife who's a waitress at Denny's. This will undoubtedly ruin his life. We'll need you to identify him."

Ronda's conscience kicked in. "You remember I told you that one of the lightbulbs in the rest room was burned out, so it was kind of dark. I didn't get a good look at his face. This man probably isn't the one." She worked the tissue between trembling fingers. "A family man, you say. They don't usually rape, do they?"

It was time for truth or consequences, Nick thought as he leaned closer to her. "It didn't happen quite the way you told us, did it, Ronda?"

"What do you mean?" she asked, her eyes downcast. "I

was raped, I tell you. The people at the hospital saw the cuts.''

He zeroed in with the final blow. "Ronda, our officers found a knife behind one of the toilet tanks." He reached for a manila envelope he'd placed on the floor when he'd come in. Opening it, he let the knife with the six-inch blade slide out onto the table. "Have you ever been fingerprinted, Ronda?"

Her hand was at her mouth stifling her sobs as tears poured down her pale face. She continued to stare at the knife.

"It's time to tell me what really happened, Ronda? Or do you want me to tell you what I feel happened?" When she didn't answer, he went on. "You've been feeling lonely because Mark works such long hours and he's tired when he is home. You had to cancel a trip you'd been looking forward to for weeks. So you thought up a plan to get his attention."

She was crying quietly now, her shoulders shaking.

"You went into the rest room, into a stall, and used this knife to knick yourself in several places, then jammed it between the wall and the tank. You tore your panties and even used something to bruise your cheek. You messed up your clothes and hair. We checked and the cleaning crew had been in that rest room earlier and left a stool behind. You stood on it and unscrewed one lightbulb. Then you left the room, screaming that someone had raped you." Forearms on the table, Nick leaned in. "Is that how it went down, Ronda?"

Eyes tightly closed, she sobbed. Nick rose and reached for a box of tissues, placed it in front of her. "I guarantee you you're going to feel a lot better once this whole thing is off your chest."

Hiccuping, she wiped her cheeks and eyes, blew her nose. "I didn't mean any harm. Please, let that poor man go back to his family. I...I just wanted Mark to...to remember why we got married. He doesn't want me to work, he's hired someone to clean the house and...and I've got nothing to do.

Day after day and late into the evening, I'm alone.'' The tears began again as she looked up. ''Am I going to get into trouble for this? I mean, be arrested.''

''Well, there is such a thing as falsely reporting a crime. And the supermarket isn't too happy about the bad publicity. But I think if we tell the manager the truth, he won't press charges.'' He slid a yellow pad and pen toward her. ''If you write out exactly what happened, I can try to persuade the lieutenant to let you go with a serious warning.''

''Will we have to tell my husband, too?'' she asked in a little-girl voice.

''I'm afraid so.''

''Oh, I'm so ashamed.'' Bowing her head, she picked up the pen.

''Just write it all down. I'll be back.'' Nick left, closing the door and stepping into the viewing room where Lou and Harris waited.

Lou clapped him on the back. ''Good work, partner.'' He shook his head. ''She had me fooled.''

''Nice job, Nick,'' the lieutenant said as he left the viewing room.

''You took a chance there, old buddy,'' Lou added, ''making up a suspect in custody.''

''Yeah, well, I had a feeling she was a decent person who didn't realize how she might wreck someone's life with that story.'' He looked through the glass at the woman painstakingly writing her confession. ''I feel sorry for her. Apparently she and her husband can't talk to each other. What kind of a marriage is that?''

''The kind about ninety percent of the population has,'' Lou said cynically. ''Men get caught up in the rat race of a job and women get involved in raising the kids. By the time he's made it and the kids are gone, they're two strangers sharing a house.''

Nick studied his partner who was thirty-seven, married ten

years with two young sons. "That doesn't describe your marriage, I hope."

Lou shrugged. "Sometimes. In case you haven't looked around, old buddy, not a lot of cops are happily married. This job drains a man. You wouldn't know, having escaped the noose so far. You're smart."

Yeah, he was smart, Nick thought, not to have married just because he was lonely. And he was lonely, unafraid to admit it to himself. Oh, his job kept him in contact with lots of people daily and his big family was always there for him with weekend gatherings. But when he went home at the end of the day to the mobile home he was living in on a wooded mountainside acreage while he slowly built his dream house, he was damn lonely many a night.

There was no one to share his small victories with or confide his problems to. No one person who waited each evening for only him to come home to her. He'd stood up in all four of his siblings' weddings and felt certain that one day he, too, would be waiting at the front of that long aisle for that special woman who would become his wife. He still believed it would happen one day. Nick was a patient man. And he'd make certain that he and his wife could talk to each other, to communicate.

Walking back to his desk and sitting down, a picture popped into his subconscious mind. She was a softly feminine woman with lovely auburn hair falling to her shoulders, mysterious green eyes that held secrets she would share only with him, and a mouth made for kissing. She was smiling, walking toward him, holding out her arms. She wanted him as much as he wanted her. He could see it on her beautiful face.

Then the picture began to fade and she disappeared, out of reach. Nick drew in a deep breath, wondering what in hell was wrong with him, daydreaming like a schoolboy.

Shuffling through the papers on his desk, he noticed a message from his sister, Louise, reminding him that their father's sixty-fifth birthday party was tonight at six at Handlebar Harry's. He hadn't forgotten, but this reminder gave him an idea. He'd been searching his mind trying to think of an excuse that Tate would accept to meet his family. This event was tailor-made.

Nick checked his watch and saw that it was only two, which meant that Tate should be at work. He dialed the number for Brennan's Book Emporium. When he asked for Tate Monroe, he was put on hold. It was a full minute before her voice came on the line, the sound of it giving him that little jolt as he envisioned her.

"Hi, there. You sound out of breath. Did I catch you at a bad time?" He hadn't identified himself on purpose, wondering if she'd recognize his voice.

Tate circled her desk in her tiny office at the back of the store and sat down, waiting for her pulse to settle. She hadn't heard from Nick for a week and hadn't thought of him more than a dozen times on any of those days. What did this man have that so many others who'd tried to get to her hadn't had? Why was it that the mere sound of his voice sent her emotions into a tailspin, despite her best efforts to put him out of her mind?

"Nick, how are you?" she finally managed to say. "I'm out of breath because I just carried a large box from the storage room to my office."

"Don't you have some muscular young man over there to haul those boxes for you?"

"I'm stronger than I look, so I don't ask."

That independent streak that he both admired and disliked about her.

"Is there something new in the case?" Why else would he call?

"No, not yet. We couldn't pick up any decent prints on the letter or the envelope."

"I rather thought that'd be the case." The man behind those threats was way too clever to get caught so obviously.

But the letter wasn't his real reason for calling. "How's Josh handling Little Miss and Mister?"

"Okay, most days. He's not crazy about the structured environment, everything planned out, the whole day run by the clock. But he's doing fine." Nick seemed to honestly like her son. Was Josh the reason for his call?

"I imagine he'd much rather stay home with Maggie."

"Yes, but her cast won't be off for several months yet, although the rest of her injuries have healed remarkably well. She's an amazing woman."

"That she is." His voice lowered, became more intimate. "How about you? How are you doing?"

His words warmed her like a caress. How could that be, a man she scarcely knew? This was dangerous, like walking in a minefield. "I'm fine. No more unexpected letters delivered. No more sightings of Mr. X, as we call him." Of course, he was checking on the case, wondering about the man in the ponytail. She was foolish to make more of it.

"That's good." He paused, searching for the right words. "My dad's sixty-fifth birthday is today and we're having a little get-together for him. I'd like you and Josh to go with me, if you don't have other plans."

Tate straightened in her chair. This couldn't be construed as anything but what it surely was. He was asking her out. Oh, he'd included her son, but nonetheless, it would be a date. And she hadn't had a date in eight years.

"Isn't it against the rules for a detective to keep company with someone who's part of a case he's investigating?"

"I've read the cop's manual twice and there are no rules against it." He leaned back, called up his most persuasive powers. "I've been wanting you to meet my family simply because they're really nice people. I've been told you don't go out much, so all the more reason you should now and then. I have a feeling Josh would fit in really well with my nieces and nephews. It's only one evening out of your life. What can it hurt?''

One evening in a social atmosphere, in front of his family, with a man whose very voice sent her heart into orbit. What could it hurt? Plenty. Still, despite the kids he'd met at the day camp, Josh had few opportunities to mingle with kids his own age.

''I don't know, Nick. I hate to leave Maggie in the evening since she's alone all day.''

''We'll take her, too. This place is a Western-style restaurant-bar, sawdust on the floor, steak and beans on the menu, a couple of guitars and a fiddle playing—good, clean fun. Maggie will love my mom.''

Tate was weakening and she knew it. ''Won't your family mind the intrusion of three strangers?''

''Are you kidding? There'll be some other friends of the family there as well. When the Bennetts get together, there's always a crowd. What time do you get off?''

He was assuming she was going. Well, why not? She wouldn't have gone out with him alone, but there was safety in numbers. ''I'm usually home by five-thirty.''

''Perfect. It's very casual, jeans and Western shirts, boots if you can handle 'em. It'll be fun. You'll see.''

Fun. When was the last time she'd had fun? She couldn't even remember. ''If you're sure it's no trouble...''

''None whatsoever. See you about six.'' Nick hung up before she changed her mind. Rising to go back to Ronda Philips, he realized he was wearing a satisfied smile.

In her office, Tate hung up the phone, surprised at how he'd convinced her so easily. But the evening would be fun for Maggie and Josh, she told herself. Reason enough to give in. She was going more to please them.

Frowning, Tate wondered when she'd begun to lie to herself.

* * *

The joint was jumping. Having lived all her life in Arizona, Tate knew there were all kinds of Western restaurant-bars all over the place. But not being a big fan of country music, and unable to afford to go out much, she'd never been to one.

That was why the first half hour at Handlebar Harry's was like atmosphere overload. The main area consisted of one large room, sawdust on the floor, groupings of wooden tables and chairs placed all around a spacious dance floor where three musicians on a raised platform kept the sound loud and hardy. Just left of the big front door was a polished mahogany bar that ran clear to the back. And behind that bar was Handlebar Harry himself, wearing a checkered shirt and white apron wrapped around his ample middle, his bald head shiny under the colored lights. He was also sporting the largest handlebar mustache Tate had ever seen.

Maggie seemed to feel right at home since her late husband had often taken her to similar places, but Josh's eyes were wide with excitement, trying to take it all in. Nick ushered them over to meet Harry first thing, then guided them over to several large round tables side by side where the Bennett clan was holding court at ringside. An assortment of children of various ages hopped down from their chairs and rushed over to meet "Uncle Nickie," making Tate aware of how popular the one single uncle was.

By the time Nick introduced the three of them to his two brothers and their wives, his two sisters and their husbands, his four nieces including six-month-old Mary Louise, and his three nephews, Tate's mind was spinning trying to remember names. When next he took her to the head of the table and presented her to his parents, Anthony and Roseanne, she noticed the love and pride in his introduction. She felt an unexpected surge of envy for these people who knew who they were and where they belonged.

Roseanne Bennett stood up to her five-two height and hugged Tate, surprising her until she realized that this woman was undoubtedly warm and friendly with everyone she met. Then Anthony, the man of the hour whose birthday they were celebrating, a big man with broad shoulders and only a slight paunch, took both her hands into his and gazed at her with the same gray eyes his youngest son owned, she felt a nervous moment.

Finally, as if pronouncing approval, Anthony smiled. "Welcome, Tate Monroe. We're glad you could come."

"Happy birthday, Mr. Bennett," Tate said, caught up in this generous family's warmth.

His arm around Josh's shoulders, Nick moved the boy forward. "Papa, this is Tate's son, Josh."

"What a handsome boy," Anthony said, shaking hands with the boy, man to man.

Nick eased Maggie forward and introduced her to his parents, pleased when his mother made room beside her place and sat the older woman next to her. In moments, they were chatting like old friends. Next, Nick settled Josh with two of his nephews who were both around his age, then leaned down to the oldest one. "Josh has a Pokémon collection that's awesome." Strolling away, he heard the boys questioning Josh about which cards he had.

They found two empty chairs alongside Nick's youngest sister, Louise, whose husband, Al, had his baby daughter on his knee while her mother fed her applesauce. Sitting down, Tate's eyes were drawn to the six-month-old with the dark curls and the huge blue eyes. "She's beautiful," she said, intrigued by the little mouth that kept opening for another spoonful. It had been so long since she'd fed baby food to Josh.

"You're beautiful," Louise said, sounding sincere as she took a moment to look at Nick's date. "How long have you known Nickie?"

"About a month," Tate answered, her eyes still on the baby.

"Hey, Louise," Nick said, placing his arm along the back of Tate's chair and leaning forward, "I'm the only one allowed to interrogate, remember?" He stage-whispered an aside to Tate. "Louise is my nosy sister. She fancies herself a writer so she pesters everyone with endless questions."

Tate recognized the affection in his voice. "One of my closest friends married a writer last year," she said to Louise. "Have you heard of Devin Gray?"

Louise's brows shot up. "Oh, sure. He writes Western mysteries. I've read him. He's good."

"What sort of writing do you do?"

"I've been working on this family saga for about three years, in my spare time. Since the baby arrived, I can't seem to find much spare time." She crammed more food into her daughter. "What do you do?"

"I manage a bookstore, Brennan's."

"How about those Diamondbacks, Nick?" Al, Louise's husband spoke across the two women, asking about the Arizona baseball club.

Just then, the waiter arrived to take their orders, preventing more conversation for the moment. Nick pointed out some especially good items to Tate. Checking them out, she noticed that each one was larger than the last.

"This seems like an awful lot of food," she told him.

"Try the petite steak, maybe," he suggested.

She did and it was so tender she could cut it with a fork. Seated alongside Nick, she let the conversation at the table swirl around her as the close-knit family kidded one another, argued about the home team's chances and laughed a lot. She hadn't seen so much laughter and genuine feelings of enjoyment at just being together in…well, maybe never.

Glancing over her shoulder, she saw, much to her surprise, that her son had caught the contagious laughter while hanging on to a hamburger so big he had to hold it with two hands. Josh seemed relaxed and happy.

This is what it would have been like, Tate thought. If she'd have chosen his father with more care, if either of them had come from the kind of loving family that embraced each member with unconditional acceptance. She sighed, pushing the guilt back where it belonged. No one could change the past, but they could learn from it and try not to mess up the future.

Tate glanced over to where Maggie and Roseanne Bennett had their heads together. What was it that Nick's mother was showing Maggie, something that looked like a pillow slip?

"Mom crochets," Nick explained, following her gaze. "She rarely goes anywhere without her sewing bag. All of my pillowcases have crochet work on them. Very macho."

Tate laughed. "I'll bet you look really cute snuggled down into a pink pillow with crocheted flowers along its edges." Suddenly realizing how quickly the picture of him in bed formed in her mind, she felt heat move into her face. What must he think of such a bold remark? "I mean...I didn't..."

Nick took her hand, smiling at her unease. "I know what you meant." He noticed that she'd eaten barely half her dinner. "Are you glad you came?"

"Josh and Maggie are having a good time, and I'm glad." She felt his fingers toying with hers, seemingly unwilling to let go.

"No, I mean you. Are *you* glad you came with me?" He captured her eyes with his intense gaze, wouldn't let her look away.

The warmth of his hand entwined with hers, the heat of his gaze, had her heart suddenly pounding and her voice thickening. "Yes," she answered so softly he had to lean closer to hear. "Thank you for asking us."

She was still thinking in the plural, Nick realized, but it was a start. The waiters were busily clearing the huge platterlike plates and serving more iced tea or pouring coffee. The guitars were once more tuning up after a break and the fiddle was lively. Folks were streaming onto the dance floor in twos and fours.

"Do you like swing dancing?" Nick asked her.

Tate couldn't remember the last time she'd danced to anything. Had to be at least ten years ago. "I'm not much of a dancer."

"Come on, there's nothing to it." He rose, still holding her hand, edging her out onto the floor.

"No, really, I don't know how." Slightly panicky, she watched as the dancers formed groupings of four and eight.

She'd taken his advice and dressed casually, a white shirt tucked into blue jeans and leather flats on her feet. Nick wished she wouldn't always tie back her hair, but he didn't feel comfortable mentioning that. Instead he stood with her as the dance began, watching. He saw that she was studying them closely, her attention riveted, so he slipped an arm around her waist and eased her closer to his side. Pleased that she didn't resist, he drew in a deep breath, saturating his senses with the scent of her, by now as familiar as anything he'd ever smelled.

Something was happening here, Nick knew, and wondered if Tate felt it, too.

Swing dancing really didn't look too difficult, Tate realized. Maybe she could...

"Come on, young lady," a deep voice alongside her said. "Let's show 'em how it's done," Anthony Bennett said, taking Tate's hand.

She sent an anxious look in Nick's direction, but he just grinned at her as he watched his father guide her onto the floor. Standing on the sidelines, he watched as Tate picked up the rhythm quickly, finally taking her eyes off her feet and giving his dad a shaky smile. God, she was beautiful.

He saw her laugh at something Papa said and the laughter made those gorgeous green eyes crinkle at the corners.

Behind him, his brother Sam spoke softly. "Nickie, you've been holding out on us."

His eyes still on Tate, Nick smiled. "Wouldn't you want to keep her a secret?"

Sam moved alongside his brother. "Her boy's a good kid. Where's the father?"

"Out of the picture," Nick answered, quoting what both Tate and Maggie had told him. If only he believed them.

The number ended and the dancers cheered while those at the tables applauded their approval.

Sam and Nick watched their father bow in courtly fashion to Tate, then make his way back to his own table. Nick saw Tate turn, her eyes homing in on him as the musicians began a slow number. He felt his brother's hand on his shoulder squeeze hard.

"Don't let this one get away, little brother," Sam said before walking away.

Nick heard Sam peripherally, but he had eyes only for Tate. She walked toward him unhurriedly, weaving her way through the chatting dancers who were pairing off, her gaze never wavering. As she came up to him, he held out his arms and she came into them as naturally as if she'd been doing it all her life.

A girl singer appeared at the microphone, something of a Patsy Cline lookalike, and began one of Patsy's heartbreaking ballads about falling to pieces.

He held her loosely, his right hand at her back as her left rested on his shoulder while their eyes stayed locked together. He was feeling too much to smile, feelings he'd been struggling with since meeting her, wondering if those feelings were reflected on his face. She, too, gazed at him seriously, as if trying to see into his mind, his heart. She made him want, she made him tremble, she made him dream.

Nick knew if he spoke his thoughts aloud, his family would think him crazy and Tate would turn tail and run. But he was as sure as he'd ever been about anything. He was in love with Tate Monroe. Hadn't he always believed he'd know when the right one came along? This was it, the real thing. She's the one, his heart whispered to him. Don't let her go.

Surely everyone in this huge room could hear the pounding of her heart, Tate thought. She hadn't been able to refuse his father, not on his birthday in front of his entire family. So she'd danced and found she was having a good time. Funny how, when you don't get out much and laugh hardly ever, you almost forget what it's like. But Anthony Bennett was a real gentleman, as gallant as his son, and a darn good dancer. He'd had her swirling and turning like a pro in no time.

But when he'd let her go, she'd swung around and found Nick staring at her with such a look of longing that she'd been drawn to him like a magnet. She didn't even question the fact that she wanted his arms around her, his warm breath on her face, his eyes telling her what his lips couldn't say. Tate shifted fractionally closer and felt his response as his arms tightened and his big hand caressed her back through the soft cotton of her blouse.

Nick was so different from the men she'd known. They'd all taken one look at her lush figure and ogled her embarrassingly, finding lame excuses to come into physical contact with her, scarcely waiting until they drove her home from a date to begin kissing and fondling. Tate shuddered at the memories, the attention she'd never sought that had caused her to reject the male of the species. Not one of them had looked behind the facade of her face and figure to the woman beneath, the real person inside the package. Not even the one man she'd trusted with her heart.

But not Nick. The most he'd done was touch her hand or slip his arm around her waist as he walked with her. He hadn't even asked her to dance; she'd more or less invited him by walking into his arms. Even now, he didn't hold her tightly, but let her make the choice of moving closer. Somehow he instinctively knew that overt moves would turn her off, but tenderness would win her.

A man, a cop yet, who could be so thoughtful, so sensitive. Would wonders never cease?

If this was wrong, if this was a mistake, if soon she'd awaken from this dream into harsh reality, so be it. For now, she was in the arms of a man who moved her more powerfully than any before him, feeling a sensual pull she'd all but forgotten, wishing this song could go on and on and on.

Nick turned her hand and pressed her fingers to his heart, placing his own hand atop hers, letting her feel the way his heart was pounding, pounding for her. His head was spinning with the sweet scent of her, yet no one watching could tell from his serious face. Tate could tell, though. He was certain she knew what he was feeling. Easing her closer, he felt her rise on tiptoe to press her cheek to his, her body swaying with his as he bent his head. There was no need for words, even if he could think of the right ones.

Don't let this one get away, Sam had advised him. Don't worry, Sam, Nick thought, touching his lips to the silk of her hair. This one's mine.

Returning from the rest room, Maggie paused before sitting back down, her eyes settling on Tate and Nick dancing. His mother was watching them, too, she noticed. Didn't they make a fine couple? Maggie couldn't help thinking. They surely danced like two people in love. It warmed her heart to see Tate finally at long last warm up to a man. And Nick Bennett was a fine man from a lovely family. If only this would work out, Maggie thought prayerfully. And if only the madman stalking them would be caught and put away.

Careful of her cast, she sat down next to Roseanne Bennett who spoke to her softly.

"She's certainly a lovely woman," Roseanne commented, wondering why her Nickie hadn't mentioned Tate before suddenly showing up with her.

"Yes, she is, both outside and inside," Maggie told her reassuringly. She couldn't blame Nick's mother for being curious. "She hasn't a mean bone in her body."

Roseanne pulled her gaze from the young people and looked at Maggie. "I'm glad to hear that. They haven't known each other very long, though, have they?"

Maggie shook her head. "Sometimes it doesn't take long."

Roseanne chuckled, then smiled. "I know. I married Anthony after knowing him two weeks. We ran away together because I was only seventeen. I thought my father was going to throttle the both of us when we finally went back." She gazed fondly at her husband of forty-three years as he swayed on the sidelines with his six-month-old granddaughter. "I'd do it again in a heartbeat."

"When it's right, it's right," Maggie said, remembering her Elroy and all their happy years together.

Roseanne's gaze slid to Josh who was playing some kind of card game with two of her grandsons at the next table. "Does he see his father much?"

"Never. That man was Tate's one and only mistake."

Roseanne nodded. "We all make a few."

The song ended to applause and a few whistles. On the dance floor, Tate and Nick stopped, eased slightly apart, each studying the other. He was the first to break the silence.

"I thought you said you couldn't dance."

"You can do almost anything if you have the right partner," she said, knowing it was true in more important things than dancing. Turning, her gaze searched the room for her son and found Josh involved with the two boys he'd eaten with. "Do you have any idea how lucky you are to have such a family?" she asked as they strolled back to the table.

"Yeah, I do." He stopped her at the edge of the dance floor. "I'm who I am because of them."

"I believe you are. Strong, honest, courageous." And sexy. Oh, Lord, she had to get out of there before her face gave her away. "I'd better get Josh home. It's getting late and I have to get him up early for that day camp before I go to work."

He stopped her from walking away with a hand on her arm. "Tate, I…"

She swung back, the mood changed. "Please, Nick. Don't let's say anything more right now."

A smart man knows when to stay, when to fold. "All right. You get Josh and I'll get Maggie."

It took another twenty minutes for the four of them to make the rounds and say goodbye to everyone. Nick's mother hugged him a long moment. "She's very beautiful, Nickie. Be careful, son."

He kissed her cheek. "I love you, Mama."

On the way to the car, Josh was more talkative than ever. "Look, Nick," he said, holding up a Pokémon card. "Charizard. It's a real special one I've been wanting. It's one of the best and Jimmy gave it to me."

"Hey, that's great." Nick unlocked the doors.

"Just gave it to you?" Tate asked as she settled Maggie into the front passenger seat where she'd be more comfortable. "Even though you had nothing to trade him?" She knew a little how the game worked.

"Yeah, he had a double." Josh buckled himself into the back seat. "Jimmy and Anthony asked if maybe I can go over to their house sometime with my collection. Can we, Mom?"

"We'll see," Tate said, climbing in beside her son, giving the standard stall answer.

Nick started the car, his eyes in the rearview mirror capturing Tate's. "I think that could be easily arranged." He shifted into gear and wound his way out of the crowded parking lot.

But Tate wasn't so sure. If she allowed Josh to get close to Nick's relatives, he'd inevitably be hurt when Nick finished their case and stopped coming around. Studying the back of his dark head, the black hair her fingers even now itched to touch, she wondered what he was feeling. Was he beginning to genuinely care or was he just a smart man who was using a clever tactic to get her into bed, then walk away?

If only she could trust him, but she was afraid to.

Maggie was dozing and Josh sound asleep when Nick pulled up in front of their home. "Why don't you help Maggie and I'll carry Josh to his bed?" he suggested.

Surprised, Tate agreed, awakening the older woman and helping her inside, telling Nick that Josh's room was the first one at the top of the stairs. She got Maggie settled and noticed that Nick still hadn't come down. She went up and stopped at the doorway to her son's room.

He'd turned down the bed, undressed the limp sleeping boy and managed to put on his pajama bottoms, leaving on his T-shirt so he wouldn't wake him by yanking it over his head. Tate watched as he settled Josh's head on the pillow and arranged the sheet and light blanket over him. Unaware she was there, he straightened and stood for a moment, looking down at the boy. Then he bent and stroked his hair before drawing the drapes and adjusting the night-light. Walking to the door, he spotted her and smiled.

"It seems you've done duty as a sitter a time or two," she commented as they went downstairs.

"Oh, yeah. The single uncle gets recruited often." At the door, he turned to her.

"You don't sound as if you mind."

"I don't. I love kids. Josh is great." He paused, wanting

nothing on earth more than to reach out, to pull her close, to kiss her. But instead, he gave her a tight smile. ''I hope you had a good time.''

''I did. We all did. Thank you, Nick.'' She waited, leaving the ball in his court.

Nick reached up and trailed the backs of his fingers along her cheek and her satin throat, feeling her pulse leap, noticing her eyes darken as they stayed fixed on his. ''Good night, Tate.'' He turned and went through the door, pulling it closed behind him. She'd probably never know that walking away from her just then was one of the hardest things he'd ever done.

Struggling with opposite emotions of relief and disappointment that he hadn't kissed her, Tate slowly slid the dead bolt home. Yes, Nick Bennett was certainly different.

Would she have stopped him if he'd have tried to kiss her? Not in this lifetime, she thought as she made her way upstairs. How had he managed to slip past all her firm resolutions?

Chapter 5

Nick leaned back in his desk chair and scrubbed his face with one hand, holding the phone in his other. "Okay, Mama, why don't you quit stalling and tell me what's on your mind?" As if he didn't know. It was the Tuesday after his father's Friday night birthday bash and his mother had called with some excuse or another every single day.

"What do you mean? I can't call my son just to say hello?"

"Come on. Fess up. You'll feel better. What do you want me to do or where do you want me to go or, God forbid, who have you invited over for me to meet?" He tried putting a smile in his voice, but this game was wearing thin. He wondered if Roseanne ever stopped to think that he was nearly thirty-four.

"I don't pick your dates. But, speaking of that, have you seen Tate Monroe since the party?"

There it was, at last. "No. Should I have?"

"You tell me, Nickie."

He was having trouble hiding his exasperation. "All right, I'll tell you. Tate is involved in a case I'm working on, as I mentioned on Friday. Maggie's home was invaded and Tate and her son live with Maggie. They don't have much family, any of them, so I invited them to Dad's party because I thought they'd enjoy being with a nice bunch of people like my family. Was I wrong to do that?"

"No, of course not. They were all three very nice. Papa liked her. He danced with her, even. But not like you danced with her. I had three friends mention to me that dance."

Nick's parents had both been born in Arizona, but to immigrant parents straight from Italy, which left them with a bit of an accent that seemed odd for first-generation Americans. So the busybodies had been calling his mother about him dancing with a woman they'd never seen before. Interesting.

"Mama, there was nothing wrong with that dance." Although he'd relived it himself more than once. "Your friends are just nosy and maybe should mind their own business, eh?"

"They're interested, that's all, Nickie. I know, your life is your own. I don't want to meddle."

But she did, anyhow, he thought. What in hell did she want from him? "I don't know what else to tell you. Tate and I are just friends, okay?"

"Okay, Nickie. Except, watching you dance, I thought you were more than just friends."

He decided to test her. "Would that be a problem for you, if we became more than just friends?"

"Oh, well, I don't know. She's lovely, that's for sure. And Josh is a nice boy. But, well, you know, Nickie. She's divorced and Papa and me, we always wanted a big church wedding for you."

Never mind what he might want. He reined in his temper, certain his mother meant well. All right, let's see how much she can handle. "Actually she's not divorced, Mama. She never married Josh's father."

"Ohhhhh."

Who said one word couldn't speak volumes? Nick thought. "Mama, I think it's a little premature to be thinking along these lines. How about we table this discussion for now? If and when things get more serious, I'll be sure to update you. Okay?"

Clearly caught off guard, his mother made some sort of noncommittal sound.

Now he was getting annoyed. "Look, I..." Someone across the bullpen was signaling to him to pick up Line Two. "I've got to go, Mama. I'll talk with you later. I love you." He clicked off, feeling a momentary guilt twinge, then smiled when he heard who was on the other line. "Hey, Eddie, have you got what I ordered?"

"Sure do," Eddie Farantino said. "Just got your message. Come by anytime and I'll have everything ready."

"Great. Thanks." He disconnected, checked his watch, then dialed a number he'd already memorized. When Maggie answered, he asked how she was feeling.

"I'm good, Nick. Tate's not home yet. She had to work late, some sort of children's storytime she's started at the bookstore."

"Maybe I'll drop by Brennan's and check it out. I have a surprise for Josh that I want to run by her."

"A surprise? How nice of you, Nick. I won't tell him."

"Is he there with you?"

"Yes. I'm much better now and he really didn't like that day camp. He minds me...he's no problem."

"Great. Maybe I'll see you later."

Hanging up, Maggie smiled. That boy wasn't about to give up on a difficult project. And Tate was certainly that. She'd noticed that, since the birthday party, Tate had been quieter evenings, more thoughtful. And Maggie would bet she knew exactly who Tate's thoughts centered around as she sat staring out the window, an unread open book in her lap.

Scooting off the couch, Maggie found herself looking forward to Nick's visit.

Dave Anderson was behind the circular Information Desk when Nick walked into Brennan's, and the assistant manager spotted him immediately. Walking over, Nick noticed that although it was past six in the evening—the hour most people were home thinking about dinner—the store was even more crowded than during his last visit. Dave pushed his horn-rimmed glasses back up his nose and smiled at Nick.

"Hello, Detective. Are you looking for Tate?"

"Matter of fact, I am."

"She's over there," Dave told him, pointing to a tiered and carpeted corner at the back of the large room. "She recently began a story hour where she reads to preschoolers. As you can see from the crowd, it's very popular."

Nick gazed past half a dozen tables of books featuring specialty reads and spotted Tate sitting on the top step. On either side of her were two children under five, their little faces turned toward her, listening hard. On the lower step and along the apron of the storybook area were at least a dozen more preschoolers. Several parents stood around in a semicircle while others hung back, browsing through books along the wall shelves.

"Thanks, Dave," Nick said, his eyes on Tate as he slowly made his way over to where she held the attention of so many little ones. She was wearing the standard Brennan's uniform of black linen slacks and white blouse with the store's emblem on the pocket. But the thing he noticed most was that her hair was loose, hanging straight and shiny to just past her shoulders. A shaft of sunlight through a mosaic window in the rear wall shone down, bringing out the red highlights in her hair and creating a visual that had Nick wishing he had a camera.

He stood just outside the adult circle, watching and listening. The story was about a gopher named Gomer who didn't like going down gopher holes, was afraid of the dark and wanted to live in the sunshine, confusing all the other little gophers. The lightly veiled message was about others making you conform and how it's all right to be different. Nick wasn't sure the young children understood, but when Tate finished and began asking questions about the story they'd just heard, he was surprised at how many had gotten the gist of it. A few had gone on to embellish the author's version.

He'd known she liked kids by how much she obviously loved her son. But to see her like this, relaxed, unaware he was watching, playing to the most natural audience in the world, he saw how much in her element she was. Tate Monroe should have a passel of kids of her own and a loving husband to go with the package.

Swallowing hard, Nick wondered if he belonged in that picture, if she'd even want him to be or want any man if what Maggie hinted at about her past life was true.

A little redheaded girl who looked to be about four, seated close alongside Tate, had launched into a story of her own and Tate listened seriously, letting her know that what she had to say was important. When the little boy on the other side of her began to squirm impatiently, Tate took him onto her lap and involved him in the story without skipping a beat. When the little girl finished, Tate stood and announced the end of Storybook Hour for this week, thanking them all for coming and informing the parents where they could find the book about Gomer the Gopher. Several children rushed up to her, offering hugs, in a spontaneous gesture of affection.

Smiling, she stroked a boy's curly hair and tied a toddler's shoe as the parents moved to collect their little ones. The parents walked away, most with books in their hands, and headed for the cashier. Brennan's had a little gold mine here, Nick thought as he stepped closer.

Tate straightened from picking up the pile of books and turned before she became aware of Nick Bennett quietly watching her. ''I didn't know you liked to be read to,'' she said with just a hint of nerves. Would she always have that quick tug, that skipped heartbeat when she first saw him?

''You're terrific with those kids.''

''I enjoy them.'' Hugging the books to her chest, she checked him out. He was wearing a white polo shirt over black chinos with gray jogging shoes. No jacket, no gun holster. ''You're out of uniform, Detective. What will you do if you spot one of the bad guys in black hats?''

He didn't think he needed to tell her that he had a .38 in an ankle holster. ''I'm off duty. Let someone else round up the bad guys tonight.''

She began walking toward the children's section and he fell in step with her, his hands in his pockets. ''And here I thought you were ever vigilant, never dropping your guard.''

She didn't seem as tense as usual around him, but rather more relaxed. ''Maybe you don't know me as well as you think you do,'' he commented, his voice teasing.

Tate stopped between two high bookcases, meeting his eyes, looking deep. ''I don't think I know you very well at all.''

''Would you like to get to know me better?'' A leading question and maybe he shouldn't have asked it, Nick thought. What if she said no?

She turned, replacing the books on the shelves. ''There are those who say we never really know another person.''

''Do you believe that?''

Tate shrugged. ''I believe that, more often than not, we see someone as we wish they were, blinded to who they really are, and then learn too late that we should have looked deeper.''

"And sometimes what you see is what you get." He'd moved close to her so that when she turned again, she was so near that she had to look up to see into his eyes. "Case in point, me. I am exactly as I seem, a thirty-three-year-old guy from a good if somewhat overwhelming family, an ordinary man with no hidden agendas." He kept his gaze fastened to hers, inviting her to probe his depths and see for herself.

Her voice was soft, low, almost intimate. "That's too simplistic, Nick. And when I think of you, the word ordinary never comes to mind."

"Do you think of me, Tate?"

She'd walked right into that one. Tate shoved the last book in place. "Sure. I wonder if you're making progress on Maggie's intruder. That is why you're here, isn't it?"

"Sort of. I have a surprise for Josh. When are you finished here?"

"I'm through now. Storybook Hour is something I do on my own after hours. What's the surprise?"

"I'm not telling. Go check out or whatever it is you have to do and let's go pick up Josh."

Still, she hesitated. "Usually, it's better if you run things by the mother before surprising the boy."

"You are the most distrustful person I've ever met. I promise you, this surprise won't hurt Josh or you. And if you truly object with good reason, we can forget it."

"All right. Give me five minutes and I'll meet you in the parking lot."

It seemed as if he'd won Round One, barely.

"But Nick, where are we going?" Josh asked for at least the third time since he'd climbed into the back seat of Nick's car. "How long before we get there?"

"It's not too far from here." Remembering how impatient boys of seven could be, he smiled at Josh's unbridled enthusiasm. "Why don't you count all the red cars you see? Helps to pass the time."

In the passenger seat, Tate thought not for the first time how patient the man was with Josh. When kids began to whine and wheedle, it was hard to be tolerant. But then, Nick had all those nephews and nieces. Or was he just trying to impress her? Which led to the question, why was he trying to impress her?

He certainly knew how to get to her, she had to admit. First, she'd gone along to his father's birthday somewhat impulsively, thinking Maggie and Josh deserved a night out, which they seldom had. And now, dangling a surprise for her son in front of her, she could scarcely say no. Oh, yes, the man knew how to get a woman to agree to things.

Tate stole a sideways glance at him, wondering why at his age he hadn't married, or at the very least, had someone steady in his life. Maybe he had, but just hadn't mentioned her. No, not that. She had a feeling that truth was a way of life for this man and he wouldn't have danced with her the way he had last Friday if he was involved. That dance that had appeared nearly nightly in her restless dreams.

He was certainly attractive. Had his dangerous job scared off women who might have been interested? That was a very real possibility. She remembered the man on the ledge, the wild fear in his eyes as he'd leaped. How could an officer face that sort of thing every day and not be affected? Yet Nick seemed to take the darker aspects of his work in stride.

Eddie Farantino was in his front yard mowing his lawn when Nick pulled up in front of the beige stucco house. He honked twice and Eddie waved.

"This is just a house, Nick," Josh commented, disappointed that they hadn't gone to some fun event like the circus, which he'd heard was in town.

"Oh, but it's a special house," Nick told him, getting out. He noticed that Tate seemed hesitant, also. He led both of them up the front walk. "Eddie, meet my friends, Josh and Tate."

"Hi, there. Come on inside." Tall and reed thin, Eddie introduced them to his wife, Lola, who was his exact opposite, quite short and considerably overweight. Tate couldn't help thinking of Jack Spratt and his wife, and found herself smiling at the private joke.

The minute Josh heard the yipping and yapping, he was no longer interested in the adults' chitchat. He looked around, searching for the source of the noise, catching Eddie's attention.

"You want to meet my dog?" he asked Josh, and just that fast opened the door to the kitchen.

A black-and-white curly-haired terrier mix came barreling through, so excited his whole body was shaking. He made straight for Josh, who went down on his knees to him as the dog began licking his face. The boy giggled and laughed, rubbing the small furry body. Everyone else disappeared for Josh as he played with the little terrier.

"I'd say they hit it off," Lola remarked, beaming.

"He's full grown, has all his shots, been neutered and he won't get any bigger than he is right now," Eddie explained, speaking to Tate. "Nick mentioned you could use a watchdog. This little guy's not what you'd call a fierce watchdog, but he makes a lot of noise if a stranger comes around."

Nick spoke to Tate as she watched her son laughing more than she'd seen in way too long. "I figured a small dog was better, so he won't knock Maggie or Josh off balance. And if someone noses around at night, his yapping will wake you."

Eddie chimed in. "I raise dogs so I know this pup's okay. I heard your son has asthma, but terriers don't shed. There's still the dander that could bother him, but it would be minor compared to the pleasure of having his own dog."

Tate had another concern. "How much do these dogs cost?"

Eddie shook his head. "All taken care of."

Tate looked up at Nick, who didn't flinch. "It's for Josh," he said quietly, then stooped down and reached a hand to pet the wiggling dog. "He's really soft, isn't he, Josh?"

"Yeah, he's great." He looked up at his mother with pleading eyes, but he didn't say any more.

He didn't have to. She could hardly deny him a pet when he hardly ever asked for anything, Tate thought. She'd settle up his cost with Nick later. "Then I guess it's unanimous."

"Terrific." Eddie stepped into the kitchen for a moment, then returned with two plastic bowls, a bag of dog food and a ratty piece of blanket. "These are his. He teethed on this blanket and now sometimes sleeps with it."

Josh had had a blanket that he'd dragged around for his first five years until Tate finally convinced him to put it away in the closet. However, she noticed that when he got upset, he took down his old blanket and slept with it. Why should the dog be different?

Bending down to his level, she ran a hand along his soft coat. "You're sure frisky."

"Do you think Maggie will mind?" Nick asked.

"No, she loves animals."

"What are you going to name him, Josh?" Lola wanted to know.

"Ralph," the boy said immediately.

"Ralph?" Tate looked at Nick who also was fighting a grin. "Where did you get that name?"

"I just like it," Josh insisted. "I always wanted a dog named Ralph."

"All right then, Ralph it is," Nick said, rising. He shook hands with Eddie. "Thanks a lot."

"Hey, no problem."

Outside, Nick settled Josh and Ralph in the back seat before getting behind the wheel. As they drove, Josh chattered away to the dog, soothing him when a turn had Ralph nearly toppling off the seat, telling him about his room and Maggie.

Listening, Tate felt her emotions twist. Such a simple thing, a dog, and look at the joy it gave her son. They'd moved around so much that she'd always felt a pet would be just one more thing to lug around, then uproot. Josh's asthma wasn't really bad, but she'd watch him to make sure the dog didn't cause him breathing problems. Sometimes, small risks were worth the pleasure a dog gave a small boy.

Because of the mistake his mother had made.

She glanced over at Nick and saw he was smiling at Ralph's back seat antics and Josh's giggles. "Thank you," she said softly.

He shifted his gaze to her, found those green eyes huge and glistening with unshed tears. Reaching over, he touched her hand briefly, then dragged his attention back to the traffic.

Seeing that her son was preoccupied with Ralph, Tate decided to ask a question that had been bothering her. "Why are you doing all this?"

Nick shrugged nonchalantly. "Because I want to." He gestured with his head toward the back seat. "Isn't it worth it to see how happy he is?"

"Look, Mom," Josh called out.

Turning, Tate saw that Ralph had worn himself out and was lying with his head in Josh's lap, dozing. Josh looked happy, so happy it choked her up. "I think he likes you," she said softly.

"Nick," Josh said, "thank you. Thank you so much."

Nick looked at the boy in the rearview mirror. "You're very welcome." As a watchdog, Ralph might fall a bit short, but as a pal to Josh, he was a big hit.

Why, then, was Tate looking at him with puzzlement in her eyes. "What?" he asked.

"I'm trying to figure you out."

"I told you, with some people, what you see is what you get. There is no deep, mysterious, hidden agenda here. I like Josh and I like his mother. Can you handle that?"

Could she? Tate wasn't altogether sure. Since this highly unusual man had come into their lives, she'd had to shift her thinking. However, the past had taught her to be cautious. She wanted desperately to believe Nick Bennett was exactly as he seemed, but she just couldn't. Not yet. He'd bear watching.

"We used to have one of these old gliders in our backyard years ago," Nick commented as he gently rocked himself and Maggie in the twilight of evening. "I wonder whatever happened to it."

"It's a shame, but I don't think they make them anymore," Maggie said. "It's such a fast-paced world that few people take time to just sit and swing or rock. A few years ago, I wanted to buy a rocking chair for my bedroom. You know, so I could sit and rock while I watch TV. I went to six stores and only found one, this padded thing with huge armrests. I wanted a simple wooden rocker, maple or the like, but apparently they're not easy to find."

They listened to a cricket's serenade for a while and rocked in companionable silence. A nearly full moon illuminated the crimson bougainvillea climbing along Maggie's tan stucco fence, the baby palm tree swaying in a gentle breeze. The unmistakable scent of jasmine perfumed the warm night air.

"Where do you live, Nick?" Maggie asked.

"I have a large wooded lot out Oracle Highway toward the Catalina Mountains where I'm building my house. Right now, I live in a mobile home on the lot until it's finished. Trouble is, it's slow going since I don't have all that much time to put into it." His dream house, the one he'd been working on for over a year. Slowly it was taking shape.

"I guess you could be there right now working, if you had a mind to," Maggie guessed shrewdly.

Caught, Nick thought, thinking that Maggie was still sharp as a tack. "You're right. Ask any red-blooded guy if he'd rather be hammering away or spend time with Tate and I know what his answer will be." He saw her smile. "You're not upset about the dog?"

"Ralph? Goodness, no. That boy needs to focus on something and the little terrier's perfect. I'm just grateful he's housebroken."

Nick heard the back screen door slam shut and saw Tate come outside. She'd put Josh to bed and changed into tan slacks and a loose black top. Her hair brushed her shoulders as she walked barefoot toward them, causing his hands to ache with the desire to touch. "Josh settled in?"

"Boy and dog both curled up and asleep. Josh was still smiling." Hands on her hips, Tate gazed up at the orange moon. "Isn't that what we call a harvest moon? What's it doing here in the middle of June?"

Slowly Maggie pushed to her feet. "We have such topsy-turvy weather in Arizona with its long growing season that even the moon's confused. If you two will excuse me, I think I'll turn in." She turned to Nick, squeezed his shoulder. "You did a really nice thing today for that boy." Then she gave Tate a hug and went into the house.

Nick patted the glider's seat. "Come join me?"

She'd half thought he'd be gone by the time she settled Josh, but here he was, looking as outrageously appealing in moonlight as he did in bright sunshine. She sat down, careful not to get too close. "Tell me, Nick, do you do this much for every case you work on?" Tate knew she'd asked him that before, but his answer had been evasive and unsatisfactory. She wanted to know the real reason, to have him state it out loud.

Were they back to this subject again? "Not really." He stretched one arm along the swing back.

"Why us, then?"

"Don't you know?"

She stiffened. "Suppose you tell me."

Nick frowned, his fingers lightly touching the ends of her hair. "Why can't you simply accept that I happen to like the three of you and let it go at that?"

"With absolutely no strings attached? I find that hard to believe. No one's that altruistic."

"If you mean what do I get out of all this, there are benefits. I think Maggie's a terrific, gutsy lady with a good sense of humor despite a not-so-happy life. Josh is a great kid who could use a little male attention and…"

"And you want to be the one to give it to him, is that it?"

"Is there something wrong with that?"

Suddenly she looked at him full face, needing to see his first, his gut reaction. "There is if you're trying to get to me through my son." She saw the flash of anger in his eyes that he quickly tamped down.

"Damn, but you have a low opinion of people, men particularly."

"With good reason."

"Yeah, I heard. Men have been trying to get you into bed since your teens. Is it so impossible for you to believe that there are men whose first thought when they meet an attractive woman *isn't* just how quickly they can seduce her?"

Tate leaned back, crossing her arms over her chest. "Let me tell you a little story. When I was sixteen and in high school, I had a best friend, Callie Hughes. We did everything together, went everywhere together, had sleepovers. Then one day, this new guy in town registered as a senior in our school. His name was Randy Owens. I was out sick with the flu for a week, but Callie met him and suddenly, they were going out together. She called to tell me she'd fallen madly in love, which girls at sixteen are prone to do.''

"So I've heard." He'd thought she would go into her relationship with Josh's father, but she had something else on her mind.

"Anyhow, I went back to school and met Callie and Randy in the hallway, their arms around each other. Callie was gushing, but Randy had a funny look on his face. A look I'd seen before. Late that same afternoon, Randy *accidentally* bumped into me, or so he said. And he asked me out. I turned him down, telling him that since I could see how much he meant to Callie, I couldn't do that. But he wouldn't give up, kept following me around, showing up at my house, at my locker. Naturally, Callie found out."

"I'll bet I can guess what happened."

"Probably. She was furious, saying I'd used my looks to lure Randy away from her, that I was deceitful and a whole lot more. The bottom line was she wanted nothing more to do with me, ever. I was crushed, because we'd been so close for years, and I'd done everything possible to get Randy to leave me alone and go back to her. Well, he did go back to her and they went together awhile, but then he dropped her. Callie still wouldn't speak to me, but Randy came around and asked me out again, now that he was free. I told him to take a hike. He surely wasn't worth the breakup of an old and dear friendship."

"And the moral of this story is…?"

"That I learned a hard lesson. No matter how close you are to a friend, they can turn on you in a heartbeat, believing not what they know about you, but what they perceive happened. And that men are terribly fickle and unconcerned about a woman's feelings." She turned toward him. "So, yeah, I guess you could say that I don't trust many people. That's only one incident. There have been others. I find it easier not to get too close. That way I won't have to deal with the inevitable split. I've learned that men don't take rejection well."

Nick studied her bare feet, the nails polished a conservative pink, as they slipped through the grass with the forward motion of the glider. "So you're trying to say that you won't allow yourself to get close to me because sooner or later I'll try to seduce you and after I've had you, I'll split? Is that the gist of it? Am I getting warm?"

Put that way, it sounded callous. "Not exactly. I..."

"No, don't deny it. That's exactly what you meant. You're so used to men falling at your feet that you think every guy past puberty is dying to get you in the sack." His temper rising, Nick tried to rein it in, without much luck.

He stopped the swing and faced her. "For every guy like Randy, there's a woman who did the same thing to a man. Don't think for a tiny minute that women have exclusive rights to being hurt. Let *me* tell *you* a little story."

Nick saw he had her attention and went on, fueled by his anger. "My brother Sam's a great guy who had an eye for beautiful women from an early age. He was twenty when he met this gorgeous blonde with huge blue eyes and a figure that would literally stop traffic. He was young and stupid, with hormones raging, and he admitted later that he'd have done anything to get her into bed. She toyed with him, used and abused his feelings for her own purposes. Thankfully he woke up in time and realized that she was nothing but a self-centered, shallow, narcissistic, cold and calculating little bitch who didn't give a damn about his feelings. So you see, it works both ways." Abruptly he stood. "I assure you I'm very much in control of my hormones and you're in no danger that I'll kidnap you and throw you between the sheets."

"I didn't mean to...I'm not..."

"Oh, sure you did. You meant to warn me, that I can stop being nice to your son because you aren't going to hop into bed with me. Well, honey, where I come from, the very least a woman does is wait until a man gives her some sign that he *wants* her in his bed.'' Turning, he walked toward the door. "Don't get up. I'll see myself out.'' Fuming, Nick just barely kept himself from slamming the screen door.

Taken aback, Tate sat there, staring at the door he'd just walked through. Well, he sure told you, lady, she thought.

Nick was finding it hard to concentrate. Shuffling papers on his desk two days after he'd stormed out on Tate, he found his mind wandering repeatedly, replaying their conversation. Earlier, the lieutenant had asked him if he had a problem when he hadn't responded to a direct question during a meeting. And his partner was losing patience with him, Nick knew.

But damn, he couldn't seem to drag his mind off Tate Monroe. What kind of hold did she have on him that he was even sloughing off at work? That had never happened to him before.

He felt an uncomfortable mixture of guilt and anger and annoyance. Guilty over the way he'd lost his temper and talked to her, considering the fact that he really didn't know her well enough to launch a full attack. Angry because others who'd come before him had formed her opinion of men and ruined everything for him. And annoyance with himself that he'd lost control, something he rarely did.

"Jorge Espinoza's out,'' Lou said, sitting down at his desk across from Nick's. Watching his partner who was intently clicking a ballpoint pen in and out and staring off into space, Lou wondered what on earth was bugging Nick. His behavior of late wasn't like the man.

"Hey, Nick!'' Lou waited until Nick finally looked over at him. "Did you hear me? Jorge Espinoza, your jumper, he's out.''

Nick's brow wrinkled as he tried to curl his brain around the here and now. "What do you mean, he's out?''

Giving an exasperated sigh, Lou shook his head. "I mean, he's out. He lawyered up and they sprung him. No priors, managed to ace the mental awareness test, convinced the judge he was just having a bad day."

"You've got to be kidding."

"Unfortunately not. Of course, he still has to appear to face charges, but they'll probably let him off, first offense and all that."

"And his wife? I suppose she's withdrawn her complaint?"

"You've got it. Typical domestic violence tune played over and over. He hits her, or his kids, she complains, they lock him up and she refuses to press charges. I'm sick of it."

Finally on the same page, Nick shook his head. "This isn't good. You know, mad as that guy was at her, he's liable to off her."

"I know that and you know that. But does Rocio Espinoza believe that? Nah." Lou leaned back in his chair and shifted his unlit cigar to the other side of his mouth.

"Damn, but I don't understand these women." Or any woman, for that matter. He had his mother on his back about Tate and Tate thinking all he wanted was a roll in the hay. "They might as well hang a sign around their necks saying, come get me."

"And he will, too." Disgusted, Lou tossed his stubby cigar in the trash can. "Oh, well. Nothing we can do till we get the call to go scoop her off the floor or wherever he ices her."

This news was doing nothing to lighten his mood, Nick realized as his phone rang. He picked it up, his voice none too pleasant. "Bennett."

"Nick, is that you?" asked a hesitant female.

Nick sat up. "Maggie? Is something wrong?"

"I think so. The man who attacked me called and left a message on our answering machine. It's...well, it's frightening. Tate didn't want me to call you. She said you couldn't do anything, but I thought you'd want to know.'' Her voice wasn't nearly as strong as the evening they'd been on her backyard glider. The evening he'd wrecked his chances with Tate.

"I do want to know. What did he say, Maggie?''

"He said that if we don't stop cozying up to the police, we would be sorry, that he'd take Josh and we'd never see him again.''

Nick's lips formed into a thin, angry line. The coward, threatening women and children. "You're sure it's the same voice?''

"Yes, positively.''

"I'll be right over.''

"Wait, Nick! Tate doesn't know I called. She might get upset.''

"She'll get over it. I'm on my way.'' He hung up, checking the duty board as he stood. "I've gotta go, Lou. Call me on my cell if something pops, okay?''

"You got it.'' Lou watched his partner all but run down the hall and out of the building, wondering what on earth had launched Nick out of his self-imposed coma.

The moment he pulled his Taurus into Maggie's driveway, Nick heard Ralph barking. As he stepped onto the porch, he saw the little dog on the couch back, barking through the window, his small body wiggling. He couldn't help smiling as Maggie opened the door. "Well, someone's glad to see me,'' Nick commented as Ralph came scurrying over, jumping up, wanting attention.

"Oh, yes,'' Maggie said, walking back to sit down, "he's a great little watchdog. He nearly scared the daylights out of the newsboy yesterday, kept barking until the kid was halfway down the block.''

Nick bent down to pet the squirming little ball of fur.

"That's his job and he knows it." Glancing around, he saw that Tate and Josh were nowhere to be seen even though it was past seven. Maybe she'd taken off when she heard he was coming over after the way he'd stormed out of there the other day. "No one else home?"

Maggie clicked off the television set with her remote as Ralph scooted up the stairs. "Josh is watching TV in his room. Tate's around here somewhere. Tate!"

Nick thought she probably was avoiding him. "Do you mind if I play the phone message?" he asked Maggie.

"No, of course not. Tate, where are you?"

Carrying a load of clean folded laundry, Tate emerged from the utility room off the kitchen. "I'm right here. Hello, Nick."

She was more subdued than usual, he thought, unwilling to meet his eyes. "I was just about to play the message. I guess you've heard it?"

"Yes." She set the laundry down on a stair step going up.

Nick hit the Play button on the answering machine.

"I warned you once. This is my final warning. If you don't quit cozying up to the cops, I'll grab the kid and you'll never see him again."

The man sounded gruff, what some would call a whiskey voice. Nick's jaw clenched at the sheer boldness of his threats. "Did you recognize him, Maggie?"

"Yes, that's the man who was in here, the one who tried to get me to talk." Her own voice sounded shaky with nerves.

Tate stood with her back to the fireplace, her arms crossed over her chest in an obviously defensive position. "I told Maggie there wasn't much point in calling you since I don't imagine just having his voice on a recording will help you get the man."

So she hadn't wanted him to come. "The recording itself won't point a finger at anyone, but when we get a suspect, we can match his voice up to this and tie the two together. That's a definite threat and a serious one.'' He played it again, just to be certain he hadn't missed anything, then reached in his pocket. ''If it's all right with you, Maggie, I'd like to take your tape and replace it with this new one.''

''Oh, sure.'' Maggie looked from Nick to Tate and back. The tension in the room was thick enough to cut with a knife. What had gone on between these two? she wondered as she saw Nick fiddling with the tapes and Tate standing silently, gazing out the front window, her expression tight.

''I'm going to play this for my lieutenant and show him the threatening letter as well. Maybe he can spare a man to keep an eye on the house.'' Although he doubted Harris would give the okay. ''Meantime, Maggie, I think you and Josh ought to stay indoors with the doors locked while Tate's at work. You have all my numbers. Call at the slightest suspicious sound. In the remote possibility I can't be found, dial 911. I hate to ask that but…''

''No, it's all right,'' Maggie answered, getting to her feet. ''We'll do whatever it takes to help you get that man, Nick.'' She smiled at Tate. ''I think I'll go to my room a while.'' So that they can talk and hopefully clear the air.

Nick slipped the tape into his pocket and walked over to Tate. It had been three days since he'd seen her and he was certain she hadn't had those shadows beneath her eyes indicating a loss of sleep that showed up so readily on fair-skinned people. He felt like a jerk for adding to her problems. ''Tate, I…''

''No, let me.'' She pulled in a breath, hoping to steady her nerves. ''I owe you an apology. You were right and I was wrong. I've been so used to dealing with men who…men who are different than you. I've gotten so jaded, it seems, that I automatically assume all men are the same. And that's unfair. You're a good guy, Nick, and you've never done anything to warrant my suspicions. I'm sorry.''

"Thanks for that, but I got a little carried away, too. And I must confess to a bit of hypocrisy in my little tirade." He watched her abandon her defensive stance, drop her arms to her sides and raise a questioning brow at him. "Maybe the reason I was so angry is that you were right about one thing. I do want you in my bed. But if that ever happens, you'll have to be the one to start the ball rolling."

Tate felt as if a huge weight had just been lifted from her shoulders. She'd agonized over their harsh parting for days and nights, finally seeing that she'd not only misjudged Nick, but she'd hurt him with her unbending attitude. She wanted badly for their friendship, their relationship, to return to what it had been before that night. No, she wanted even more.

She took a small step closer to him, a giant step in trust. "I do find you attractive, as if you couldn't tell, especially after that dance."

"That dance." Nick's lips twitched. "It seems my mother's getting calls from several of her friends who'd watched us dance. She wants to know what's up with us."

Before this, her first reaction would have been to deny there was an *us*. But if she were to be as honest as he was, then she had to admit there definitely was an us. "What *is* up with us, Nick?"

He took the final step between them, closing the gap, taking her hands in his. "My viewpoint? Well, on the one hand, we have here a beautiful woman who's afraid to trust because of her rocky past. On the other hand, we have a man who's been looking a long time, who never could settle for second best, who wants this woman but he's willing to wait until everything's right in her world."

Her emotions flooded, Tate leaned into him and felt his arms go around her and tighten. How good it felt to let herself be held by strong arms, to absorb his strength, to feel safe. Her hands curled around his shoulders as he pressed her head close to his heart where she heard the steady beating. For

Chapter 6

Nick pushed the Stop button on the recorder and looked at the lieutenant to gauge his reaction.

Leaning back in his chair, Harris frowned. "It's sure as hell a threat, but who is he?"

"No one seems to know." Although Nick had a sneaky hunch that Tate recognized the voice the way she'd kept her eyes averted yesterday when they'd discussed the tape. "Obviously he's the guy who wrote the letter." Which was resting on Harris's desk blotter. Nick had approached him with both, hoping the lieutenant would take this matter more seriously now that he had two separate threats.

"Do you have any leads on this guy?"

Nick shook his head. "A few hunches, but no solid leads. I was hoping you could assign someone to keep an eye on the house. We have an older woman who's been attacked and has trouble getting around, a young woman who works days and a seven-year-old boy who, for reasons I haven't determined yet, someone wants to kidnap. They're like sitting ducks in this old house."

The lieutenant was wearing red suspenders today, but the bright color hadn't improved his spirits. "I agree, but I simply don't have the manpower, Nick. I can get the area patrol car to drive by now and then, but that's it for now." He narrowed his eyes, studying his detective, noting that his decision didn't sit well with Nick.

Nick Bennett was one of Harris's best cops. He'd been with the Tucson Police Department for ten years, working throughout the system, hopping from Juvi to Narcotics to Homicide, making detective three years ago. He had a good record, a clean one, with three bravery citations. If once in a while Nick didn't follow procedure, he apparently led a charmed life because those incidents had all turned out well. So far.

Nick let out a frustrated breath. "That's what I thought you'd say."

Harris watched Nick pick up the letter and pocket the tape. "Are you personally involved with these people, Nick?"

Nick shrugged, keeping his expression bland. "I like them, if that can be labeled personal involvement. I think Maggie Davis is one gutsy little lady and I'd like to do something to take that worried look off her face, which has just healed from a brutal home invasion. The boy doesn't like to attend day camp, sensing something's wrong, though he doesn't know what."

"And the woman, Ms. Monroe? Isn't it odd that she wouldn't have an idea who might be after her son?"

"Yeah, it is. I think she knows something, but she's afraid to speak up. The same guy who beat up the old lady knocked Tate around several years ago, on the record. And we never found him then, either."

"And you can't get her to open up to you? Nick Bennett, who could probably negotiate world peace if he put his mind to it?" The lieutenant's tone was surprisingly light-hearted for a serious man.

"Not so far, but I'm working on it." He nodded his thanks and started for the door.

"Nick," Harris called, signaling him to turn around, "I hope you're not thinking of doing something crazy here."

Nick frowned. "Like what?"

"You tell me."

"I'm following the rules, Lieutenant. But what I do on my own time is nobody's business." With that, he opened the door and left the office before Harris could come down on him.

Seated at his desk, Nick drummed his fingers on the scarred wood surface, his mind traveling in many directions. He was warmed by Tate's apology and knew it was heartfelt. He'd managed to let her know he cared about her, not just her body, although that certainly was part of the attraction. He'd be a fool to protest otherwise. But he cared for the whole woman.

He'd told her the truth, that he'd waited a long time, dating any number of women through the years, yet always ending things before they became too serious. He knew exactly what he wanted—a union like his parents had. Though he got annoyed with them occasionally, he loved his folks.

Perhaps more importantly, he'd seen how, after forty years of being together, Anthony and Roseanne Bennett still loved each other deeply. They'd had their hard times, of course— two miscarriages that Nick knew of, a bout with breast cancer for his mother which, so far, hadn't returned, and the failure of an early business for his father. But through it all, there was affection, devotion and deep commitment.

Exactly what he wanted for himself and the woman he would make his wife.

Nick wasn't sure just how, but he'd always believed that when he met that special someone, he'd know. No bells going off or whistles blowing. Just a feeling inside that this was his soul mate, corny as that might sound to others.

And the day he'd met Tate Monroe, he knew he'd found her.

I want you in my life, she'd told him. In her life was where he planned to be and to stay. If he couldn't get help from the department, he'd take the matter into his own hands and do what was best for Tate and Josh and Maggie.

But first, he had to pick up a surprise for Maggie. And then shop for something special for Tate. Josh had Ralph and now it was the ladies' turn. Whistling, he left the bullpen.

Tate fidgeted in the passenger seat of Nick's car as he drove toward the desert. She wasn't at all certain she was up to the task ahead. "I'm not sure I can shoot a gun," she confessed. "I've always criticized parents who kept guns in the house and then were shocked when their kids found them and got hurt."

He'd known she'd balk at handling a weapon, but he felt it was necessary. "First, I'm going to show you how to shoot this gun so you'll be comfortable with it. Second, we're going to explain to Josh that he's never, ever to touch the gun or the bullets, should he somehow run across them. He's a good kid. He'll listen. Next, it's going to be locked in your nightstand, the key on a chain around your neck. How much safer can we make it?"

"Not having one at all?" She caught his look and backed down. "All right, so I'll learn how to shoot. Do I need a permit for it?"

"In Arizona, you don't need a gun permit unless you intend to walk around with the weapon concealed. After two death threats, it would be no problem getting one if it came to that. However, the most important thing is that you should know how to use the gun and that you've been given safety instructions. That's why we're going out for Lesson One."

The sun was still quietly sinking in a somewhat cloudy sky even though it was close to seven. It was beautiful out, about ninety degrees, but with very little humidity. But Tate was too keyed up to appreciate the scenery. Maybe a change of subject would relax her, she thought.

"It was wonderful of you to give that bentwood rocker to Maggie and set it up in her bedroom. She hates watching TV from bed." She'd noticed that Maggie had had tears in her eyes at his thoughtfulness. "She's nuts about you, you know."

"That's because I'm a hell of a guy." He grinned at her.

He'd remembered that his mother had his grandmother's bentwood rocker stored up in her attic and had asked if he could have it. She'd agreed, though she'd given him the third-degree about who it was for and what was the story. He'd talked only of Maggie, but he hadn't fooled Roseanne. Wisely though, she'd not mentioned Tate.

Nick turned onto a dirt road leading to a deserted trail. About a quarter of a mile in, he spotted what he was looking for and stopped his car. "This is the place."

Tate got out, looking around. A few wild cactus plants were scattered here and there, some mesquite and a couple of dried-up old logs. "You've been here before?"

"Yeah," he said, opening the trunk and taking out a cardboard box. "I could have taken you to a shooting range, but they're usually noisy and crowded. I often come here to practice. So do several cops I know." He carried the box to where the logs were stacked atop one another just so, creating a short wall. Taking the cans one by one from the box, he lined them up on the top log a foot or so apart, then turned to where she was standing. "See that mesquite bush?" he asked, pointing. "That's a hundred yards. Next one's at fifty."

He walked back to the trunk and took out the gun he'd gotten for her. "This is a Smith & Wesson five-shot snubby. You could use a .38 like mine, but this is even lighter and it'll fit in your purse if you ever feel the need to take it with you. That's when you'd have to get the gun permit.''

Tate's brows rose at that thought. ''Should I be that afraid?''

''Sometimes having a gun handy is more for self-confidence than anything else. It gives you an added measure of safety. I really hope you never have to use it, but if worse comes to worse, I want you to know how.''

Tate drew in a long, shaky breath. *You can do this,* she told herself.

Standing with her at the hundred-yard marker, he handed her the gun. ''Let me see how you'd hold it if you were to shoot at those cans.''

Gingerly she took the gun in her right hand. ''It's loaded, right?''

''Yes, but the safety's on right now.''

She relaxed fractionally. Trying to recall every gunfighter movie she'd ever seen, Tate gripped the gun in her right hand, raised her arm and took aim at the first can, closing one eye to get a bead on it. ''Like this?''

''Not quite.'' He stepped up behind her, placing his hands on her elbows. ''Loosen up. The tension should be in your wrist and hand, not throughout your whole body.'' Close behind her now, his hands slid along her arms, adjusting her fingers. ''Your left hand should lightly grip your right wrist to keep it steady, not in a death hold, but firmly. If you grasp it too tightly, you'll cause the shot to jerk to one side.''

Tate was having trouble controlling her trembling hands, not necessarily because she was nervous about the gun. Nick's large frame was molded to her, his legs glued to hers, his arms around her, his chin all but resting on her head. She felt his warm breath on her face and felt her stomach muscles quiver. She swallowed hard. ''I see.''

''Now, leave some play in your stance.'' Leaning into her, he touched first one leg, then the other with his bent knee, getting her to correct the way she was standing. "Line up your head so that your eyes are directly across from the target you've chosen." Placing his cheek along hers, he aligned their upper bodies.

Out so far into the desert, the temperature was beginning to drop, yet Tate suddenly felt warm. She had on only a white shirt over jeans, but beads of moisture slipped down between her breasts. She could feel Nick's five o'clock shadow brush against her cheek and his heart beating steadily against her back. The overpoweringly masculine scent of him was playing havoc with her concentration. She shifted her feet nervously, hoping he'd attribute her restlessness to her hesitancy over guns.

"Are you ready?" he asked.

"Yes."

"Remove the safety." He pointed to it. "Then go ahead and shoot."

Tate did as he instructed, taking careful aim at the twenty-eight-ounce empty can of tomato sauce and pulled the trigger.

And missed by a mile. "Damn!" she whispered before glancing up at him.

Nick's lips twitched. So, the lady had a bit of a temper. "Don't get discouraged. It takes practice and that's what we're here for." He walked her to the fifty-yard line, thinking the other too difficult for her first time. "Okay, let's try again."

But when he stepped close to surround her again, she lowered the gun. "Look, why don't I try this on my own? You…you make me nervous." Which was an understatement if she'd ever uttered one.

Nick moved back and waved his hand, indicated she should proceed.

Drawing in a deep breath, Tate again assumed the position. She shuffled her feet until they felt just right, corrected her grip the way he'd shown her and took careful aim.

When the bullet pinged off the can, knocking it onto the ground, she let out a victory yell.

"Easy, hotshot," Nick said. "One hit doesn't a marksman make. Let's see some more." Five cans remained standing.

Tate managed to hit two more making it fifty-fifty, not a bad first performance. He had her shoot two more rounds and she lost some of her nervousness as she became familiar with the weapon. Walking back to the car, he praised her. "You're doing great. If we can manage to practice a couple times a week, you'll be a pro in no time." He stashed the cans he'd picked up in the box and set the box in his trunk before locking the gun in as well. "Does your nightstand drawer have a lock on it?"

"No." Tate brushed back her hair with both hands.

Nick saw that she'd left her hair loose tonight. Soft bangs fell on her forehead while a breeze played with the auburn strands. His hands itched to run his fingers through, to feel free to touch.

"We should stop at a hardware store and I'll pick one up. I can install it tonight."

Tate paused at the side of the car, leaning onto the door. "Did something happen? Is that why you're stepping up protection?"

Nick stood looking at her, at the way the setting sun turned her hair to burnished copper. She was the best reason for his need to protect, but he couldn't tell her that.

"I talked with my lieutenant and they don't have the manpower to put Maggie's house under surveillance, other than the occasional drive-by. I want to check the other locks on the back door and windows. The house is old. They probably need changing."

Josh's safety was of paramount concern to Tate. She'd find the money somehow. "I'll pay you back."

"I'm not worried." He moved a fraction closer, brushed a strand of hair off her cheek and tucked it behind her ear and watched her eyes turn a deep green with awareness. "I want to run something by you."

That was new, she thought. He usually took the bull by the horns. "What's that?"

"Do you think it would be all right with Maggie if I slept on the living room couch some nights?" He'd thought it through and decided this was the only way to protect them during their most vulnerable hours. "I doubt that the guy in black will return in the daylight hours since he's aware Maggie's talked with the police and he's probably seen my car there."

"You have an unmarked car."

"Guys like him have a way of finding out things. And darkness changes things, makes someone out to do harm bolder. Let's face it, we have an old woman who maybe doesn't hear as well as she used to, a young woman who's probably tired and sound asleep and a small boy. Ralph does his job, but he's a small dog and wouldn't do much harm if someone actually got in. The house is a piece of cake for an experienced man."

Talk about your rock and a hard place. On the one hand, it would be comforting to know an officer of the law was downstairs guarding the house. On the other hand, could she even go to sleep knowing Nick was right below her, lying on Maggie's couch, all alone while the house slept? "But I thought that was why you were teaching me to use the gun, so if someone showed up at night, I'd be ready."

"It is, but tell me. Do you feel ready to go face-to-face with this guy, should you hear something suspicious? Would you feel confident enough to go downstairs and investigate?"

Tate swallowed around a huge lump. "Not yet, but..."

Nick reached up and stroked along her silken cheek, watching her luminous eyes. "Why should you when I can sleep there as well as at home?" Especially since right now home was a trailer with a narrow bed and few amenities.

She was wavering, but trying to be fair. "I can't ask you to give up the comfort of your bed for us."

"You didn't ask. I offered. I'd feel better knowing you're safe." He stroked along her throat and felt her breathing change.

For long moments, they stood there, gazing into each other's eyes, hearts beating faster and faster, becoming breathless. Nick waited, giving her the choice.

"Are you ever going to kiss me?" Tate asked in a voice so husky she scarcely recognized it.

Slowly Nick shook his head. "I told you, if you want me, you'll have to make the first move."

The corners of her mouth twitched as Tate struggled with nerves. "I don't know. I'm a little rusty at this." Actually she'd never had to make the first move. Every man she'd ever known had been willing and eager long before she'd thought it through.

"It'll come back to you." Nick's pulse was pounding, his body hardening. If she didn't do something soon, he'd lose all control and break his own promise to himself.

Eyes open, Tate went on tiptoe, laid her hands on his chest and touched her mouth to his experimentally. It was a mere brushing of lips, a tentative exploration. She drew back, her eyes meeting his, beseeching his.

"Is that how you like to be kissed?"

"Well, I..."

"Or like this?" Gathering her close, he played with her, pressing gentle butterfly kisses to her cheeks, her eyes, her ears, the corners of her lips, along her throat. Building, building, feeling the tension in her as she moved her arms to enfold him, still holding lightly. He made the rounds again, slowly, softly. In moments, he felt the change in her, her patience gone.

Tate pulled back. "Mmm, not exactly. How about like this?" Rising on tiptoe again, she wound her arms around him, pressed her body to his and took his mouth. All the pent-up needs from years of self-denial went into her kiss as she danced her tongue inside, thrilled when he responded. Hadn't she known kissing this man would be like this, like an explosion of riotous colors behind her closed eyelids, like the Concord taking her on the ride of her life, like a runaway train.

Suddenly she felt Nick take over, his mouth slanting over hers, taking her deeper, his big hands roaming her body as she marveled at his touch.

And the way he made her feel. Glorious. Enraptured. Every inch a female.

He was so tall that he had to bend to her, molding his solid body to hers. He was so strong, yet he took care not to crush her. She felt the sensual tug deep inside and recognized desire for the first time in years.

The shock of it was that she hadn't seen this coming, this overwhelming need, this warm flush of physical awareness. This one man had methodically broken down the walls she'd painstakingly built to keep herself from being hurt. He'd rushed past the barriers she'd erected over nine long, lonely years.

Most astonishing was the fact that she cared for him, cared about him, and that surely was unplanned, unexpected, un-believable. How long had she been saying that never again would she trust a man? She'd repressed any and all male/female feelings, buried her desires, denied her needs. But they were out in the open now—alive, thrilling, frightening.

Nick's head was spinning from the taste of her, the close-up scent of her, the sweet, soft sounds she made deep in her throat as her hands bunched in the cotton of his shirt at his back. He'd expected shyness, hesitancy, a touch of reserve—like that first tender kiss. Instead she'd knocked his socks off, kissing him back fully, completely. He'd often thought of her as a wounded bird, but she didn't kiss like one, but rather like a woman who made his heated blood race through his veins.

Later, he couldn't have said how long the kiss lasted. But suddenly he knew, as he found his fingers wandering around the front toward the soft pillows of her breasts, that if he didn't stop soon, he wouldn't stop at all. He'd promised himself he'd go slowly and this was anything but.

Pulling back, breathing hard, he stared into green eyes still hazy with passion unexpectedly aroused. "It seems we have a choice here," he said, his voice shaky. "We can take this to my back seat or check in to the first motel we can find. Or we can cool down for now and wait until our surroundings are more...romantic."

Tate was having difficulty regaining control—over her body, over her emotions. She was embarrassingly aware that he'd been the one to stop, not she. What did that say about how needy she was?

She took a drunken step backward, hoping she didn't look as disheveled as she felt, and dragged both hands through her hair. "I honestly thought I'd been kissed before." She raised her eyes to his. "I was wrong."

Nick smiled and eased her back into his arms, but he held her lightly. He couldn't help thinking that there was a great deal of passion locked inside her slender frame. She'd fooled him, throwing herself into the kiss, holding nothing back. He'd been seconds away from slipping his hands under her shirt and closing his fingers around her full breasts that had pressed against his chest. "Lady, you pack one hell of a wallop."

"Ditto." She breathed in deeply, feeling as if air was in short supply. "Thank you, for having the good sense to stop. I'm not sure I would have. I wouldn't want our...I mean..."

"You wouldn't want our first time to be in the back seat of my Taurus. Me, either." He tightened his hold, capturing her gaze. "But soon, Tate. Real soon, there will be a first time, and many more after that."

She searched his eyes, then her own heart. Yes, she wanted that, too. This time, with this man, she'd walk into this with her eyes wide-open.

"You're definitely not a quickie-in-the-back-seat type of gal."

She smiled at that. "You must have read my mind."

"Sometimes, I almost think I can."

"Really? What am I thinking now?"

He pretended to contemplate a moment before answering. "You're thinking, why doesn't he kiss me again before we go, just to make sure that first one wasn't a fluke?"

Her smile widened. "Oh, you're good. You're very good."

He kissed her then, keeping the brakes on, going for thorough but tender. Her response was instantaneous and avid. In some lucid part of his brain, he wondered how Josh's father had ever let her go. But his loss was Nick's gain.

Now that he'd found her, now that he knew she wanted him, too, he couldn't lose her. Nick's troubled thoughts swam around in his cloudy brain as an unexpected fear set in. Fear that he wouldn't be able to keep her and Josh and Maggie safe. Fear that whoever was out there would take away this woman who suddenly meant a great deal to him.

His lifelong reluctance to share his feelings out loud coupled with a natural policeman's reticence kept him from saying the words. But he could show her. Suddenly, the kiss changed and became none too gentle, none too patient. His mouth ravished, conquered, claimed ownership of hers. His hands at her back molded, crushed, kneaded. Finally, after an instant of shock, Tate responded in kind.

He was kissing her the way every woman dreams of being kissed—masterfully, possessively, excitingly. He left no doubt in her mind what he wanted, Tate realized. He wasted no time on the niceties, on romance, nor had she expected either. He was a rugged man in a dangerous line of work, and his rough edges would never all be smoothed out. It shocked her that she who hated every aspect of danger would be drawn to a man who lived in a world of daily peril.

But there was more in this kiss. Without a word being spoken, Tate understood why his mood had shifted, why there was an undercurrent of desperation in the way his mouth ruthlessly took ownership of hers. The stalker had jumped into his mind and fear had come with him. The fear she'd lived with for so long now. Having reached out to Nick and acknowledged that she wanted him in her life, he suddenly was afraid that the stalker would make sure that never happened. Tate didn't know how she could identify his feelings so readily, but she was sure she was right.

With his body so closely aligned with hers, the evidence of his desire so prominent, Tate knew it would be so easy to let him make her forget. But she mustn't allow herself to overlook the man with the ponytail and the even bigger man behind him. It was time to be as truthful with Nick as he'd been with her. She needed to tell him everything as soon as the moment was right. For now, she'd reassure him the only way she knew how—by accepting his bruising kisses, and understanding his desperation.

She was different somehow, Nick thought, wilder, more abandoned, unapologetic about her desire for him. Hunger raged through his system and had his head reeling. Her slender arms wound around him and his heart thundered a welcome.

This was what he could lose, the woman he'd just now found. This seemingly fragile yet very strong woman who'd taken over his mind, his senses, his life. The loss of this woman could very well bring him to his knees and it stunned him to realize it.

In the distance, thunder rumbled a warning of an evening

storm, underscoring the turbulence Nick felt. He eased back from Tate, more shaken than he'd have thought possible.

It was Tate's turn to reassure, to soothe. "Don't," she said softly. "Don't think about all the terrible things that could happen. Think instead that we'll get through this."

Surprised, he looked at her. "How do you know what I was thinking, what I was feeling?"

Puzzled, she shook her head. "I'm not sure. I just know. The way you kissed me felt like…like…"

"Like suddenly I realized I could lose you, that he could win?"

"Oh, Nick, no. We won't let him win."

He leaned against the car, trying to sort out his thoughts. "You remember the man on the ledge whose baby I grabbed before the guy fell into the net? He's Hispanic so the ACLU got into the picture and when he passed the psych exam, some smart lawyer got him out on bail awaiting trial. So what does he do? His wife called in this morning. He's stalking her. Very carefully, not too close, but always there. She's scared to death."

Nick straightened, took her hand and guided her to stand between his legs. "I've handled lots of stalker cases before. I was beginning to think stalking's become the great American pastime for some of these creeps. Some we've caught before they did any real damage. Others outmaneuvered us and managed to kill their victims." His hands stroked up her arms and settled on her shoulders. "But since knowing you, since learning to care for you, suddenly it's not a textbook case anymore. It's up close and personal. As a cop, I'm not supposed to be afraid. But I am, of losing you."

She gazed into eyes a deep pewter-gray. "That's not going to happen. You won't let anything happen to me or Josh or Maggie."

Nick was aware how far she'd come. "I hope you're right." He thrust shaky fingers through his hair. "I want so badly to get this man out of your life. If only I could get a solid lead, his license plate number, his picture. Something.''

Tate stared up at thick gray clouds shifting across a darkening sky. When had the sun gone down? She felt a shiver take her and knew what she had to do. "I know who he is," she said quietly.

Nick's eyes stayed on her face, registering no surprise. "I kind of thought you did."

"But you didn't push me to tell you."

"I felt you would when you were ready. I didn't think it would do any good to try to pry it out of you."

How well he knew her already. Tate let out a trembling sigh. "It's a long story, one I'm not sure you'll believe."

"Try me."

"All right, but not here. And not right now. It's a long story. I'll tell it to you, but give me a little time to sort out my thoughts, will you?"

He'd waited this long, he could wait a bit longer. "Okay." He kissed her forehead, then opened the passenger door for her. When he'd settled himself behind the wheel, he turned to her. "You didn't answer me about whether it was all right if I spend the night on the couch."

It would be even more difficult for her now that he'd kissed her, now that she knew how much he could make her feel, to know he was on the couch one story below her large double bed. But she'd handle it if he could. "I'm sure Maggie will sleep better with you in the house."

Nick thought he'd read her mind, her misgivings. "I might be a little restless, knowing you're so close and I can't touch you."

Tate took his hand, leaned over and kissed him gently. "You'll manage. And tomorrow's another day."

Chapter 7

The couch was old and lumpy. Nick beat down the pillow into a more comfortable shape and tried to ignore whatever was jabbing into his lower back. They didn't make sofas with springs anymore, did they? What else could it be?

Knowing he wouldn't rest until he found out, he got up, pulled off the sheet Tate had so neatly tucked into place and yanked up the middle cushion. A toy truck. Probably Josh's, lost some time ago. Who knew how long it had been there?

Fixing his bed again, Nick felt too restless to sleep, unable to turn off his mind. Josh had been asleep in his room before they'd returned from Tate's first shooting lesson. Ralph had barked, then come down to investigate but, recognizing their familiar scents, had scampered back up to sleep alongside Josh's bed. Maggie had been nodding on the couch in front of the television, but she'd awakened and heartily approved Nick's plan to stay on premises most nights. She'd gone off to her room. That had left him and Tate alone.

They'd sat on the backyard swing and had an iced tea,

talking about anything and everything except those kisses out in the desert and the mysterious man in black. He'd gained her trust and confidence by not pushing and he wasn't about to begin now. So when she'd yawned and said she had to get up early tomorrow, he'd watched her make up his bed, disappointed but patient. She'd brushed her lips across his quickly, as if afraid to really kiss him knowing the banked fire between them could flare up in a moment. And there were others in the house. She'd gone upstairs, looking as reluctant as he felt. Minutes later, he'd heard the shower turn on.

He'd checked both doors and the downstairs windows. Maggie had the air-conditioning on, but the temperature was set quite high since her old bones liked to be warm, she'd explained. Nick had removed his shoes and shirt, stretched out in just his jeans. His .38 was tucked in his ankle holster and he decided to leave it be.

There was a night-light on in Josh's room, plus a low wattage bulb burning in the upstairs hall. Maggie had left the dim stovetop light on, probably in case she got up during the night. The old air-conditioning unit creaked and moaned as the air whooshed on. He padded barefoot into the kitchen and ran himself a glass of water from the cooler. Sipping it, he peered out the window above the sink. The leaves of the eucalyptus tree swayed in a light night breeze. Shadows chased each other under a half-moon. Unfortunately, the street lamp was three houses down, offering no light into Maggie's yard. Maybe, since he was up anyhow, he should take a look around outside to reassure himself that no one was lurking around.

Slipping his shoes on, Nick went out the back way. The yard was good sized and somewhat overgrown with bougainvillea trailing up the stucco fencing, pink rhododendron flourishing in a corner bed, an orange tree with the fruit still green and a smaller lemon tree. Lots of places to hide, he thought as he strolled around cautiously. The plants really should be cut back, the trees trimmed. He walked to the back gate, saw there was no lock on it and made a note to get one tomorrow. Of course, a lock was no deterrent for someone determined to get into the yard, especially with a fence most anyone could easily scale, but it would be a start.

Hands in his pockets, he thought about the small lock he'd gotten at the hardware store on their way back. Tate had shown him the way to her bedroom where he'd drilled the hole into her nightstand drawer and installed the lock. He'd also looked around at her large double bed, a cheery yellow comforter covering it, two fluffy white pillows at the brass headboard. The furniture here, like everything downstairs, was old and well used by countless renters, but it was kept up and clean.

On the dresser he'd studied a picture with four divided snapshots, all of Josh at various ages up to the present. Even as a baby, he hadn't looked much like Tate with his round face and blond hair, even with those green eyes. His looks had to be a legacy from his father. Nick felt he was getting closer to knowing who the man was.

Tate had gone downstairs and after he'd finished with the lock, he'd stood staring at her bed, wishing he could join her there, see all that gorgeous auburn hair spread out on the pillow, watch those green eyes turn opaque with desire. For him.

Out by the fence, Nick shook his head and dragged his errant thoughts back to the here and now. He stood perfectly still, scarcely breathing, an old cop trick. Only then could you pick up on movements foreign to the scene. But after several minutes, he couldn't sense anyone else in the area.

The house to the left of Maggie's was also a two-story with no lights on to be seen. On the other side was a smaller bungalow, also dark. Maggie had told him a widow named Berta Stone lived there alone with her cat since her husband died last year. As he studied it, the floodlight flashed on, illuminating the whole yard. Wondering what had set off the sensor, Nick rushed to the fence and peered over. A wild rabbit was calmly munching on the new growth of lettuce in Berta's small garden.

Smiling, he strolled back toward Maggie's house, pausing to glance up at the second floor. What he saw had him stopping in his tracks. Tate's bedroom was the largest one, stretching from the front of the house to the back. He could see her unmistakable figure silhouetted behind sheer curtains, and it looked as if she wasn't wearing anything. He saw her grab what looked like a towel, bend over and dry her hair. Fascinated despite feeling like a voyeur, he moved a few steps closer.

Now she was applying lotion, it appeared, propping those long legs onto a chair, smoothing on some cream she squirted into her cupped hand. Nick found himself swallowing as she spread the lotion all over herself. Fortunately for his state of mind, her back was to him or he might have lost it completely when she got to her breasts. His vivid imagination filling in the blanks was bad enough. Finally finished, she picked up a gown or some sort of long shirt and pulled it over her head. By the time he saw her disappear from sight and turn off the light, his mouth was cotton dry.

Quickly he went back inside, locking the back door. That was enough torture for one night, he thought, draining the glass of water he'd left on the counter. Maybe he wasn't the only one who'd stood watching Tate through that window at night, unknown to her. He needed to talk her into hanging some heavier drapes or, at the very least, getting some room-darkening shades.

Nick kicked off his shoes and again stretched out on the couch, taking up every inch despite the extra-long length. Squirming to get comfortable, he decided a man his size wasn't meant to sleep on a sofa. Nevertheless, he closed his eyes.

Lights from a passing car coming in through her streetside front window danced across her ceiling as Tate lay in bed, wide-awake. She'd thought the long tiring day plus a hot relaxing shower would have done the trick. Not so.

She'd been right to suspect having Nick in the house was a double-edged sword. Maybe if he hadn't kissed her senseless just hours ago, she could stop thinking about him, but even that was doubtful. Her skin tingled all over, not from bathing but from the memory of his hands skimming along her arms and pressing into her back. Reaching up, she traced her lips with a fingertip, remembering his mouth touching hers, drawing from her the most marvelous responses. Thank goodness Maggie had been groggy with sleep when they'd returned or she surely would have noticed Tate's lips swollen from rough kisses she'd welcomed like a desert walker welcomes rain.

She turned over and kicked off the sheet, her restless body unable to lie still. It was going to be a long night, she knew. Probably few would believe that after her experience with Josh's father, she'd managed to suppress, to bury, to stifle any and all sexual impulses. Ruthlessly she'd ignored that part of herself, certain she could erase those fierce nighttime longings, calling it mind over matter. And she'd done a marvelous job of it.

Until Nick had entered her life and changed it forever.

One touch, one heartfelt kiss, and she wanted more. So much more. Josh's father had been older than she and light-years more experienced. But even so, it hadn't been sex that had drawn her to him. It had been the caring, which too late she learned had all been an act to get her into his bed and keep her there until he was through with her.

Tate sighed, trying to forgive the lonely twenty-year-old

she'd been back then—naive, foolishly trusting, unsuspecting. She'd been such easy game for a man with no scruples, playing right into his hands, too unsophisticated to see where their liaison would lead. To nowhere except heartache.

But she'd learned, she'd survived and, although she'd paid dearly for those months of bad choices, she had a wonderful son that, please God, no one would take from her. Since meeting Nick, she at last had hope that if anyone could stop the boy's father, he was that man.

The phone rang just then, startling Tate. Automatically she reached toward the nightstand, then stopped. Nick had told her not to answer the phone, that either he would get it or they should let the machine take it. After two rings, there was silence. The answering machine was programmed to pick up after four rings, allowing slow-moving Maggie time to get there. Apparently Nick had answered.

She glanced at the clock. Eleven o'clock. She had few friends in Tucson, having moved around so often. Neither Molly nor Laura would be calling this late. Maybe someone was calling Nick. As a cop, he had to have left their number with his precinct. No one at Brennan's would phone her at this hour, either. Curiosity had her rising.

Tate glanced down at the old football jersey she was wearing that came to just above her knees. The only robe she owned was flimsier than her present outfit. She decided to go downstairs and see who'd called. Feet bare, she left her room and padded down the carpeted stairs.

He was lying on the couch, his arms raised, his hands beneath his head, watching her approach. She might have known she wouldn't surprise him. He always seemed on ready alert. She stopped several feet from the couch. "I heard the phone."

Nick sat up, his eyes caressing her. The glow from the upstairs hallway filtered down, gently backlighting her, the kitchen lamp chasing away more shadows. She had on some sort of University of Arizona nightshirt and her hair hung to her shoulders in soft waves. Watching her through the window had been nothing compared to viewing her this close.

He cleared his throat. "I took a chance and answered. No one spoke, but I could hear breathing before they hung up. If it was our guy, I wanted him to hear a man's voice here late at night so he'd know the three of you weren't alone."

"Oh, I see. Then you think it was him?"

Nick shrugged, making room for her on his couch bed. "I don't know. Do you get many breathers?"

"Breathers." She shook her head, taking his lead and sitting down, not too close. "I've never encountered any when I'm home, but I don't know if Maggie has during the day. I'll ask her tomorrow."

Realizing the couch was a little uneven, she looked at him. Then wished she hadn't, as her eyes were drawn to his wide chest liberally sprinkled with dark hair. "This bed isn't too comfortable, is it?"

"It's fine." He waited, wondering if she needed to talk. "You couldn't sleep?"

She shook her head.

"Me, either."

Tate studied her hands intertwined nervously in her lap. "If the call was from who I think it was, it seems he's running out of patience. And that's not good news."

Nick decided to plunge in. "Isn't it time you told me who he is and why he's doing this to you?"

Her eyes downcast, Tate nodded. "Past time, I think."

He moved closer, took one of her restless hands in his. "Just take your time and start at the beginning. You know nothing you can tell me will change the way I feel about you. I'm here for you, Tate."

His words touched her more than he could ever know. She felt his arm slip around her shoulders as he eased her close to his solid chest. For just a minute, she let herself absorb his strength. Then she straightened, reached for a tissue from the box on the end table and swiped at her eyes. "If I'm going to do this, I think it would be better if you don't touch me right now. You...you're very distracting."

"Okay, whatever you say." Nick scooted back, giving her some space.

Tate drew in a breath and began. "I've already told you a little about how things were with me in my teens. I'd learned early not to trust guys. I hadn't planned on going to college, but my dad insisted. He was such a wonderful man, both mother and father to me and my brother. Steve's in San Diego, a career navy man. He joined at eighteen and got his degree through the service. But Dad had painstakingly saved this money and he was determined that I get a good education. He was a tailor for this high-fashion men's store. For years, he worked double shifts, almost ruining his eyesight."

She stole a glance and took courage from the intense way he was listening. "By then, Dad had sold the house we'd grown up in and rented a little apartment, contending that I couldn't have the whole college experience if I lived at home. So he paid my tuition plus room and board at Maggie's, which was considerably less than if I'd have lived in a dorm. I'll be eternally grateful, too, because here is where I met Maggie and Molly and Laura."

She was dragging this out too long, Tate realized, trying to delay the tough stuff. "I'd taken odd jobs for spending money, trying to ease Dad's burden. In my junior year, I went to work on the political campaign to elect Adam Weston as the youngest senator from Arizona. He was a popular and successful attorney and very ambitious. Even more ambitious than I'd realized, I was to learn. And he was ten years older than I."

Tate glanced at Nick, but his face was carefully expressionless. "Adam was, *is,* quite handsome and very charismatic, the all-American boy type, tall, well built with blond hair and blue eyes.''

Listening, the reason she had been so silent so far hit Nick like a ton of bricks. A U.S. senator was Josh's father. That was one he wouldn't have guessed in a million years. Small wonder she'd been so frightened. From what he'd read, Weston was a powerful man, heading several important committees, a go-getter on the way up.

''Adam is very charismatic, especially when he wants something,'' Tate went on. ''Or someone. That year, he wanted me. I still didn't trust men, but he pursued me zealously. Despite my misgivings, I was too young and inexperienced to be immune to his charm. We began dating and very soon after, we became lovers.''

She was coming to the hard part and, although it all had happened so long ago, Tate felt as if it were yesterday. ''If I'd have been just a little smarter, I might have caught the early-warning signs, but I was wearing some pretty heavy rose-colored glasses.''

Nick wanted to interrupt her, to tell her to stop blaming herself for falling prey to an experienced seducer ten years her senior, but he didn't speak up, allowing her to tell her story in her own way.

''You see, Adam insisted we keep our relationship secret until after the election. He had a ready list of reasons. The rest of the staff, mostly young and female, might be jealous. The press would dog my steps and make my life miserable. We wouldn't have any privacy. So, naively, I agreed. I didn't even tell Maggie or my roommates.''

Tate forced herself to get it over with. ''Just about the time I learned I was pregnant, Adam won the election. I was elated, thrilled to be a part of his victory, sure we could come out of the closet at last. But suddenly, he was traveling to Washington and other places out east, never phoning me, not returning my calls, always unavailable, according to one of his many aides.

"Finally, I took a home pregnancy test just to make sure, and decided I'd have to find Adam somehow, go to him and explain, still sure he'd be happy about the baby and me. Before I could, I read in the newspaper that he was engaged to marry the daughter of a politically connected senator from the East Coast." She let her last statement hang in the still night air.

Nick wanted badly to take her in his arms, to try to make up for all the pain she'd suffered, but she held herself erect, watching her hands shred a tissue in her lap.

"Like a bad novel, innocence ended for me that day. The worst part was telling my father. Though he was wonderfully supportive, I knew I'd disappointed him. He offered to help me put the baby up for adoption, but I was determined to have my child and never tell anyone who'd fathered him. Adam didn't deserve to know. However, I couldn't hide the pregnancy, so I confided in Maggie and my roommates. They were wonderful. Laura and Molly helped me keep up my classwork and when Josh decided to make an early appearance, all three of them helped deliver him right here in my room upstairs. From the first moment I saw him, I vowed he was mine and no one else's. I swore I would shield him from any harm."

She let out a long, shuddering sigh. "Unfortunately that wasn't as easy as I'd hoped. After graduation, Maggie took care of Josh while I worked my way up to manager at Brennan's. They've been so good to me, putting up with my comings and goings. I began saving some money, hoping to get a small house for Josh and me, knowing Maggie was getting older. And then, the bottom fell out of my world again."

Nick had been waiting for this. He moved a little closer, but he didn't touch her, didn't speak.

"When Josh was almost four, I'd taken him shopping. I

remember it was around Christmas and all the stores were decorated. I took him into Brennan's to show him off. He was such an adorable little boy, so loving and carefree.'' Regret moved into her eyes as she continued. ''We were just walking out of the store when this tall man walked in. I looked up and recognized him immediately. Senator Adam Weston.

''My heart stopped. His smile, the public one, slipped a little and he had the decency to look a shade guilty, but he did remember my name. I tried to push past him, anxious to get Josh away because, as you've probably figured out, he looks a great deal like Adam. Well, no one ever called Adam stupid. I wasn't quite fast enough. He took one look at Josh and he knew. I left without another word as if the hounds of hell were after me. Little did I know they soon would be.''

Tate shifted in her seat and looked at him. ''Are you getting bored by my little tale of woe yet?''

''Hardly.'' Because she was nearing the end, he took her hand again, and this time, she didn't pull away.

''It seems that Adam had everything he'd ever wanted— wealth, power, the possibility of one day moving up to perhaps the presidency, and a beautiful wife. Except that I learned that his wife couldn't have children.''

''How'd you find out?''

''From the great man himself. He arranged a private meeting, threatening me even then and all but physically forcing me to go. That's when I learned about his wife. And, having seen Josh, his perfect little replica, Adam wanted him. And what Adam wanted, Adam went after and usually got. But not this time. He offered me an outrageously generous amount of money to hand over my son. When I refused, he upped the ante. I believe he was truly shocked when I told him that no amount of money could buy Josh. He was furious when I walked out on him, yelling after me that he would make my life so miserable, I'd eventually give in. Well, I haven't given in, but he has made my life miserable.''

Tate threaded her fingers through his, glad this was almost over. "The harassing began right after that meeting. He sent one of his so-called aides—more of a bodyguard than an aide really—by the name of Rafe Collins to visit me. Thank God, Josh wasn't with me at the moment. Rafe is the man in black with a long ponytail, a thug who used to be a boxer and gets off on intimidating women.''

"He came to your apartment and more or less beat you up?''

"You know about that? Oh, I remember. I'd called the police so it's on record. Their advice was to file a restraining order. Can you see the clerk's face now if I told her that Senator Weston was harassing me and sending his henchman to intimidate me? Right!''

"Maybe the embarrassment of having to explain would have stopped him,'' Nick suggested mildly.

"You don't know Adam. Besides, it would be my word against a United States senator. Who do you suppose they'd believe? I had no proof Rafe had been sent by Adam.''

"You're right.'' Nick was thoughtful, digesting all he'd heard. "So that's when you and Josh disappeared for a while.''

"Yes.'' She hesitated a moment, then decided it should be all or nothing at all where trust was concerned. "My mother has a sister who's married to a rancher up in northern Arizona. It's lovely country, but quite isolated. In the winter, the roads can become impassable. They have a phone, but it doesn't always work when the weather's bad. We went there and stayed quite a long while. No one knows about my aunt Helen so I felt safe again.''

"Why did you come back?''

"My father had a heart attack. Maggie got word to me. I came back, had Maggie watch Josh and I spent ten days at the hospital, but a second massive coronary took him. I hadn't heard from Adam or any of his people in over two years, so I decided to stay, hoping he'd forgotten or given up. Maggie had grown older, more frail. I felt she shouldn't be alone. Besides, it was time for Josh to go to school. Up there, the school's some distance away, over an hour's bus ride each way. I didn't want that for him.''

"And then it began all over again, right?"

Tate nodded, leaning her head against the couch back, feeling drained. "I don't know how he found out we were back. I tried to keep a low profile. He must have had someone in Tucson checking." She rubbed a spot above her left eye, hoping to forestall a headache. "I'm so tired of moving, of looking over my shoulder, of being afraid."

Nick moved close, gathered her into his arms, holding her loosely, kissing the top of her head as she lay her cheek on his shoulder. "You don't have to be afraid anymore. I'm going to take care of this. Maybe not today or tomorrow, but soon." He pulled back to face her. "Do you trust me?"

"I've never told anyone the whole story like I did tonight. Does that show you how much I trust you to help?"

"Thanks. You won't regret it." He smoothed her hair back. "There's one thing that puzzles me. Why do you think he's never kidnapped Josh up to now? I mean, surely with his connections, he's had means, motive and opportunity."

"I think because I told him once that if that ever happened, I'd notify everyone—the police, the newspapers, TV, the senate chamber if I had to—and blow everything sky high. I believe he knows I meant every word. His career and quite possibly his marriage and his lofty plans would be over. So he thinks his one chance is to persuade me to give up Josh, that I'll tire of the harassment and the fear. What he can't seem to get through his thick head is that hell will freeze over before I let him near my son."

"Has Josh ever asked about his father?"

"Not until he started school and most of his friends had dads who lived at home. I told him that his father had to leave us, that those things happen sometimes and that I'd be both mother and father to him. I even went to a father-son luncheon they had earlier this year. He seems satisfied with my explanation so far, but I know one day he'll want to know more. I'm not looking forward to that day."

"You have nothing to apologize for. You've done nothing wrong."

"Except make a lot of poor choices, giving in to Adam being the major crime."

Nick touched two fingers to her chin, turned her face toward his. "It's not a crime to be young, to fall in love."

"I suppose not, but I wonder if my son will agree." She sighed noisily. "I often think I'd like to visit high school seniors and tell them my story, anonymously, of course. To explain how one bad decision can change your life forever. Women are so vulnerable in their teens and early twenties. Especially, like me, if they have no mother to guide them and a father who was methodically working himself to death and had very little time left over."

"You were looking for someone to love you and instead found someone who used you. And now, he's trying to do it again."

Looking sad, she nodded. "But let's not excuse what I did so readily. I take full responsibility. No one held a gun to my head and told me to go with Adam. I have to live with the results of that bad decision every day. I have so much guilt over having to uproot Josh, haul him up north, then back here. He didn't see me get hurt, but he saw my face and it scared him. Now, it's happened again with Maggie. I'm surprised he's not having nightmares."

"Kids are far more resilient than we give them credit for. Josh seems much happier since Ralph arrived."

"Yes, the dog helped a lot. I should have thought of a pet for him myself."

"Hey, why are you beating yourself up so much? You're only one person. Besides, Josh knows he's loved by you and by Maggie. That's most of what a kid needs right there."

Tate shifted her head so she could study him for several moments. "You seem always to know the right thing to say at the right moment."

He smiled, then his mood sobered as he reached to cup her face in his big hand. "You deserve good things in your life, Tate. You're a beautiful person, inside where it counts. I wish you'd stop blaming yourself for your past mistakes. We're all human and we make mistakes. But we learn from them, as you have." He ran his hand down her silken cheek to her throat where he felt her pulse pick up speed. "I hope I can bring good things to you."

"You already have. If anyone can get this monkey off my back, I believe it's you. I've carried it alone so long. You can't know how good it feels to have someone in my corner."

Nick leaned into her, nuzzling her, his mouth finally settling over hers. The kiss was almost lazy, lips brushing lips while his hands encircled her. He wanted to show her that it didn't have to be all flash and fire, that slow and seductive could be arousing, too.

Tate returned the gentle pressure, her eyes closing as she let the floating feeling take her. Her pulse stirred, awakened, came alive. His beautiful mouth skimmed down her throat as his clever hands shifted and closed over her breasts. She sucked in a deep breath, almost a gasp, as she felt her own response build. It had been so long since she'd allowed a man this kind of intimacy.

Only the thin jersey was between her flesh and his gently stroking fingers. She felt the heat take over, warming her blood, making her restless. Then his mouth replaced his hands, drawing on her through the cotton material, and she all but lost it as a moan escaped from between her parted lips. She buried her hands in his thick hair, pressing his head closer, wanting more.

Nick was breathing hard, wondering why he was putting himself through this a second time in one day. There was no way they could finish this on the couch with Maggie asleep two rooms over and Josh upstairs. Yet as he shifted his attention to her other breast and felt her nipple tighten into a hard bud at first contact, all rational thought fled from his mind. All he could think was that Tate was here, in his arms where he'd imagined her so many times, warm and willing.

Tate knew she should stop him and she would, in just a moment. Just a moment longer to feel his wondrous mouth turn her brain to mush, to enjoy his seeking hands wandering over her body, to allow herself to dream that this would never end. Finally she drew him to her by placing her hands on his cheeks and brought his mouth back to hers.

He'd ignited a fire in her that was no longer a slow burn but a raging inferno. She let him deepen the kiss as she squirmed closer to his strong, hard body. Needs she hadn't recognized in years fought for dominance over her hazy mind. Not even as a teenager had she necked on a couch, shamelessly pressing herself to the one man who'd unleashed a sleeping tiger.

Nick tasted traces of a minty toothpaste and inhaled the fragrant lotion he'd watched her apply to her body through the backyard window. Her tongue was dancing with his now as he mimicked the act of love. Maybe they could go upstairs to her room and...

Suddenly Tate pulled back, cocking her head to listen above the hoarse sound of their breathing. "It's Josh," she said when she again heard the coughing sound. She pulled back and jumped up, straightening her clothes, looking with dismay at the wet spots on the front of her jersey where Nick had tasted her breasts. "It's his asthma. I've got to go to him, give him his inhaler."

"Sure, all right," Nick said, sitting back heavily, waiting for his thundering heart to slow down to normal.

Tate blew her bangs out of her eyes as she hurried up the stairs. Saved by the bell, or rather, the cough. As she rushed to her son's bedside, she couldn't help wondering what might have taken place had Josh not awakened just then.

Chapter 8

They needed a break—from the stress, the worry, the tension. Saturday morning, Nick woke up early in his bed on the couch and went into the kitchen to put on a pot of coffee, thinking he'd take all three of them out somewhere today. Four, if you counted Ralph who came bounding downstairs, greeting him with lavish licks, then hurrying out into the backyard through the door Nick held open.

It was a happy coincidence that both he and Tate had the same Saturday off. A drive in the country would be nice. He was on his second cup when Tate came down, already showered and looking morning fresh in white shorts and a yellow top, her feet bare. He returned her somewhat shy smile as he rose from the kitchen table.

Glancing first at Maggie's closed door, he took her in his arms. "Did you sleep well?" he whispered in her ear.

"No," she answered honestly. "I thought about you all alone down here..."

He nuzzled her fragrant neck. "I'd rather have been up there with you."

"Me, too." She kissed him lightly before moving to the counter and pouring herself a cup of coffee.

"Do you have a lot planned for your day off?" Nick asked.

Tate took a couple of sips and felt the caffeine dance into her system. "Not really. A couple of errands. Why?"

"I thought I'd go home and clean up, then come back and take everyone for a long drive, like up Mount Lemmon. We can check out the shops, have lunch, just relax for a day. I think Maggie and Josh could use a little time away from the house. What do you say?"

She looked at him over the rim of her cup. "Do you think it's safe?" She knew she didn't have to explain what or who she feared.

"It is when you're with me." He slid his pantleg up, revealing his ankle holster and gun. "I'll be armed, just in case, but after hearing who's behind all this, I doubt he'll make a move in a crowd. Even Rafe, if he got caught, could be traced back to the good senator. Might get messy."

She believed him, believed he'd keep them safe. Mount Lemmon held some bad memories for her, but with Nick, she'd be all right, and they all could use a day off. "Then I say let's go."

"Great. You get everybody ready. I'll be back by, let's say eleven. Okay?"

"Okay." She walked him to the door, saw he'd neatly folded the bedding he'd used. When he tugged her into his arms for a kiss at the doorway, she had a question for him. "And how did *you* sleep?"

"Who, me? Like a baby." He opened the screen door. "One who's got colic, a bad cold and is teething." He gave her a smile before sliding behind the wheel and taking off.

Tate closed the door and leaned against it. A leisurely day driving and strolling around, acting like tourists. Like people who hadn't a care in the world. She could pretend, for a little while, that she was one of them.

He'd gotten his Taurus washed and, except for a rather elaborate radio system and the flashing red light he could clamp onto the roof if needed, the car looked like any other on the road. Nick chose a roundabout route, driving for the sheer pleasure of sight-seeing, even though he'd lived in the area all his life and so had his passengers. Taking it slow, he drove around the University of Arizona campus first, commenting on how much it had changed since he and Tate had attended.

"Jeez, Mom, how'd you ever find your classroom?" Josh wanted to know, confused by the many buildings.

"They give you a map and eventually you memorize where everything is." Seated in the back with him and Ralph who had two paws up and was busily gazing out the window, Tate smoothed back his hair. "We need to get you a haircut, young man."

"Nick says he cuts hair," Josh informed her.

Her eyebrows rose as she sought Nick's eyes in the rear-view mirror. "Is that so?"

Nick shrugged. "My dad used to cut all the boys' hair to save money. He taught me, so now I do the nephews. I told Josh and he thought it'd be a good idea if I cut his."

"I see. You two ganging up on me?" she asked, but she was smiling.

"It appears that Nick walks on water," Maggie interjected, "wouldn't you say, Tate?"

"Just on lake water," Nick answered, grinning. "I haven't tried the ocean yet."

He turned onto the road leading up Mount Lemmon. "I'm surprised you haven't been up here, any of you. It's a real popular spot."

Tate's smile slipped. "I was here once, several years ago," she said very quietly.

Watching her in the rearview mirror, Nick got the impression the trip hadn't been pleasant. He couldn't help wondering if the memory had anything to do with Senator Adam Weston.

The area with the shops was crowded with tourists so it took Nick some time to find a parking space. They all climbed out as he attached Ralph's leash to his collar. "Loop your hand through this twice, Josh, so he doesn't get away from you," Nick instructed.

"I've got him." Josh moved ahead of them on the crowded sidewalk.

Nick offered his arm to Maggie who was moving a little slowly today. "Are you all right?" he asked her.

"I'm just fine," the older woman informed him, but she let Tate hold her other arm as they strolled along.

"Josh, wait for us," Tate called out, uneasy at having him too far ahead. She glanced at Nick and saw his cop's eyes scanning the crowd, looking for anyone familiar or someone who looked as if he didn't belong. She relaxed fractionally as they stopped in front of a store selling Western artifacts.

By the time they'd walked one side of the street of stores, then back along on the other side, everyone was hungry. They ate at a crowded little outdoor luncheon café while Ralph napped in the sun, his leash tied to the fence post next to their table.

Afterward, wanting to walk off his lunch, Nick suggested a stroll up the mountain, which had well-marked trails. Maggie opted to wait at street level, sitting down on a bench with Ralph by her side. As the three of them started up the path, Nick thought that Tate seemed a little nervous, but he decided she was just concerned over Josh.

"Stay right by us, Josh," Nick told the boy. "It's really easy to slip off the path and, in some places, it's a long way down.'' He positioned the child between himself and Tate as they climbed.

They passed other climbers, some going up and some already coming back down. The sun was hot overhead, though it had been fairly cool at the outdoor restaurant with the mountain breezes. Tate removed her sweater and tied the sleeves around her waist.

''I used to come up here a lot when my brothers and I lived at home. It's a great place to get some exercise.'' He glanced at Tate's face and saw that moisture had beaded on her brow, whether from the sun or the physical exertion he wasn't sure. Each step seemed to require an extra effort on her part.

They came to a small plateau that looked out on where the trail wound around itself. Across the way, the path narrowed and overlooked a steep ridge, the gulley below rocky and dangerous. A small stream snaked its way out of sight, the water clear enough to count the stones at bedrock.

Nick noticed that Tate was standing very still, gazing across the chasm, her eyes narrowed, her lips pressed together. He stopped, pointing out some shiny stones to Josh who immediately stooped down and began picking through them. Returning his attention to Tate, who hadn't moved, Nick slipped his arm around her. ''What's wrong? Tell me.''

For a moment, she didn't move, just swallowed hard. ''I was here once before, over there where that rock forms a sort of ledge.'' She felt a shiver take her, unable to hide her reaction.

''Tell me what happened.''

''He'd stopped his limo outside Brennan's and waited for me, insisting I get into the car and talk about Josh,'' she explained, her eyes on the gully below, her voice low. She knew she didn't have to explain who *he* was. ''Rafe was driving and they brought me up here. It was twilight and there was no one else around. We stood over there and we were quarreling and...and...''

Nick tightened his arm around her. "It's all right. I'm here. You're safe now. Tell me what he did."

"Adam knew I was terrified of heights, so he had Rafe pick me up and dangle me over the precipice. And he stood there and laughed at my fear. When Rafe set me down, Adam told me to remember how that felt, that if I didn't start co-operating with him about his son, he'd have Rafe finish the job next time. He'd make it look like an accident and no one would question a senator's word." Tate shuddered and turned into Nick's arms.

"You believed him, of course."

"Wouldn't you?"

Gently Nick made her face him. "Honey, plenty of important lawmakers have gotten in hot water for abusing their power. Being a senator isn't a free license to do as you please. We'll get him. I want you to stop worrying."

"I wish I could."

"Hey, Nick, look!" Josh came running over, all excited. "I think there's diamonds in this stone."

Nick kissed Tate's forehead lightly, then turned to her son. "Mmm, that's a beauty, all right. Only I think it's more apt to be quartz than diamonds." He saw that the boy had a whole handful of shiny stones, washed clean by the stream. "You can take those home. Are we about ready to go back?"

"Can't we climb up there?" Josh asked, pointing to the higher path.

"No!" both Tate and Nick said in unison, causing the boy to look at them wide-eyed.

Nick softened the refusal. "I'll bet that ice-cream stand is still open. What do you say we get a cone before driving home?"

Josh brightened. "I want chocolate with sprinkles."

"You got it." Taking Josh's hand, his other hand curling

around Tate's fingers, he led them back down. Though he was trying to be upbeat for Josh's sake, inside Nick was seething. What kind of man would hold a woman over a precipice, then laugh at her fear? A man drunk with power, a threat to society.

Senator Adam Weston had to be stopped.

Nick leaned back in his desk chair at the precinct, thoughtfully considering the information he'd gathered from a variety of sources like the newspaper archives, magazine articles and the Internet. To all outward appearances, Adam Weston was a *wunderkind.*

His father had died when he was eight and his mother had raised him, an only child she doted on. She'd started a small restaurant, called it Hattie's on the Hill, and worked round the clock to make a go of it. By the time Adam was in his teens, she had enough saved to send him to a prestigious prep school back east.

Adam did his part, carrying a *B*-plus average, excelling in basketball as well. In his final two years, he improved his grades to 4.0 and made all-American in his sport of choice two years running. He applied at Harvard and got accepted.

By then, Mrs. Weston had two more restaurants and bought a big house in the foothills of the Catalina Mountains. She joined a country club where Adam learned to play golf and met more people who could advance his career. He went on to Harvard Law, making his mother proud. He was sought after by several very good law firms, settling on Tremaine, Emory and Whitfield, the biggest, the best. When he decided to run for political office, the firm was behind him, knowing it would add to their prestige.

Though Adam won his senatorial seat by barely squeaking by, it might just as well have been a landslide according to the enormous party Mrs. Weston threw in celebration. Nick was sure that Tate and the others who'd worked to get him elected hadn't been invited.

After a whirlwind courtship, according to the article Nick had located in the back files of the *Arizona Daily Star,* Adam married Angela Templeton, only daughter of Senator and Mrs. Roger Templeton of Connecticut, shortly after starting his first term. The in-laws had a lovely home built for the newlyweds next to theirs overlooking Long Island Sound, though Adam listed his mother's home as his primary voting address since he'd been elected to represent the good people of Arizona.

According to his voting record, Adam walked the fence, just liberal enough so his constituents wouldn't abandon him, yet conservative enough for the old guard. A careful man is the junior senator from Arizona who doesn't get "home" as often as he wishes to see his beloved mother, according to one interview.

The interviewer ended with speculation as to just what position Adam was being groomed for by his powerful father-in-law. It was simply a matter of time before the entire country would know the name Adam Weston.

Right, thought Nick as he straightened, but perhaps not for his political contributions. After what he'd done to Tate, especially the way he'd treated her on Mount Lemmon, he'd like just ten minutes alone with the guy. There had to be a way to flush the man out without endangering either Josh or Tate or Maggie.

"Hey, Nick," Lou called from across their two desks facing one another as he hung up the phone. "We got a 911 from Jorge Espinoza's wife. He's there with a gun." Rising, Lou reached for his jacket from the back of his chair.

"Damn!" Nick said, shrugging into his own jacket. "I just knew this was going to happen." Racing after Lou, he followed him outside.

* * *

They were too late. Nick knew that as they approached the apartment building and saw the meat wagon waiting. The uniformed officer first to arrive met them as they hurried to the entrance. The kid was new, looked about twenty-five, his face ashen. "I never saw anything like it," he said, taking deep breaths. "So much blood everywhere."

"Take it easy," Nick told him. "Sit down and put your head between your knees." They didn't need a cop to pass out on the scene.

His partner was an older, experienced officer with a full mustache and face that had seen too much sadness. He came toward them carrying a baby in a blanket. "Guy killed his wife, then turned the gun on himself," he said wearily. "But, as luck would have it, he only winged his arm." He glanced toward the EMS. "Hey, over here," he called out.

"Where is he?" Nick asked.

"In the ambulance with my partner, handcuffed."

"Anyone else in the apartment?" Lou asked.

"No one." The cop handed the baby over to the paramedic. "I heard they have a son, but I don't know where he is."

"He's still in the hospital," the paramedic said. "He's got internal injuries from when his father punched him out a while back." Her face registered anger and sadness as she carried the baby over to the EMS wagon.

"Let's have a look," Nick said, dreading the whole thing.

"Once these guys start knocking their wives and kids around, they never quit," Lou commented as they climbed the stairs. "Not until one or both of them are dead."

Exactly what Nick was thinking. Adam hadn't made a move in quite a while, nor had Rafe Collins been spotted lately. He knew better than to believe they'd given up. And he was scared to death that one day he'd get a call telling him that all three in Maggie's house had been wiped out. The warped SOB might decide that if he couldn't have Josh, he was going to see to it that Tate didn't, either. Wrapped in his political cocoon, Adam apparently felt invincible.

There had to be a way.

Nick found himself genuinely liking Tate's former roommates and their husbands. At his request, she'd arranged for both women and their spouses to come down to Tucson so he could talk with them informally. He'd been tied up at the precinct with paperwork on the Espinoza murder and had joined them and Maggie after dinner, allowing Tate a chance to talk privately with her friends. He'd arrived just in time for dessert and coffee. Despite the work it took to put on a big dinner, Tate seemed more relaxed and smiling than perhaps he'd ever seen her.

Sipping his coffee and listening to the friendly bantering, Nick studied the new foursome seated around Maggie's big oak dining table. Molly Shipman Gray, the one they called the brainy one because of her high IQ, was an attractive, slender blonde who patiently handed pieces of cookie to her eighteen-month-old son wiggling on her lap. Nick had liked Molly's husband, Devin Gray, immediately, a man with powerful genes since both of their children had inherited his black hair and green eyes and none of Molly's fair good looks. Devin was a fairly well-known author, but he downplayed his celebrity. Tate had mentioned reading his Western-mystery novels and enjoying them. Nick made a note to pick one up.

He also noticed that Josh had overcome his shyness with the Grays' eight-year-old daughter Emily and even now, they were on the couch playing Pokémon. Too bad the Grays didn't live closer, he thought. Josh could use a friend nearby.

Dr. Sean Reagan, a tall, sandy-haired obstetrician, was finishing a story about a woman who'd thought she had a large stomach tumor only to deliver an eight-pound baby girl. Sean's wife, Laura Marshall Reagan, was the rich one, though you'd never know it from her down-to-earth attitude. Laura was willowy with shoulder-length black hair and warm blue eyes. She'd just learned she was pregnant and the two of them were overjoyed.

Although both Molly and Laura were attractive, Tate was stunningly beautiful in a white pantsuit, her auburn hair hanging loosely to her shoulders, her green eyes sparkling. But then, perhaps he was prejudiced.

Everyone smiled at the end of Sean's story as Maggie got up to pour fresh coffee all around. Nick thought that the older woman looked happy tonight to have her little family around her table. Then the mood sobered, almost as a cue for Nick to explain why he'd wanted this impromptu meeting. He started by asking Tate how much she'd told her friends before he'd arrived.

She glanced over and saw that Josh was absorbed with the game and the television was on, further blocking out their conversation. "I told them who the father is and the name of his so-called aide."

"Aide my aunt Tillie," Sean spoke up. "That guy tried to kill Laura by forcing her off the road with his car." As if to reassure himself that his wife was all right, he reached to take her hand in his.

"So I heard," Nick said. "Did you report that incident to the Scottsdale Police?"

"Yes," Laura answered. "But I couldn't get the license plate number—he was alongside me and behind—so all I could give was a vague description of the car. A long, black limo-type vehicle. The windows were tinted so I couldn't make out the driver. The police said it simply wasn't enough to go on."

Nick caught Tate's look, knowing she recognized the car's description. "The driver was probably Rafe, doing Weston's dirty work. That same car and that same man have been spotted across the street here and once at the park watching."

He kept his voice low, his eyes drifting to Josh to make sure he wasn't listening. "I need to know if either of you have had any other contact with him."

"A man with a gruff voice called our home several times looking for Tate," Molly offered. "But when I put Devin on after he became insistent, and he more or less told him off, he never called again. Apparently realizing there was a man on the scene, he backed off. I imagine he's the same man, right?"

Tate answered. "Yes, Rafe has a gravelly voice. He left plenty of messages for me."

"For me, too," Laura said. "We also think he's the one who broke into my condo some months before Sean and I were married, and ransacked it thoroughly."

"Did you fill out a police report?" Nick asked.

Laura shook her head. "At the time, I was having trouble with my ex-husband and I was sure he'd done the damage. But later, Sean confronted my ex and determined it wasn't him. That was several weeks later and I didn't call the police because I thought there'd be no point since I had no proof it was him."

"There was also a previous incident where he messed with the brake line of Laura's car," Sean interjected, "causing her to go into a skid and slam her Bronco between two trees during a snowstorm. Fortunately she wasn't badly hurt, but she could have been killed then, too."

Frowning, Nick looked at the notes he'd been taking. "Is that when she wound up in the hospital?"

"No," Sean corrected. "That was the *second* incident, when he banged into her rental car with that black limo on a stretch of road in Scottsdale, forcing her car off the road into a gully. That happened right after Laura told him she didn't know where Tate was and wouldn't tell him if she did." His remembered anger had his face hardening. "How long is this bastard going to keep this up? He's obsessed."

Molly reached over to place her hand over Tate's, realizing how badly her friend felt that because of their friendship, both women had been put in harm's way. "What I'd like to know is, what on earth would Weston tell his wife in the event he got the boy?" She looked at her husband a long moment. "We've been through something similar, where suddenly a child you didn't know you have shows up. Let me tell you, it takes some adjusting."

"It sure does," Devin added.

"That forced meeting I had with Adam after he first saw...saw me with the boy," Tate said, unwilling to speak her son's name in case he overheard and began listening, "he told me his wife can't have children. Undoubtedly he's sweet-talked her into accepting a child of his from a former relationship. He's good at that."

"Has he heard of adoption?" Sean wanted to know.

Tate's eyes were downcast. "You have to know Adam. He wants what he considers his and, apparently, he'll stop at nothing to get his way."

"This Rafe Collins," Molly began, looking at Nick, "can't you have the police pick him up for stalking?"

"Yeah, we could, provided there are witnesses. And, if he's got priors, the charge goes up to menacing, which is a serious felony. The reason we haven't picked him up is that we're after the big fish and we're hoping this guy leads us to him. If we lock up Rafe, Adam can replace him easily enough. Money talks."

Devin had an idea, one he decided to run by the others. "Nick, as a detective, I know you have to follow certain rules. But what if you left your badge home one day?" He glanced over at Sean, hoping he'd go along. "What if the three of us paid a little visit to the senator? Maybe we could *persuade* him to back off permanently."

"I'd like nothing better," Nick answered, and saw that Sean was in agreement, too. "If I thought that would work,

I'd be the first to go confront him. Unfortunately, when you're dealing with a U.S. senator, you have to walk a fine line. He's got a list of privileges longer than my arm. And he's got automatic credibility because of his position. Up against that, we're whistling in the wind.''

''So, you're saying it's hopeless?'' Laura asked, more than ever afraid for her friend.

''Hell, no,'' Nick answered quickly. ''What I am saying is that we need to stay within the law, if possible.'' He looked at both men, studying their faces. ''Of course, if that fails...'' He let the thought hang in the air. ''Let me say this much. I've promised Tate I'd get this guy and I intend to do just that. I appreciate your offer, both of you, and if it comes to that, believe me, I'll call on you.'' He allowed himself a small smile. ''Tate's fortunate to have such good friends.''

Seated next to him, Tate blinked rapidly, then slipped her hand in his. ''Aren't I just,'' she answered, looking into his eyes.

Handing her fidgety son to his father, Molly caught the look that passed between Tate and Nick. So that's how it was, she thought. It's about time Tate fell for one of the good guys. And from where she sat, Nick Bennett more than fit the bill.

Across the table, Laura slid her gaze from Tate and Nick to glance at Molly. The two friends smiled, each thinking the same thought, pleased for a friend who'd had way too much trouble in her life so far.

Maggie hadn't said much all evening, pleased to listen to the young people, but seeing Tate take Nick's hand in a gesture that spoke more than words ever could, she had to join in. ''I believe in Nick, that he'll make those two terrible men pay for what they've done to Tate.''

''And to you,'' Tate reminded her, giving her a quick hug. ''Let's not forget that Rafe broke in here, too.''

"The bastard likes to beat up women," Sean muttered. "I'd like a few minutes alone with him."

"Get in line," Devin added, rising with his son. "Listen, I hate to end this, but this young man's ready for some shut-eye and we've got a two-hour drive ahead of us."

The goodbyes, the hugs and promises to keep in touch, took a while, but by eight o'clock, the Scottsdale visitors were gone. Josh was upstairs showering and Maggie was in her room, putting her feet up and watching one of her favorite programs. In the kitchen, Tate loaded the dishwasher while Nick helped clear the table.

"I like your friends, Tate. They seem like good people."

"I knew you would," she said, rinsing dinner plates. "I knew if you met them, you'd realize they wouldn't harm us in any way."

"I never really suspected them, but I wanted to know what kind of brushes they'd had with Rafe." He dropped silverware into the dishwasher tray.

"Twice, he could have killed Laura," Tate mused. "Why? I wonder. Okay, so she wouldn't tell him where we were. How would killing her accomplish anything?"

"Sometimes a guy like Rafe just gets frustrated with getting nowhere, unable to come up with answers, reporting failure to the guy paying him. Or, it could be he just meant to scare her into revealing your whereabouts and he went too far, forcing Laura's car off the road."

Tate added soap and closed the dishwasher before turning it on. A heartfelt sigh drifted from between her parted lips as she leaned wearily against the counter. "When is this ever going to be over?"

Nick hung up the dish towel, turned and took her in his arms. "Soon. I promise you. I don't want to take the law into our own hands, not as things stand. He's going to make a move, a mistake. Then we'll get him and put him away for a long while. Confronting him now might just make matters worse. I hope you trust me on this.''

''I do.'' She snuggled closer, very aware that only here, in his arms, did she feel safe. However, all evening, she'd sensed something bothering Nick. Easing back, she looked up at him. ''Did you have a really bad day? Is that why you were late?''

Nick let out a frustrated sigh. ''You could say that.'' He told her about the Espinoza case, leaving out the details about the carnage he and Lou had found in that small apartment.

''Oh, Nick. That poor woman. And those two children, having to grow up knowing their father killed their mother. Who's going to care for them?''

''Mrs. Espinoza has a sister in Phoenix. She's on her way down to take the baby temporarily until the courts can decide what to do. The boy's still in the hospital.'' He shook his head. ''Such a waste.''

All the violent things he'd seen and done were there behind his serious gray eyes, Tate thought, reaching up to stroke his dear face. But he managed to keep his demons at bay most of the time. She wished she could help him more. ''Did you eat anything? I can fix you a ham sandwich or...''

Nick shook his head. ''I'm not hungry. Let's just go sit on the couch so I can hold you. Just hold you.'' He stroked the backs of his fingers along her silken cheek. ''You're all I need right now.''

Arms around each other, they strolled into the living room.

Nick grabbed the bag of Kentucky Fried Chicken from the passenger seat and got out of his car that he'd parked in front of Maggie's. He was glad this day was over, though it hadn't been as bad as yesterday. He and Tate had sat on the couch until nearly midnight last night, taking comfort from each other, until he'd fallen asleep. He vaguely remembered she'd fixed his bed and taken herself upstairs. He'd left before she'd come down this morning, driving off early since he'd had to go home to shower and change before an eight o'clock meeting.

Frowning at the empty driveway, he wondered why Tate wasn't home since she usually was by six. He gave two quick knocks on the door and heard Maggie invite him in. "Dinner in a bucket," he called out as he entered the living room.

"Oh, bless you, Nick. I'm sure Tate won't feel like cooking tonight." Nervously Maggie ran a hand through her white curls. "Her car broke down so she's going to be late."

Just what they needed, Nick thought, setting down the food. "I'll call and tell her I'll pick her up. Is she still at Brennan's?" he asked, walking toward the phone.

"I think so. She called about ten minutes ago and said she was waiting for the tow truck to arrive." Seemingly agitated, Maggie wrung her hands repeatedly.

He got ahold of Tate quickly and told her he'd be right there, all the while watching Maggie squirm and fidget. He hung up, his curiosity aroused. Walking over, he toyed with his keys. "Is something else wrong here, Maggie? You seem a little…frazzled."

Maggie glanced out the front window almost furtively, then up the stairs. "I don't want Josh to hear. We saw the black limo out front a while ago."

Nick went on alert. "How long ago? Was it there long?"

"Oh, about an hour ago. I let Josh go out on the front porch. I feel sorry for him, cooped up in here all day, you know. I was sitting right here watching him play with his toy cars. Suddenly the black car drove up and stopped right across there." She pointed a trembling finger.

"Did the driver get out?"

"No, I don't think so. I hurried to the door and got Josh inside. Just to be sure, I sent him up to his room to watch TV. Then I drew the drapes over the window. I kept peeking out and about twenty minutes later, the car was gone." Flustered, she looked ready to cry. "Oh, dear. I shouldn't have let him outside. Tate's going to be upset."

Nick sat down and patted her shoulder. "Yes, she's going to be upset that the car was here, but not because you let Josh on the porch. You did nothing wrong. Don't worry." He got up, walked to the door. "You didn't tell Tate?"

"No. She had enough to worry about with her car and all."

"It's okay. I'll tell her. Now come lock the door after me, Maggie, and neither one of you go outside. We'll be back shortly. Don't worry, okay?"

But the poor little soul looked as if she couldn't help worrying, Nick thought as he drove to Brennan's. He got there just as Tate was signing the tow truck slip. She saw his car and walked over, looking hot and tired.

"Of all days for that silly car to break down," Tate said, getting in and sitting down.

Nick drove out of the lot, his suspicious mind at work. "What's wrong with it, did the man say?"

"The battery. Totally dead. He's taking it to the station and putting in a new one. It should be ready in a couple of hours. They're a little backed up."

Okay, so at least it didn't sound like a tampering. "I'll take you over after dinner. I picked up a bucket from the Colonel with all the trimmings. It's too hot to cook tonight."

Leaning her head on the seat back, she smiled at him. "You're wonderfully thoughtful. Thank you."

Nick hated to take the smile from her, but she had to know. "Maggie had a little problem today," he began.

Tate frowned. "What kind of problem? Is Josh…"

"He's fine. The black limo came by, stopped in front of the house and just sat there. Josh was on the front porch."

Tate sat up. "Oh, no. What was he doing on the porch? I told Maggie that he's not to go outside and…"

"Don't blame her. She already feels bad enough. Josh was

getting cabin fever so she let him out, just on the porch, watching from the couch by the window. Damn, but wouldn't you know that's just when that jerk came by."

"How long was he there?"

"Not long."

His radio crackled once and he heard his call letters. Nick turned up the volume and grabbed the mike. "Bennett here. What's up?"

The dispatcher came on. "We got a call, Nick, about an explosion of some sort, near your friend's house."

Nick's instincts went on alert. Della, one of the dispatchers, was a neat gal, one he often kibitzed with. "Give it to me," he told her, knowing she was doing him a favor by calling him on this.

"Squad car's on the way plus fire department. Thought you'd want to know…401 Mesquite Drive."

"What?" Tate said, startled. "That's Berta Stone's place next door to Maggie's."

Tight-lipped, Nick spoke into the mike. "I'm on it. Thanks, Della." He hung up, stuck his red light onto the roof and turned on the siren as he stepped on the gas.

Tate's heart was in her throat. "It's him. I know it's him. We're never going to be free of Adam. Oh, God."

Chapter 9

Yellow crime scene tape was once more stretched across the yard on Mesquite Drive, only this time it encompassed two houses, Berta's and Maggie's. Seeing that, Tate sucked in a fearful breath, her fist going to her mouth to keep from crying out as Nick pulled in behind the white police car with its red light still flashing. She opened the door before he'd come to a full stop, glanced at the fire truck and several curious neighbors who'd come out to watch, jumped over the wide hose leading to the backyard and rushed into Maggie's house.

Right behind her, Nick hurried to catch up, hoping to prevent her from walking in on a bad scene if there was one. He heard her frantically calling for Josh and Maggie, but no one answered. Wild now, Tate ran upstairs to check, praying she'd find her son playing in his room, oblivious to the danger.

Nick went to the back door and saw Maggie with her arm around Josh seated on the swing while a tiny woman with salt-and-pepper hair paced the patio. His leash tied to a tree, Ralph barked his annoyance at being restrained. "They're out back," Nick called to Tate, then stepped outside. He saw the fire truck hose, turned off now, lying on the grass, in a puddle of water. The stucco fence between the two houses was in ruin, large and small chunks scattered all over, singed with black soot. A couple of firemen stood talking with the officer who was taking notes.

"Maggie, what happened?" Nick asked, wanting her version before he talked with the officials.

"Oh, Nick, I'm so glad you're here." Her voice trembled as her arm tightened around Josh whose big eyes stared up at him. "I honestly don't know what happened. One minute I was watching TV and the next, there was this terrible sound, like an explosion, and the house shook. Josh came running downstairs and we huddled together, not knowing what was going on until we heard Berta here calling for us." She turned to include the little lady. "Berta Stone, this is Detective Nick Bennett. Berta lives next door."

"I don't know what happened, either," Berta said, "except our fence is ruined."

Just then, Tate came running out, paused long enough to see that both Maggie and Josh were alive and unharmed, then ran over to the swing and hugged both of them, squeezing hard. "Oh, thank God, you're both okay."

"Mom, I was so scared," Josh admitted, his voice shaky.

"Oh, honey, I don't blame you." Her heart still pounding, Tate held him close.

Needing some answers, Nick walked over to where the officer was talking with the firemen. He listened a moment, then stepped in and flashed his badge since he didn't recognize the men. "Can someone tell me what happened?"

The taller fireman spoke up. "Some kind of amateur incendiary device exploded. Someone apparently stuck it on top of this fence. A prankster, probably a kid."

Nick didn't think so. He'd had his suspicions on the drive over. Just today, the black limo had been seen out front. Maggie had said she'd drawn the drapes and the little widow next door may not have been around. It wouldn't have taken long to jump the fence, plant the device and take off.

The officer closed his notebook. "At least, no one was hurt."

"The bomb, if you can call it that, was homemade, not highly powered, inexpensive, unsophisticated. That's why I think some kid did this," the fireman went on. "You know, these kids get on the Internet and learn how to make these bombs. Might even be someone in the neighborhood who lives nearby and could watch all the excitement he caused. They get off on that."

Or it could have been a warning, Nick decided. It had to be. With Weston's connections, Rafe could have gotten ahold of a deadly bomb if he'd wanted one. No one had gotten hurt because they hadn't wanted that, had intended to warn them, to let them know they meant business. Even if Berta Stone had been working in her little garden or if Maggie had let Josh play in the backyard instead of the front porch, the most that could have happened was that they'd have been hit by flying debris.

Watching the fireman drag his hose back to the truck, Nick struggled with a rush of anger. Something had to be done. The next time, it might be more than a mere warning.

"Thanks," he told the uniformed officer. "Turn in your report on this, will you?"

"Will do." He followed the firemen out of the yard.

Erasing his glum look, Nick walked back to the little group on the patio. "Mrs. Stone, you can report this to your insurance company and they'll probably help with the fence repairs. Maggie, if you'll do the same, they'll work together."

"My garden was looking so good," Berta said sadly as

she walked back to her yard, gingerly stepping over the rubble.

"No one was hurt," Nick said, stating the obvious. "That's the important thing. Maggie, if you and Josh go inside and get dinner on the table, Tate and I will be right in."

Maggie made her way to the door. "Josh, you set the table while I dish the chicken and fixings, okay?"

When the door closed behind them, Nick sat down on the swing next to Tate and looked at her ravaged face. "I have a suggestion," he said quietly.

She let out a tremulous sigh, fighting the urge to scream out her frustration and fear. "What would that be?"

"I think we both know who set that device on the fence. We need to get Josh someplace safe for the time being until we can round up the bad guys. Can you get in touch with your aunt and uncle up north? We need to get him out of here tonight."

The roomy white Crown Victoria wound its way along the highway heading north with Nick behind the wheel, Tate on the passenger side and Josh buckled in in the back seat as he lay sleeping, his dog curled up at his feet. It was just past eleven and the sky was clear under a half moon.

Nick had made some quick arrangements, asking Lou to drive over so they could take his car, leaving his Taurus in Maggie's driveway, hoping to throw off anyone driving by into thinking he was in the house. Lou's wife had followed in her car and driven his partner home after Lou assured Nick he'd handle things at the precinct until he returned, even though Nick had talked with the lieutenant and brought him up to date. Harris wasn't happy, but he'd reluctantly given his okay.

After dinner, Nick had sat down with Maggie and Josh, explaining the situation without overemphasizing the fear factor. Maggie could readily see the need to get Josh to

safety. Nick had called in a favor from a female police officer, Sally Cummings, and had gotten her to agree to stay
the night with Maggie just in case. After all, Rafe had broken
into the house and beaten the older woman, so he couldn't
in all good conscience leave her unprotected.

Although Josh was reluctant to stay up north without his
mother, Tate had managed to tell him in such a way that he
accepted her decision. Fortunately he was an adaptable kid
and remembered staying at Aunt Helen and Uncle Joe's ranch
a while back where he'd enjoyed the horses and helping out
in the garden.

Tate had hurriedly packed his things, letting Josh choose
what he wanted to take, like the raggedy blanket he sometimes slept with, his Pokémon collection and, of course,
Ralph. When Nick was certain they weren't being observed,
he'd bundled the two of them into the Ford along with Josh's
belongings and Ralph. They'd started out at nine and now
had another hour to go.

Glancing over at Tate, Nick saw that she was holding herself tightly in check, staring out the windshield unseeingly,
her arms wrapped around herself protectively. She was too
quiet, too tense, almost robotlike and had been ever since
they'd heard the bomb report. He couldn't blame her, but her
state of mind worried him. After they dropped Josh off, he'd
work on easing her mind.

"It's Barkley, right? Your aunt and uncle. Helen and Joe
Barkley, didn't you say?" he asked, trying to draw her out.

She knew what he was doing, trying to penetrate the icy
fear that clutched at her. If only he could. "Yes."

"Is it a horse ranch they own, or cattle?"

"Both."

"Do you know how to get there once we reach St. Johns?"
She'd told him the ranch was almost to the eastern border of
Arizona just before New Mexico.

"Yes, I know the way." *Please,* she prayed, *let him leave me alone. Doesn't he know that if I let myself think, I'll fall apart and I can't do that in front of Josh?*

Nick recognized the barely suppressed emotion in her voice and decided that leaving her to her thoughts might be better. They rode the rest of the way in silence, through the flat countryside. Nick had never been up this way and he had to admit the widely spaced ranches afforded a great deal of privacy. Acre after acre of farms and grazing land where cattle lay in grassy fields and corrals fenced in a variety of quarter horses. It was quiet and peaceful. A man could get away from the stress of city life with its crime and traffic and myriad other problems up here, Nick thought. He'd always been an urban creature but he had to admit, the country had its own appeal.

Tate stared out the window, but saw nothing, her thoughts turned inward, her nerves stretched tight as rubber bands. She and Josh had spent nearly two years here once upon a time, and it had been a fairly uncomplicated interlude. But that's all it had been, an interlude, a break in the norm, unreal. Even if her father hadn't died, she'd have had to go back sooner or later. She couldn't live like that, in hiding. It wasn't fair to Josh.

She loved the country, but to visit, not to live in. She wanted close schools, museums, nearby bookstores for herself and for her son. But most of all, she wanted to be free, to come and go as she pleased, without fear. Would that day ever come? Tate wondered.

The Barkley spread was substantial with two barns, several outbuildings and the farmhouse two stories high, white clapboard with a wraparound porch. Lights were on downstairs as Nick pulled up in front, noticing that it was exactly midnight.

Helen Barkley came down the front steps to greet them, a tall slender woman with auburn hair lightly streaked with white that she didn't bother tinting. Still an attractive woman, her warm green eyes were welcoming as she hustled them inside. Nick could see that Tate had inherited Helen's good looks, thinking that in twenty years, she'd look very much like her aunt at fifty.

Tate hurriedly introduced Helen and Nick as he took Josh from the back seat and hefted him in his arms. The boy didn't stir.

"I've got the bedroom next to ours all made up for Josh," Helen said, leading the way upstairs as Nick carried the sleeping boy, Tate following with Josh's small bag. A subdued Ralph trotted alongside.

Nick laid the boy on the single bed and tugged off his shoes, then stepped back while Tate removed his jeans and tucked the covers around him. "No use waking him to put on pajamas," she commented, smoothing back Josh's hair.

"He won't wake up frightened, will he?" Helen asked.

"No. I explained everything to him." Well, almost everything.

Just then, Josh opened his eyes, looked a little disoriented, then spotted his mother. "Are we here?"

"Yes, honey." Tate leaned down, kissed the downy soft cheek and hugged her son to her as an emotional wave engulfed her. She'd never spent a night without him since he was born. "Nick and I have to leave, but Aunt Helen and Uncle Joe are in the room next door. Okay?"

"Okay, Mom." He waited until his mother stood, then in a gesture that surprised everyone in the room, held out his arms to Nick.

"So long, sport," Nick told him, moved that the boy would want to hug him. "Remember, we'll be back for you as soon as we can."

"I know. Bye." Curling up with his blanket, he closed his eyes.

Tate saw that Helen had left a night-light on. She patted Ralph's head as he jumped up on the foot of the bed. "You take good care of him for me, Ralph," she whispered, then followed Helen and Nick downstairs.

"Are you two hungry?" Helen asked. "It's a long drive and…"

"Not for me," Tate answered. She'd only picked at the chicken dinner earlier and knew she couldn't swallow a thing even now. But men could always eat, she supposed. "How about you, Nick?"

"I'm fine, thanks." He gazed around the big living room, spotting some great antiques and wished they were here under better circumstances, for he'd like to look around. "You have a great place here," he told Helen.

"Thanks." She followed his gaze as he studied an old clock. "We drive around weekends sometimes and hunt out antiques. You should come back when you have more time."

"That would be nice." He glanced at Tate, noting her anxious expression. "We really should get back."

"Yes, Aunt Helen," Tate said, her voice husky to her own ears. "I hate to just drop Josh and run, but we both have to work tomorrow and…"

"I understand." Helen patted Tate's shoulder as they walked out onto the porch. It was cooler this far north, but not cold, with a night breeze that brought with it the scent of nearby honeysuckle. "Now, don't you worry about a thing. Joe has his shotgun if anyone comes nosing around, and he's not afraid to use it. Josh loves it here and we're so glad to have him. Joe goes to bed early, you know, about eight, on account of he gets up at five. But he's real excited about having Josh here. And I've baked his favorite cinnamon buns. You remember, Tate, how he loves those buns?"

Tears threatening to fall, Tate nodded, then accepted the older woman's hug. "I hate to have to impose on you again."

"Now, you stop that. We're family." She leaned back, brushed a tear from her niece's cheek with a weathered hand that had seen a fair amount of work through the years. "You're both welcome here anytime." As Tate stepped back, Helen looked up at Nick. "And your young man, too."

Nick had heard Tate explain the situation to Helen on the phone, but he felt he had to add his own reassurance. "Thank you. This is only temporary. We're working on getting that man out of Tate's life for good." He slipped his arm around Tate's waist, felt her trembling. "We'll be back for Josh as soon as this is over."

Green eyes so like Tate's studied his face a long moment, then Helen smiled. "No hurry."

Unwilling to risk talking with her emotions so high, Tate simply nodded, gave her a final hug and got into the Crown Victoria. She saw Nick bend down to hug Helen as well before getting behind the wheel. How easily he'd fit in, hugging Josh, then Helen. He was a man people trusted instinctively, she decided. Through damp lashes, she watched her aunt waving from the porch as they drove off.

"She's good people," Nick commented as he swung onto the road. "You resemble her."

"She's been more of a mother to me than my own ever was. They're twins, both really beautiful. Only my mother used her beauty for her own selfish interests and Aunt Helen downplays hers. So different even though they're twins."

"Then you're like Helen in more than just looks," he told her, but wasn't sure the compliment registered. He saw that exhaustion had stroked with a broad brush over her features.

Letting out a ragged sigh, Tate leaned her head back and closed her eyes, wondering if she'd done the right thing. Already she missed Josh terribly. They'd never been apart because no matter how often she'd felt the need to move, to stay one jump ahead of Adam, she'd always taken Josh with her. This time, Nick had convinced her that they needed to flush both Adam and Rafe out, to force them to make a move, and Josh needed to be somewhere safe. The very thought frightened her, but she had to trust Nick on this.

She angled her head to look at him. Concentrating on driving, his hands on the wheel, he was looking straight ahead, his mouth a somewhat grim line. Tate wondered what he was thinking.

He felt her eyes on him and glanced over. He reached to cover her hand with his, needing the contact. "Are you all right?"

No, she wouldn't be all right until Adam was gone from her life for good and Josh was back with her. But for now, she'd pretend, for his sake, that she was doing fine. "Yes." She saw him turn his attention back to the road though he left his hand on hers. "Nick?"

"Mmm?"

"Thank you."

His only answer was to thread his fingers through hers and give her hand a squeeze.

Weary to her very soul, Tate closed her eyes.

Two hours later, Nick had reached a decision. He'd been glancing over at Tate for miles now, making note of when she'd finally given in to fatigue. He'd also noticed what a restless sleep it was, her face moving into a frown, her body language indicating an unhappy dream. Twice she murmured something incoherent, then had almost shouted, "No, don't!"

There were dark smudges beneath her lovely eyes and her skin was pale. She was undoubtedly drained, not so much physically as mentally and emotionally. The bomb scare and having to be parted from her son for the first time was taking a terrible toll on her. He couldn't take her back home until she'd truly rested.

Using his car phone, he dialed Maggie's number, hating to wake her, but he felt it was necessary. She picked up quickly, whispering a groggy hello, even though Nick had instructed her to let the policewoman take the calls. Probably instinct.

"Maggie, it's Nick. Listen, we dropped Josh off and we're on our way back." He spoke softly, not wanting Tate to awaken. "I wanted to tell you that I'm taking Tate to my place for tonight. It's late and I think she'll rest better this way. I hope to talk her into missing work tomorrow."

"That's a good idea, Nick. She's all right, then?"

"A little tense, taking a nap right now. Is everything okay over there? No surprises?"

"No surprises. We're fine. Sally's a lovely woman."

"Great. I'll call you sometime tomorrow." He pushed the disconnect and stole a glance at Tate. Her head was moving restlessly as she muttered in her sleep. When she started to moan as if frightened, Nick touched her arm. "Tate. Wake up."

Startled, her head raised. "No, please, no," she said, her eyes open but unfocused, obviously still back in her dream.

"You're dreaming," Nick told her as he turned onto the dirt road leading to his mobile home. It was long and narrow, but he planned to clear more trees, widen and pave it once his house was finished.

He saw that Tate was wide-awake now, looking scared as she shoved both hands through her hair. "Are you all right?" he asked.

She let out a huff of air. "The dream, more of a nightmare, really. It was horrible." She bent forward, wishing she could erase the mind pictures.

Nick pulled into the carport attached to his double wide trailer, shut off the engine and turned to her. "Tell me about it."

"I just want to forget it."

"Damn it, Tate, when will you ever truly trust me?"

She shuddered, her eyes downcast. "We were up on

Mount Lemmon and this time it was Adam who dangled someone over the ledge. I couldn't see who he was holding at first, but I could hear Adam laughing. Then I recognized his victim. It was Josh and he was crying for me, holding his arms out to me.'' Her shoulders hunched as she struggled with the memory. ''He kept calling *Mommy,* and I couldn't reach him.''

Nick reached for her, but she raised her hands, holding him at bay. ''No, please. I need to work this out myself. This is *my* problem, not anyone else's.'' Angrily she swiped at tears wanting to fall.

He sat back, feeling deflated, yet trying to understand. ''I know you've always handled everything alone. But you're not alone anymore. Let me help. Let me carry some of this load with you.''

Slowly, she swung around to face him, trying to see his eyes in the dim moonlight coming in through the windshield. ''Why?'' she asked, her voice hoarse. No man had ever wanted to help before. She was suspicious of such an offer, certain there had to be strings attached. Yet he'd been nothing but kind and caring.

Tate felt confused, lost down an unfamiliar road.

He wasn't sure how to answer her, wasn't sure she was ready to hear his reasons, if he could verbalize them. He took her hands, found them icy cold, rubbed them in his. ''Let's get out of the car.''

She looked out the window as if just realizing they'd stopped. ''Where are we?''

''At my place. I called Maggie. It's three in the morning. There's not much night left, but we're spending it here.''

''No, I want to go home. I need to go to work. I have to be strong and…''

His mouth took hers, ending her protests. He'd wanted to be gentle, to take care of her, but she kept pushing him away. He could think of only one way to stop her.

At first contact, he felt her stiffen, resisting him or herself, he wasn't certain which, then slowly she relaxed a little. His arms gathered her closer, tightening his grip. Almost immediately, he felt the heat bubble up from within her. Nick deepened the kiss as desire awakened within him.

He'd kissed her before, Tate thought, his mouth at times hard, almost cruel, yet this time, she found his lips incredibly soft as they coaxed a response from her. His hands were roaming her back, his solid chest pressing into her breasts. She welcomed his touch this time, with no thought to pushing him away. Senses reeling, she forgot everything except the way he made her feel, and kissed him back.

Reality intruded when she felt his fingers move to the front of her blouse to pry open her buttons. Breathing hard, she touched a hand to his chest to put some distance between them while she waited for her brain to clear.

"What are we doing, out here in the middle of the night, in the middle of nowhere?" she asked him.

She was no longer fighting him, Nick noticed, but rather she looked confused and a little stunned. "I can drive you home or you can come inside and we can finish this. Your choice. Go or stay."

Tate felt her heart lurch. He was leaving it up to her. Was there really a decision to be made? Hadn't she wanted this man since almost the first day she'd met him?

Forever was not an option with her mixed-up life. But didn't she deserve some joy, some pleasure? Something to remember during the long, lonely nights alone. Maybe if she at least had some good memories, she could be strong. For Josh and for herself.

"Stay," she whispered.

Nick climbed out, walked around, opened her door. Still she sat there, looking lost. He took her hand. "Come with me."

Like an obedient child, she followed him up the two steps

and inside where he tossed his keys on the table. He locked the door and bent to her, his mouth taking hers greedily. She responded, as he'd suspected she would, hungrily, avidly, everything forgotten but this man and this moment.

Her arms were around him, her hands diving into his hair. She moved against him and he thought he'd surely explode.

He couldn't wait, not this first time. He couldn't kiss her deeply enough, couldn't hold her close enough. He was struggling with a sharp, urgent need that threatened to take over. His hands were everywhere, trailing along her rib cage, moving to the front and fumbling with the row of buttons. His mouth never left hers as he all but shoved her slacks off while she toed off her canvas shoes.

Passion rose in Tate like a tidal wave. She was as feverish as he, pushing his jacket from his broad shoulders, then jolting when her hand touched his gun holster. She heard him swear softly against her lips as he worked his way out of the harness and tossed it aside.

"The bedroom," she murmured, groping along the opening of his shirt, the need to touch his flesh overwhelming.

"Too far," Nick muttered, knowing he'd never have the patience to make it. Shedding his clothes and hers, he drew her over to the carpeted area in front of his couch. His fingers thrust into her hair, sending the gold clip she'd used to tie it back flying. His knees weakened, so he shifted her to the floor and followed her down, thinking the couch too narrow.

Tate moaned low in her throat as her hands caressed the hair of his chest, then moved to encircle, to stroke his back. She arched as his lips claimed first one breast, then the other, drawing on her flesh deeply. Mind spinning, she pressed his head closer while her hips shifted restlessly.

There was only a hint of illumination drifting in through the slatted blinds, but Nick's eyes had adjusted to the dimness. He thought she looked incredibly beautiful wearing only streaks of moonlight, her auburn hair spread out on the

carpeting, her eyes darkening as her arousal deepened. He'd
wanted to go slowly, to treat her like the lady he knew she
was, but needs hammered at him. When her clever hands
roamed lower and closed around him, he knew he didn't have
much time.

"Tate, I want you so much," he whispered close to her
ear, his voice hoarse. "I don't think I can wait."

Tate wanted no lazy loving, either. "Don't wait. I want
you, too. Right here, right now." Desire had her squirming,
had her aching. As she felt Nick's fingers slip inside her, she
closed her eyes and let the wondrous feeling take her.

This was what she'd needed, this mindless retreat from
herself. The outside world was kept at bay for this small
measure of time. There was no madman stalking her, no danger to her son, no separations to break her heart. Here and
now, if only temporarily, she felt wanted, loved, safe. This
was the only reality in a world gone mad.

She felt his body tremble as he hovered over her, his dark
eyes shimmering with passion. Could any woman resist being
wanted this wildly? she asked herself. Then he was on her
and in her, his thrusts deep and sure. The climb was faster
than she'd ever known, more frantic. In moments, her body
rippled with pleasure and her mind went blank as wave after
wave of white-hot pleasure rocketed through her. Seconds
after, she heard Nick whisper her name as he reached the
summit with her.

Long minutes later, Tate lay quietly listening to Nick's
harsh breathing slow, holding him still locked within her. She
was a little dazed at how easily he'd managed to send her
flying. In the distant past, she'd often had trouble getting
there, and Adam, it seemed, had always been in a hurry. In
her youth and inexperience back then, she'd assumed the
problem was hers and that she'd never find the patient lover
she apparently needed. Yet with Nick, she'd exploded almost
violently moments after contact.

It had been more like an episode of hot, reckless sex than tender lovemaking, Tate thought. Slowly she smiled. It had been the single best experience she'd ever had.

He shouldn't have been surprised at her sensuality, Nick thought, since every time he'd kissed her, she'd been passionately responsive. Tate was a woman a man made love *with* not *to*, a greedy participant who'd shattered his control far more easily than he was comfortable acknowledging. She'd made him forget everything but her and his helpless attraction to her.

Which might present a problem.

Rising on one elbow, he gazed down at her. Her eyes were soft and dreamy, her mouth slightly swollen from his kisses. "How do you feel?"

"Amazed, astonished, astounded. And that's just the *A*'s."

That made two of them. He wondered if such an unbridled passion, such a feverish need for completion that they couldn't make it some thirty feet to his bed, was old hat for her. Or was she used to more tender encounters, candlelit bedrooms, champagne and sweet preliminaries. "I guess, on a romantic scale, that didn't even make it to five."

"Maybe." She raised a hand to touch his cheek. "But on a sensual scale, it shot off the chart."

He smiled at that, then sobered quickly. "I didn't use anything," he confessed unnecessarily. This hadn't happened to him since his teens, this craving that had overruled good sense and all reason.

"I know." Tate brushed back her feathery bangs. She'd never in her life grappled on the floor with a man like some wild woman. How was it he could bring her to that? "I wasn't prepared for…it's never happened for me like that before. So blindly, so fiercely. I couldn't think."

Nick didn't want to admit that it had never happened quite that way for him, either. Rolling to the side, he took her with him, keeping their lower bodies locked together. He struggled with a belated self-anger at his stupid haste, his careless loss of control. Not wanting to upset her, yet needing to know, he braced himself to ask a very important question. "Do we have a problem or are you on the pill?"

"We're okay. I've been on the pill since Josh was born." She hadn't wanted to risk another pregnancy with a chance encounter, although there hadn't been any. But Nick hadn't known that when he'd maneuvered her down, hadn't stopped to ask or to think, like she herself. She could scarcely blame him for what she was guilty of, also.

Through his relief, Nick noticed her frown and trailed his thumb down her cheek, then along the fullness of her lower lip. He felt too good to completely withdraw as small after-wave tremors from her teased him. "Are you sorry now?"

With just that light, gentle touch of his finger, he had her full attention again. Though his eyes were on hers, his other hand closed over one breast, the movement a caress. Deep inside, Tate felt him hardening with renewed desire, and felt her own astonishing response, as savage as the first time.

Fragments of a conversation she'd had recently with her landlady came back to her. It had been Maggie's wedding anniversary, which she'd been celebrating alone since her husband's death, and she was waxing sentimental. They'd been discussing great loves and Tate had commented that Josh's father had certainly not been the love of her life, though maybe at twenty, she'd thought so. Maggie had commented that perhaps Tate had never felt an attraction so deep, so strong that all else be damned. Tate had agreed, had doubted she ever would.

But now, lying here on his living-room rug with Nick Bennett buried deep within her, after incredible sex yet already wanting more, Tate felt that intense attraction now.

"Sorry?" she repeated. Tate shook her head. "How could I be sorry when no one's ever made me feel the way you do?"

He didn't say anything, but she saw the tension leave his face just before he gathered her closer to kiss her deeply. This time he explored her mouth unhurriedly, then shifted his hands to wander her body, all the while watching her reaction to his touch. Leisurely he investigated every curve and hollow he'd missed on his previous speedy journey, searching out all her sensitive spots as Tate felt her breathing go shallow. He was once more throbbing within her and she was no longer able to lie still.

Nick shifted her until she was on top of him, then thrust upward, letting her know he was more than ready. Tate settled her mouth on his and let him lead the way.

Later, much later, Nick turned to find Tate watching him. "We could move to the bed," Nick suggested halfheartedly.

"Oh, I don't know. I'm growing quite fond of this rug." She gazed around the small living room, her eyes by now accustomed to the dimness. A fairly large mobile home, she guessed, and very compact. One couch, one chair, one end table and lamp, a television set and a bookcase. A Pullman kitchen at the far end and, she supposed, a bedroom and bath down the hallway. Enough for a bachelor pad, she decided.

He saw her take inventory and felt the need to explain. "This is temporary. A lot of my furniture's in storage. Tomorrow when it's daylight, I'll show you the house I'm building about three hundred yards from here. Slow going but one day it'll be finished."

"You like to work with your hands?" she asked, although hadn't he quit the family building business?

Lying on his side, he propped his head with one hand and toyed with her hair with the other. "When it's for myself like this, I don't mind the work. I want it to be just so. But I don't want to do it day after day, especially to others' specifications. I don't like to cut corners and settle for inferior products to save money. That's why I wait until I have the money to continue, then I work on my place. When it's finished, it'll be all paid for.''

"I envy that, a place of your own.'' She sighed, brought back to the present in a rush. "I want that for Josh and me, one day.''

"And you'll have it, too.'' He touched her chin, turning her head toward him. "Please, let me help. Don't shut me out. I think you must know, there's something pretty strong between us.''

"I don't know. I...'' He was so close she could see his jaw shadowed with a day's growth of beard, could smell the warm, masculine scent of him that further clouded her already foggy brain. She needed some answers and wondered if he'd give them to her straight. "In the car, I asked you why, why you wanted to help me and my son, and you didn't answer. I know you don't go this far in all your cases. Why are we special?''

Nick couldn't believe she was still asking. "Adam Weston did more than abandon you with a child. He ruined you for any other man. You can't trust any man and you won't let yourself believe that I might have an unselfish motive for wanting to help you carry that heavy load.'' His voice was heavy with disappointment.

Slowly Tate got to her feet, feeling terrible that she'd probably hurt him again, but unable to stop now that she'd started this. "What is it, then? Why do you want so badly to help us?''

He stood, then turned to her and framed her face with his big hands, capturing her eyes, holding her still. "Because I love you, Tate Monroe, and I've never said that to any other woman.''

Tate licked her lips, felt her heart pounding, her knees weakening. That was one she hadn't thought of. "I...you're right. I'm having trouble believing that. No one's ever...I mean, love was never mentioned and...''

"Why do you find it so hard to believe? Is it because you're so ugly and I'm so handsome? Or are you a rotten mother who doesn't care about her son? Maybe you take advantage of your sweet little old landlady, never helping her? Do you kick dogs and tear the wings off bees? What is it that you think makes you unlovable?"

Stunned speechless, she just stared at him.

"All right, let's forget your looks, though I find that damn hard to do with you standing naked in front of me. Maybe I love you because you've put up with so much, yet that bastard hasn't been able to break your spirit. Or maybe because you'd crawl over broken glass for your son. Or perhaps because you stay with Maggie to help her, not the other way around, even knowing that Adam could find you there."

His thumbs caressed her cheeks as he saw her eyes grow moist. "Yeah, because of all that. And because you're the best thing that's ever happened to me, a woman who's warm and loving and loyal to a fault. You give me reason in this insane world to get up in the morning and face another day full of killers and rapists and thieves. You make me want to hurry up and finish that house so I can bring you and Josh and Ralph here to live with me. So we can be a family, like I've always wanted. And maybe like you've wanted, too."

He stepped back, dropped his arms. "But if you still feel that sex is all I want, I'll drive you home and leave you alone."

Tate closed the gap between them, put her arms around him and looked up at his deep gray eyes. "I'm sorry, Nick. Sorry for not believing, for not trusting. For so many years, I've forced myself to back away from my feelings. The men I've known, none have been like you. You're the one who's special. Please, I didn't mean to hurt you."

"Are you sure? I don't want you agreeing with me for all the wrong reasons."

"There's only one reason I'd ever be this intimate with

another man ever again. I care about you. I have for a long time now, but I'm still afraid to trust my feelings. Once, years ago, I thought I cared for Adam, although we never talked about how we felt. I assumed he cared about me, too, and that was a huge mistake. I was in love with the idea of an important, popular man choosing me. I was very wrong and I've paid for that lapse in judgment.''

He was softening. How could he not when she'd said she cared for him, when she looked so contrite. ''You were young. We're all allowed a few mistakes.''

She draped her arms over his shoulders. ''Yeah, well, mine was a whopper.'' Slowly she pressed herself close to his body, watched his eyes darken. ''This doesn't feel like a mistake. It feels right. I know you're nothing like him. But you're going to have to be patient with me.''

''This feels right for me, too.'' Bending his head, he touched his lips to hers lightly. But in moments, it wasn't enough for either of them. He drew her closer, deepened the kiss as his hands kneaded her back and shoulders. He felt her breath hitch as she returned his kiss, as her tongue moved into his mouth, as her breasts rubbed against his chest.

Nick pressed into her, backing her up until she reached the far wall. Holding her there, he kissed her mouth and her cheeks, down along her silken throat. Never would he have enough of this woman.

At least with this, Tate felt herself on firmer ground. Making love with Nick was a joy she'd never thought she'd find. But confessions of love were something else again. How could she trust her heart to a man she'd known a mere few weeks?

Growing impatient, Nick bent to pick her up in his arms and carried her to the back where an accordion door led into the one bedroom. His bed dominated the small room with space for only a nightstand. He laid her on the mattress and quickly joined her.

The hall light had been left on, a dim glow drifting into the room. Nick lifted his head, his eyes devouring her. "I won't tell you how beautiful you are," he whispered. "Too many men have already done that."

"No one who matters," she answered. "Tell me what you see."

"Perfection. Absolute perfection." His hands settled on her breasts as she sucked in a deep breath, her eyes fluttering closed. He caressed her gently, then more sensuously, before lowering his mouth to her. He drew on her and she jackknifed as sensations flooded her system.

His breathing ragged, Nick buried his face in her neck, murmuring hot, hungry, exciting things into her ear. Her eyes were half closed as she lay back, absorbing each new sensation, as with lips and teeth and tongue, he pleasured her. Anticipation bubbled in her because now she knew what he could bring to her. Now she knew and wanted to visit again that place that only he could take her to.

She was giving him the gift of herself, Nick knew, one she didn't part with easily or often. He would do the same, hoping to chase away her bad dreams, her pain, the bruised look around her eyes. He wanted her to think only of him.

Tate wanted more, wanted to give to him what he'd brought to her. Her hands thrust into his hair and her mouth settled on his as her body began to move, reaching for him, drawing him to her. He knelt over her and slipped inside as if they'd been lovers for years.

He'd known—not guessed, but known—it would be like this with Tate. He caught her hands, stretched them over her head and gripped her fingers tightly in his. Now he increased the rhythm, moving within her, watching her climb with him.

"What are you thinking?" he asked, needing to know her mind.

"That I want you," she answered, her breath heaving.

"You've got me," he answered, feeling her heart slam

against his, feeling the damp, slick slide of her skin against his.

The hunger inside him was like a living, breathing thing, the strong streaks of desire that he'd tamped down all too often were screaming again for release. Her eyes stayed on his, those brilliant green eyes, and he watched them change, darken, and finally disintegrate as they exploded together.

Shuddering, whispering his name, Tate closed her eyes and let go of the world, feeling certain this man would be there for her when she came back.

The return was slow, languid, lovely. She kissed his shoulder as he lay atop her, and tightened her arms around him.

"I must be crushing you," Nick said, easing from her.

"No, you're not. Don't go." She didn't want this closeness to end, didn't want to leave this wondrous world for the real one.

But he shifted anyhow, drawing her with him so she lay alongside, facing him. His eyes seemed to take inventory of her face and a soft smile played on his marvelously sensual mouth. "I never expected to feel this way," she confessed. "All those years, I met a lot of men, and never wanted any of them to touch me. I did everything I could to stay uninvolved. But you...you just..."

"Tore down all those big walls you so carefully built?"

Tate smiled. "Something like that."

"Let's leave them down, Tate. No more barriers between us, no more secrets. Promise me."

She nodded, hoping she could keep that promise.

Chapter 10

They hadn't closed the blinds the night before, their minds on other things. So the morning sun came pouring in the bedroom window at five, awakening Tate, catching her slightly disoriented. She was lying on her back in a fairly small bed in a really small room, she noted. A quick glance around brought memories rushing back, and heat moved into her face. She turned toward the man who was taking up three-fourths of the space.

Nick. He was on his side, the pillow scrunched under his head, his hair mussed by her hands, his jaw shadowy with his morning beard. He looked like a young boy, his face relaxed and unlined, almost carefree, like Josh so often did. Only there was nothing little-boyish about his arm curled around her, his fingers grazing one breast.

She lay there, a myriad of emotions flooding her. This was the very first time she'd ever awakened in a man's bed, with the man still in it. The times she'd been with Adam had been stolen hours, furtive, with a clandestine air that had made it seem exciting at the time. Thinking back now, the hours she'd spent with him, the ease with which he'd maneuvered her into his bed, shamed her.

It wasn't the same with Nick, she knew. He'd excited and intrigued her from the beginning. She knew only too well what trusting your heart to a man can do to your emotional well-being. There was no question that she'd wanted Nick to make love with her last night. The first time so that he'd make her forget her fears. But after that, she'd wanted him because he made her feel so much, and what she'd felt had been thrilling.

For hours last night, she'd let herself dream that this was how it could be, how it would be from now on. With a heart full of longing, she let herself believe that Nick meant all the wondrous words of love he'd murmured to her in the throes of passion. Yet now, watching him sleep in the cold light of dawn, she wondered if he'd awaken with regrets, wanting to be rid of her as soon as possible.

Tate frowned, knowing she was doing it again, thinking negatively, something that had become too much a habit. When you're not used to good things happening to you, should they finally happen, you question them and yourself. Maybe, if she began to look on the positive side, things would work out.

In a perfect world, Adam would forget about trying to get Josh or Nick would catch him making a mistake that would force him to stop. Josh would come back and they could live without fear. And maybe there'd be a future for her and Nick.

But then, when had it ever been a perfect world?

She raised a hand to touch his hair ever so gently, just to reassure herself this wasn't a dream. He was a beautiful man, a wonderful man. But she had no right to lead him on. Had no right to take his love when she wasn't free of the demons that tormented her.

She'd made love with him and accepted his words of love,

but nothing had really changed. Her son was still miles away, needing protection from his own father. Adam was still plotting a way to take Josh from her, increasingly terrorizing them all with bombs and letters and telephone threats through a vicious thug he called an aide. Adam thought that being a member of the U.S. senate made him invincible, immune from the rules and laws that governed ordinary citizens. And maybe he was.

For years now on and off, he'd been stalking her, hounding her, menacing her. As much as she knew Nick's intentions were based on his belief in himself and his ability to get Adam, yet she couldn't buy into his blind faith. Because nothing had changed in her life as far as the danger aspect went. She was still on the run, constantly looking over her shoulder, an unwilling target of a madman.

Adam had to be mad to think she'd ever let him have Josh. As before, it was up to her to protect her son. Nick's scheme, of waiting around to flush Adam out, was viable if you didn't consider what a toll waiting would have on her nerves. It was more than waiting for the other shoe to drop. It was waiting to see where Adam's henchman would plant the next bomb or sabotage the next car. This cat-and-mouse game was going to drive her crazy.

Sighing, she eased out from under Nick's arm, gathered up her clothes lying where they'd been flung all over the living room and went into the bathroom. She badly needed a shower.

The flow wasn't the greatest, but the water was hot and steaming. Tate stepped under the spray and was just beginning to lather up when the shower curtain slid back. A devilish grin on his face, Nick joined her, ducking his head under the water.

"Let me do that," he said, taking the soap from her. Lost in her troubled thoughts, she wasn't much in the mood for fun and games. But all Nick had to do was touch her and she forgot what she'd been thinking. The moment he started soaping her skin with those big hands, Tate knew it was going to be a very long shower for both of them.

The hot water ran out before the two in the small shower stall were finished playing. When it began to run quite cool, Nick shut off the spray and grabbed two towels, handing one to Tate. "This is a first for me. I haven't ever showered with anyone," he told her, rubbing dry his wet hair.

"Nor have I. Pretty tight quarters, but we got the job done."

He bent to kiss her neck. "Mmm, did we ever."

Tate hated putting on yesterday's clothes, but she had no choice until she could get to Maggie's and change. However, she looked with some trepidation at her blouse where two front buttons were missing.

"I seem to recall someone in a hurry to get this off me last night," she commented, holding up the blouse.

"It was worth a new blouse, which I'll get you." He opened the closet to reveal a small dresser. He found a blue T-shirt and handed it to her. "Here, try this. It's too small for me."

It was still miles too big for Tate, but she put it on anyhow, then went out to the tiny kitchen and looked around while Nick shaved and dressed. She spotted the coffeepot and searched the cupboards until she found coffee. By the time Nick joined her, the coffee was dripping and Tate was seated at his small kitchen table sipping orange juice.

"I hope you don't mind that I made myself at home," she said as he bent to kiss the top of her head.

"*Mi casa, su casa,*" he said, taking the juice she handed him.

A nice thought, my house is your house. But it wasn't really her house and she'd have to get going very soon. Glancing at him, she noticed that Nick was wearing jeans and a snug black polo shirt. "Kind of casual for work, or aren't you going in today?"

"I'm not going in and neither are you." Before she could protest, he took her hand, squeezed her fingers. "After the last twenty-four hours, we deserve some downtime, and today is that day. What time does your store open so you can call in?"

She stared at him a long moment. "Are you always this bossy this early in the morning? Nick, I have a job to protect. They've been awfully understanding of all the time I've taken off as it is. I can't take advantage."

"Then quit the damn job and marry me." He'd spoken without thinking, but found he meant every word. "I'll adopt Josh and then let's see the good senator try to pry him away."

"Whoa, here." Tate brushed back her hair, trying to keep up, to stay calm. Rising to give herself a bit of time, she went to pour them both coffee.

Marriage. Good Lord. She hadn't thought, hadn't dreamed of marriage since her disastrous affair with Adam all those years ago. And those had been the unrealistic dreams of someone young and infatuated for the first time. She'd been a girl, but she was a woman now. One who had to face facts, even if they weren't to her liking.

Her hands shook so that she almost spilled both mugs. She sipped the hot brew, staring out the small window. How do you tell a man who's not only said he loves you, but has asked you to marry him that none of that is possible just now, without hurting him badly? Tate asked herself.

"Did you hear me?" Nick asked.

"Oh, yes, I heard you. I heard you loud and clear." Frowning, her green eyes settled on his as she came up with a viable argument, one she felt he should accept. "I can just see your mother's face when you tell her that you're going to marry that woman you danced with, the dance that apparently set all her friends to talking. The woman with the son, the one who never bothered to marry his father. Oh, and don't forget to tell her that Josh's father is now stalking both mother and son, and you as well, setting off bombs, sending threatening letters, forcing cars off the road. I just know she'll be thrilled at your news.''

''Are you marrying my mother or me?''

''Neither. Nick, don't try to tell me that how your family feels isn't important to you, because I saw how close you all are at your father's birthday party. You can tell me their feelings don't matter, but I know that's not so.''

He drank a long swallow of coffee, trying to come up with the right words. ''All right, so my family's important to me. But I've gone against their wishes before, by joining the police force instead of knuckling under in the family business. Besides, what makes you think my mother won't understand about your past once we explain it to her? She's a really good person, Tate. You need to give her a chance.''

The question was, Tate thought, would Mrs. Bennett give her a chance, or would Tate have to keep proving herself worthy of her son over and over? But she wasn't able to say that to Nick nor was she ready to even consider marriage at this point in time. ''Look, I'm not about to put myself between you and your mother. You've known me, what, three weeks? Four? And her all your life. I don't want to cause a rift.''

He studied her face, thinking she was skirting the issue. Was there another reason? ''Is it because of Josh? You don't feel he'd accept me?''

''Are you kidding? Did you see how he raised his arms for a hug when he was groggy with sleep last night? He's been nuts about you ever since you got him Ralph. No, Josh isn't the problem.''

''There is no problem, except in your mind, Tate.''

She shook her head. ''Nick, we're rushing this. Let's just

go on like we have been, get to know each other better, and then, once this is over, if it ever is, see where we stand."

But Nick wasn't satisfied with that. "I want you to answer me just one question. One."

She sighed, met his serious gaze. "All right, one."

"Do you care about me, honestly care, and would you consider spending the rest of your life with me?"

"That's two questions disguised as one."

"Don't fudge the issue. It requires only one answer. Go ahead. Answer me, Tate."

She dropped her gaze. "You don't play fair."

"I'm not playing here. I'm dead serious. Answer me."

"It's not as simple as that. I can't answer that question just now. My life's too complicated and..."

"Complications always exist. You have to decide what it is you want."

She moved away from him, unable to think clearly when he was touching her. "You seem to have forgotten something. Adam is not going away. Maybe he never will." She swung toward him, deciding to reveal another terrible fear.

"I have this recurring nightmare that maybe Adam will wake up and realize that I won't ever give Josh to him. So instead, he'll go to court, establish paternity and petition for custody since he's a senator with a solid marriage, a stay-at-home wife, a lovely home, an impressive job."

"The courts tend to favor mothers. It's not that easy, taking a child from its mother."

"Oh, no? If you were the judge deciding between a father like the Adam I just described and a mother who manages a local bookstore, rents a couple of rooms in a fifty-year-old falling-down house with a frail old lady and drives a car held together with spit, glue and prayers, which way would you decide? Adam can give Josh everything. What can I offer him?"

"The most important thing of all—love. And a history of

being there for him for all his seven years. Also let's not forget that Rafe Collins, who is on Adam's payroll, committed several criminal acts. Breaking into Laura's place, messing with her brakes, forcing her off the road and beating up Maggie.''

''All without proof.''

''Not so. Maggie could identify Rafe, even though he wore a ski mask. That ponytail, his voice on the tape.''

''You don't know Adam. He'd clean Rafe up, get him a designer haircut, put him in a five-hundred-dollar suit. As to the voice on the tape, it may sound like Rafe, but Adam would parade half a dozen other men in who sound the same.''

''Hey, who's the cop here? If we wanted to start a lawsuit on Collins, we could, right now, and we'd win. The only reason we haven't is we're trying to flush out the head man.'' He drained his mug, turned to pour more coffee for both of them.

''Be that as it may, we really don't know how this is going to end up. Or when. It's true, I care about you, Nick. But I don't have the energy to think about a future when the past is closing in on the present. I'm having trouble holding myself together. It's all I can do to get through each day.''

''This will end and end soon. And everything will be all right, you'll see. I promise you.'' He set his mug down, took hers and did the same before pulling her into his arms. ''I don't mean to rush you, but I need to know if I have a chance here.''

Tate saw the hope in his eyes and hated disappointing him. He could ask her to walk on water and she'd try. But there was more involved here than their feelings. ''Did last night give you a clue about your chances, about how I feel? Making love with you was mind-blowing, but I've lived without sex for a lot of years and I could again. How I feel about you is much more than sex, much stronger. But those feelings are going to have to be put on hold.''

"Do you trust me?" Without trust, there could be no love.

"I trust you to get proof on Adam and put him away." What other choice did she have, at this point? He was a good cop; she knew that. She'd sent away her son so Nick would have free rein to do his thing. She prayed he wouldn't take too long.

Nick frowned. "You trust me to take care of Adam for you. Okay. But what about trusting *me*? As a man, as someone you care about, trusting me with your feelings, certain I won't hurt you?"

Tate didn't want to be in this conversation right now. "I'm doing the best I can here, Nick. Don't ask for more than I can give right now, please. I need time."

It wasn't the answer he wanted, but it was the one he was stuck with for now, like it or not. He tamped down on his impatience, remembering his thoughts that night he'd watched her dance with his father. *She's the one. Don't let her go.* Just because he knew that Tate was meant for him, didn't mean that she felt that way, too. Not yet. But she would. "All right. I'll give you time." And hope she didn't take too damn long.

Thinking they both needed a change of scene, he opened the door of his mobile home. "Come on. Let's take a walk. I want to show you my house."

Tate really didn't want to go. She wanted to see his house, but not just now when she was so stirred up. But she knew he was hurt by their conversation, by the way she'd put him off. She also knew he was proud of his house so she walked outside with him.

He'd chosen his spot well, she thought as he pointed to the far boundaries. The lot was wooded with a variety of trees—birch and pine, eucalyptus and palo verde. Two tall saguaro cactus stood like sentinels, both with two arms stretched skyward, one on either side of the house. Toward the back, she spotted the wood fence he'd put up enclosing his property and the stream that flowed lazily along over rocks made smooth by the gurgling water.

They walked up the path to the front door. A purple jacaranda bush was in full bloom and two varieties of bougainvillea graced the side yard, one pale pink and the other flaming red. The scent of honeysuckle perfumed the air as Tate breathed in deeply. A mourning dove sang its sad song from somewhere in the trees. Something brown and furry skittered across the side yard, drawing Tate's attention.

"What was that?"

"A baby coyote. We probably frightened him. The mother and four or five of her young live over there," Nick told her, pointing off to the right. "She's usually with them, very protective. The father's around here somewhere, too. They're a nice little family." He inserted a key into the lock and swung open the solid oak door with its beveled glass window, inviting her to go inside.

The foyer was Italian tile, that much she recognized. Straight ahead was a winding stairway, the wood banister beautifully carved and gleaming. "Don't tell me you did this?" she asked, moving to run her hand along the smooth surface.

"Yeah, I did. One of my hobbies." Hand at her back, he guided her into a room off to the left that had two walls of bookcases built in, several with glass doors, and a fireplace at the opposite end. "The den or library, whichever."

"Do you have enough books to fill all those shelves?"

"Them and lots more. I noticed you have quite a few, too. Something we have in common, the love of books." He led the way to the dining room with its crystal chandelier and a generous window that looked out onto the sloping backyard. "I plan to clear back there and put in grass, plus a pool one day."

The kitchen was mostly unfinished, floor bare wood and no appliances yet, though the places where they would be were marked. The cupboards, a warm oak, were in. "You must like to cook. This looks like it'll be a dream kitchen."

His arm slid around her waist, drawing her close. "Do you like to cook?"

"When I have the time."

"I can picture you in here, making dinner while Josh and I take a swim out back. There'll be a large patio off the family room..." He walked her over, stopping in front of the French doors that opened to the back. "The lot stretches half an acre in both directions so there's plenty of room for a horse or two. Maybe a tennis court. Josh would like it here, don't you think?"

She saw what he was doing, mentally moving them in, and she felt the tension build. "What little boy wouldn't?"

He showed her the laundry area, two baths, one off the kitchen, the other opening to the backyard for the swimmers. Then he carefully led her up the uncarpeted stairs, pointing out three bedrooms, each with their own bath, then the master suite at the far end.

"This would be our room," Nick said, pushing open two wood doors, also carved, the detailing beautiful.

The room was huge, Tate noticed, with a raised platform that would easily hold a king-size bed and nightstands, a television niche across from it, and several windows to let in the light. An enormous walk-in closet was off to the right.

"And here's my pride and joy," Nick said, moving to a wall switch. Pushing it, he looked up and Tate watched the ceiling panel open over a skylight. "I admit I had to have help installing this. It's pretty tricky."

"It's...breathtaking." What else could she say? Despite her best effort to stay untouched, unmoved, Tate found herself mentally decorating the room, adding homey touches, picturing the two of them in that big bed, staring up at the stars at night with Josh safely tucked in his own bed next door.

A dream was what it was, Tate reminded herself. And like so many other dreams, out of her reach, at least for now.

Nick walked her through the archway into the master bath with its sunken tub outfitted with jets to make it into a whirlpool and the glassed-in shower. Two walls were windows, looking out on the tops of trees, no neighbors nearby to interfere with privacy. In the distance, she could see a ridge of mountains. "It's lovely, Nick. You've done a wonderful job."

"Oh, I'm not finished yet. I've got lots of ideas. I'd like to talk them over with you, when we have time, of course. And colors. I haven't picked out any yet. What are your favorites?"

Tate turned from the view and saw how alive his face was, his silver eyes shining. Dear God, how could he just forge ahead with plans for a future when a dangerous man could very well change her life, or even end it if he became desperate enough?

"I...I think it's a little premature for me to be picking out colors in your house." She checked her watch, saw that it was already seven. "I need to go to Maggie's, Nick. I'll have just enough time to change and get to work on time."

A frown creased his handsome face. "I thought you were going to play hooky today, that we'd spend the day together."

"It's a lovely thought, but I can't, really. We're shorthanded at the store. It wouldn't be fair." She left the room, started down the hall.

Growing angry, he trailed after her. "You're exhausted. You hardly slept at all last night. Can't you give yourself a break?"

"Nick, please!" She stopped at the top of the stairs and faced him. "I have to go to work. Please don't make decisions for me. Just drive me to Maggie's.'' She started down the stairs.

They were in the Ford before Nick spoke again. "I'm sorry if I seemed to bully you, Tate. It's just that I'm so nuts about you and Josh, and I believe you care, too. I really don't see the point in waiting."

Staring straight ahead, Tate drew in what she hoped was a calming breath. "Nick, up until now, you didn't push. I wish you'd have stayed that way. This sort of thing, it's our whole future. It can't be rushed. As I told you, I need time. Please understand."

"I'll try." He started the car, turned around and drove down the bumpy dirt road.

She hadn't seen this side of him before today, this impatience bordering on insistence, this wanting his own way. Even as a young girl, Tate had hated to be hurried into making a decision, especially a life-altering one. She hoped this tendency of Nick's to want to take over wasn't an ingrained habit. She'd lived alone with only Josh too long to bend to someone else's will without serious thought.

Maybe she didn't know Nick Bennett as well as she thought she did.

Tate came down the stairs and turned to Maggie, already enthroned in her favorite spot on the couch in front of her picture window. "I hate to hurry off, but I don't want to be late," she said, fastening her watch. "We're shorthanded, as usual."

Maggie's keen eyes studied the younger woman's face. At first, knowing that Tate had spent the night with Nick, she'd hoped her young friend would return with a rosy glow, something she hadn't seen in years. But instead, there was a sadness in Tate's eyes that bothered Maggie. "Are you all right, dear?"

"Yes, just rushed. Want me to pick up something for dinner on the way home tonight?"

"If you like. How did Josh take to being left with your aunt and uncle? He didn't put up a fuss, did he?"

Realizing she hadn't taken the time to bring Maggie up-to-date, Tate sat down a moment. So she'd be a few minutes late. She owed Maggie the courtesy. "Actually he was asleep when we arrived, but he woke up long enough to say goodbye. I think he'll be fine. He likes it there, the horses and all. Helen and Joe are thrilled to have him, thank goodness. I'll call them tonight."

"I noticed Nick didn't come in, just dropped you off. I suppose he had to hurry off to work, too, eh?"

Eyes downcast, Tate searched her handbag for her keys. "I imagine so."

"What's his house like?"

"It's going to be lovely. I had no idea he was so talented, although he'd said he'd worked in the family business while going to school. You should see the carved wood banister and the front door. Beautiful work. Of course, it's not done yet. He has a lot of finish work to do, and decorating."

"A big house?"

"Yes, four bedrooms, six baths, if you can believe it. And there's a skylight in the master bedroom that opens electronically. Pretty fancy." She stood and smiled at Maggie, unaware that the smile didn't reach her eyes.

"What's wrong, honey?" Maggie asked. "And don't tell me nothing's wrong because I can see it in your eyes."

Maggie always could read her like an open book. With a heavy sigh, Tate sat down again. "It's all too much too soon. He...he told me he loves me." She caught her lower lip between her teeth, trying to stay in control.

Maggie looked confused. "And that upset you?"

"Upset me, shocked me, surprised me. Maggie, he's known me less than a month. He walked me through his house, saying things like, Josh would love the pool, and this would be our bedroom. Mentally moving us in with him. Don't you find that a bit strange? And way premature.''

"Oh, I don't know. I think it's kind of sweet.''

Maggie was a romantic. "He told me this sweet but highly suspect story about always believing that he'd know the right woman for him the moment he met her.''

"And that woman is you?''

"Apparently. But, despite this...this somewhat over-whelming attraction, we don't really know each other. And there's Josh to consider.''

"Josh adores the man.''

"Well, okay, but what about Adam? He's not going away, is he?''

"Maybe he is.'' Maggie reached for the newspaper along-side her, folded to a picture and story beneath. "Read this.''

Hesitantly Tate took the paper. The picture was a recent one of Adam and Angela, his wife, in formal attire taken in front of a fireplace. The article went on to say that Senator and Mrs. Adam Weston had recently purchased a large home in the Catalina foothills near the senator's mother's home. They plan on keeping their east coast home as well as their apartment in Washington, but this new house will be their permanent address since they're soon adopting a young boy.

"Adopting a young boy,'' Tate whispered, her blood run-ning cold. "Oh, Lord.''

Maggie frowned. "That's good news, isn't it? I mean, I know he'll be right here in Tucson, but if he adopts a boy, that must mean he's given up on getting Josh, don't you think?''

Fear had her heart beating in overtime. "Or that Josh is the young boy he intends to pass on as his adopted son.''

Maggie looked stunned. "Oh, no, dear. He can't do that, can he?''

"I don't know. What if he went to the courts, proved by

blood samples that he's the father and took Josh away from me? I'm sure Adam knows several judges who owe him favors. They'd rule in his favor and...I'd lose my son." The very thought had her voice trembling.

"Maybe you should call Nick," Maggie suggested.

"And say what? I can't prove that's what Adam has in mind. Nick said he wants to marry me and adopt Josh."

"That sounds like a wonderful solution to me. That is, if you love him. Do you love him, Tate?"

She leaned back on the couch, closing her eyes. "I don't know. He's a terrific guy, one who deserves better than a woman with a carload of baggage she's been hauling around for years."

"Now, you stop that! You're pretty terrific yourself, and I should know. Don't be putting yourself down. Nick Bennett would be darn lucky to get you."

Loyalty...it was wonderful. Tate sat up and smiled at her friend. "Thanks for that. But you have to admit, my life is full of complications. Why should Nick take on all that?"

"Personally I can think of only one reason—because he loves you."

She wanted to believe that. Oh, how badly she wanted to believe that Nick Bennett loved her. And while she was wishing, she might as well wish he'd wave a magic wand and make Adam and all his pals disappear. But the truth was, she'd stopped believing in fairy tales quite a while back.

Studying Adam's picture again, Tate wished she knew exactly what he was up to.

Rising, she tossed the paper down. "I'll have to think about this. But for now, I've got to get going. Can I get you anything before I leave?"

"No, honey, I'm fine."

Tate picked up her keys just as the phone rang. Her heart fluttered once, then again, thinking Nick was on the other end. What would she say to him? The ride home had been quiet, both of them lost in thought. The sky had darkened with the threat of rain and thunder had rumbled, matching Tate's mood. When he'd stopped the car in front of Maggie's, neither one of them made a move to kiss goodbye, rather surprising after the passionate night they'd spent together.

Bracing herself, Tate answered the phone.

"Tate, is that you?" a deep, cultivated voice asked.

Her heart lurched as she recognized Adam's deep tones. For a second, she longed to slam the receiver down, then decided that was too childish. Maybe she could learn his plans if she appeared to cooperate.

"Hello, Adam." Tate saw Maggie's eyes widen as she overheard.

"I see you haven't forgotten me."

"That would be difficult since you keep sending your long-haired assistant to remind me."

He chuckled deep in his throat. "Still feisty, I see. I'm glad to hear you haven't lost your fighting spirit. I always admired that about you."

"Is that why you called, to compliment me?"

"Not quite."

"What do you want, Adam?"

"The only thing I've ever asked you for—my son."

"He's not a *thing* and you'll never have him. As a matter of fact, if you don't stop harassing me and stalking me and hurting my friends through that thug assistant of yours, I'm going to take Josh and we're both going to go so far underground you'll never, ever find us." So much for cooperating, but the man knew exactly which buttons to push to make her react.

The voice became chilled, dangerous. "Are you threatening me?"

"No, that's your department. I'm only telling you how it will be and I'm dead serious."

"Now, you listen to me. This is the last time I'm doing this, appealing to your sense of fairness. I've had papers drawn up whereby, for a very tidy sum, you hand Josh over to me so that Angela and I can adopt him. He'll become Adam Weston, Jr. He'll have everything he'll ever need— the best education, friends in high places, trips abroad, lessons in sports, music, the arts. One day, he'll follow in my footsteps, become *someone*. I can give him all that, Tate."

There was only silence on the other end, so he continued. "As compared to what you can give him, living in that broken-down house with that pathetic old woman on the pittance you earn at your bookstore. You won't be able to afford city college for him, much less Harvard, like we can. He'll be lucky to get some minimum-wage job driving a pizza delivery truck under your guidance. Be reasonable, Tate. Think of the boy, not yourself. Be generous to him, not selfish. Give him this chance."

Tate's grip on the phone was so tight her knuckles turned white. Tears of frustration swam in her eyes, but she ruthlessly blinked them back. She wished with all her heart that what he was saying wasn't more than a little true. What could she offer Josh?

Feeling he was gaining on her, Adam went on. "These papers are quite legal. You relinquish all parental rights and I sign off on any child support from you. You turn him over to us and you need never see him again. And Tate, I promise you, I'll take very good care of him."

He'd thought of everything, hadn't he? The only reason Adam wanted Josh was to turn him into a little clone of himself, so he could show him off. He didn't know Josh, didn't love him. This was like a business deal to him, papers drawn up nice and neatly, sign away your child and here's your check.

The bastard.

With difficulty, she found her voice. "Would you raise him to be like you, Adam?" she asked quietly.

Smelling victory, Adam put a smile in his voice. "Yes, yes, exactly. Basketball, college, Harvard Law. I'd introduce him to the right people, groom him slowly for politics. He is, after all, my blood. Then, when it's time to choose a wife, he'd have his pick of suitable mates. The good life, Tate. And speaking of that, you wouldn't have to work anymore, either. Not with the money I'm giving you. You could relax, travel, see the world."

"I see."

Adam took that as an acceptance. "Good, good. I'd like you to meet with me at my attorney's office tomorrow at eleven. Bring your own attorney, if you like, of course. I'll have the check and you produce Josh. You must know, as I do, down deep inside, that this is the best decision for our son."

"Adam?" Tate said, her voice cool, collected.

"Yes?"

"Go to hell." She slammed the receiver down and collapsed into the desk chair, her stomach heaving. Unable to control her body, she hurried to the downstairs bath and lost her morning coffee.

Moving slowly, Tate brushed her teeth and applied a cold cloth to her face. Finally she walked into the living room and told Maggie about her conversation with Adam.

"Oh, that terrible man," Maggie said. "Can't he see that taking Josh from you would devastate the boy?"

"He sees only what he wants to see." She brushed back her hair, trying to think, to plan. Adam had decided to do this legitimately, which had to mean he couldn't operate outside the law because he had no idea where Josh was. That, at least, was good.

Should she take a chance, leave everything and everyone here, go join Josh at Helen and Joe's? As much as she wanted to protect her son, she had no right to expect those two lovely people to take them both in indefinitely. Besides, she had a hunch that with Adam's resources, if she made him angry enough by skipping out now, he'd find them sooner or later.

Where could she go, what could she do, to escape him?

"What are you going to do, Tate?" Maggie asked gently.

"I honestly don't know." Wearily she walked to the phone and dialed Brennan's Book Emporium. Her assistant, Dave Anderson, answered on the second ring.

"Hi, Dave. It's Tate. Listen, something's come up and I've got to take a personal day. Can you handle things?"

"Of course. Are you all right?"

She doubted she'd be all right ever again. "I just have something I have to take care of. If I can, I'll check in later, okay?"

"Sure, Tate. You can count on me."

Thank goodness for that, she thought as she hung up.

Maggie shifted on the couch. "Tate, dear, please call Nick. He'd want to know about that phone call."

So he could do what, pressure her even more intensely to marry him and let him handle her problem? A part of Tate, the soul-weary part that had carried this burden alone far too long, wanted to phone this minute and hand everything over to Nick, to accept the safety net of his strong arms.

But not the independent part, the hard-fought, hard-won side of her that knew this was her problem, her mistake in choosing Adam in the first place, and her dilemma to solve. Although her throat ached with tears, she refused to give in to them. She wasn't some helpless little flower needing a man to take care of her, to make everything right. Josh, his safety and well-being, was her responsibility and no one else's.

She had to think, to find a way out.

Tate tossed her keys into her handbag, left both on the table. "Maggie, I'm going for a walk. A long walk. I need to think things through. Maybe I'll call Nick later." And maybe not. If she decided to leave, it would be best if she made a clean break. Though he owned a large part of her heart, she'd adjust somehow. She'd handled tough decisions before.

Maggie glanced out the window, saw the heavy rain clouds gathering. "Honey, it's going to rain any second."

Tate gave her a tight smile. "It's summer, a warm rain. I won't melt. Don't worry about me, Maggie. I'll be okay." With that, she went out on the porch and closed the door behind her.

Maggie watched her young friend hurry down the steps and start along the sidewalk, head bowed, hands in the pockets of her slacks. Even if thunder hadn't rumbled overhead just then, she'd have begun to worry. Tate shouldn't be alone right now, out walking when she was so upset, with a storm about to begin.

Hating to interfere, yet seeing no other way out, Maggie picked up the phone.

Chapter 11

"How in hell did this guy get a gun in jail?" Lou asked, crouching down behind a large trash container alongside his partner in a filthy alley in South Tucson.

"I doubt that it was smuggled in," Nick answered. "Security's pretty tight at Pima County Jail, for visitors, that is. I don't doubt that he got it right there from some con."

They heard shuffling noises, then a crashing sound as a trash can down at the far end was upended, its sickly sweet contents spilling onto the alley floor. The rain beat down in a steamy spray, soaking the two cops as well as their prey hiding somewhere ahead of them. Then it was quiet again. Too quiet, Nick thought.

After dropping Tate off, he'd decided to go in to the precinct after all. There seemed no point in going back to his mobile home and brooding. He'd checked in and tried catching up on the paperwork all cops hate when Lou got the call. Jorge Espinoza had escaped.

They'd rushed out, but it had taken them nearly two hours

to pick up Jorge's trail. Apparently he'd hijacked a car and forced the driver to take him to South Tucson, his old neighborhood. From there he'd set out on foot, according to the frightened driver. Finally Nick and Lou had spotted him on a deserted street walking fast, tucked close up against a section of old, abandoned warehouses. Jorge's survival instincts on alert, he'd glanced over his shoulder, seen them and ducked into the first alley.

Only he hadn't known it came to a dead end with a back wall fifteen feet high, further caged in by three-story buildings on either side.

"Where do you suppose he was headed?" Lou whispered, shifting to a more comfortable crouch.

"Probably looking to connect with some of his old pals who might hide him. Or someone to bankroll him so he can make it to the Mexican border. He's got relatives there. I'm sure he didn't like jail, waiting for his trial and knowing he'll get convicted and sent to prison. His buddies undoubtedly told him that jail's bad enough, but prison is the worst."

"He should have thought about that when he decided to stalk his wife and kill her." Lou had no patience with domestic violence offenders.

Nick used his small flashlight to check his watch. "We've had him cornered here twenty minutes. He can't go anywhere. Does he think we're going to walk away?"

Lou shook rain off his hair, then glanced over his shoulder, his eyes searching the eerily quiet street. "He might be waiting for an accomplice. I wish we had some protective gear so we could rush him. But damn, he could put a hole right through us." Jorge had fired two shots at them when they'd first entered the alley, fortunately missing both of them. "I don't think he's an expert with guns, but he could get lucky."

"We're not taking that chance. Where in hell's the backup we radioed for?"

As if in answer, they heard a siren coming closer.

Nick frowned. ''They had to show off and make a lot of noise, spooking Jorge even more.''

Minutes later, two older officers got out. Lou went to meet them while Nick kept guard, explaining the situation and grabbing the gear. He put on a bullet-proof vest and hurried back to Nick, handing him the other one. The two officers stood guard at the mouth of the alley, guns drawn, watching the street for any unwelcome visitors.

Nick finished fastening the vest and came to a decision. ''We can't stay here all day. I'm going down there, see if I can talk him in. I got to him once before.''

''The hell you did. He jumped, remember? Would've killed his baby if you hadn't grabbed her.''

''This is different. I think he's just scared. You notice he hasn't fired any more shots? Maybe his gun's jammed or he's out of ammo.''

''Yeah, and it could be it has a forty-shot clip. That vest can't protect all of you. He can still take you out, one shot to the head. Don't be stupid.'' Lou's voice was low, annoyed. ''Let's wait him out. He has to make a move soon.''

He was no hero, but Nick also knew that if Jorge showed himself now, he'd die. Maybe he could prevent that. Nick stood. ''I'm going. You guys keep me covered.''

Slowly, his gun in his right hand down at his side, he started down the alley. Rain fell on him, but he couldn't get any wetter than he was. He blinked, trying to keep his vision clear. ''Jorge, it's me. Nick Bennett. You remember, I was on the ledge with you? I'm not going to shoot. Come out and talk to me.''

The voice came from behind a large, soggy cardboard box, that Nick could barely make out in the dark alley. ''Don't give me that crap. I'm done for and you know it. Only if you guys don't back off, I'm going to take all of you with me.''

"You got twenty-five to life hovering over you for killing Rocio. You do this and it's the gas chamber for sure. Is that what you want?"

"What I want is to go home, my mother's place in Hermosillo. I won't bother nobody ever again, man. Just let me go there." His voice quivered with nerves, emotion, fear.

"Can't do that, Jorge. But I'll put in a good word for you at your trial. Worst thing you can do is kill a cop, Jorge. They'll hunt you down like a dog. Is that how you want to be remembered by your son?"

Nick heard shuffling sounds again, as if the man had stood up, but it was too dark and the rain too heavy for him to be sure. He gripped his .38 tighter, ready to squeeze off a shot if it came to that. "What do you say, Jorge?"

"I say, get the hell out of my way." Gun blazing, Jorge came running at Nick.

Nick felt the thud of a bullet hitting his vest, but the vest held. He raised his arm to shoot, but a shot from behind him slammed into Jorge's chest and felled the big man. Managing to get off one more shot that went wild, Jorge lay in a crumpled heap, the blood on his shirt mingling with the rain.

Standing over him with his weapon still drawn, Nick saw there was no need. The bullet had ripped into Jorge's heart. As Lou came over, Nick looked up. "Thanks, buddy. I owe you."

Lou signaled to the two officers. "Call the meat wagon."

"What a waste," Nick commented. "Once upon a time, he had a nice wife, two little kids and a good job. What makes a guy go crazy like that?"

"Stalkers are a breed apart," Lou said, holstering his weapon. "They get to feeling that if the woman won't do what he wants, she deserves to die. Or they feel that if they can't have the victim, then no one else will have her, either. Then they're still unhappy and usually either kill themselves or let a cop do it for them."

Nick's thoughts flew to Adam Weston, a man who seemingly had everything, yet was willing to risk losing it all by stalking his son and the boy's mother.

"The pitiful part is that they never give up until one or both of them are dead," Lou commented.

Experience with stalkers bore out Lou's observation, Nick knew. He ran a hand over his face, swiping off the rain while a cold chill that had nothing to do with the weather raced up his spine. *They never give up until one or both are dead.*

Something had to be done about Weston before Tate got hurt. Nick hoped she'd listen to him. After the way they'd parted this morning, he wasn't sure.

He shouldn't have pushed her, talking about marriage and adopting Josh. She was too upset over Adam to think about a future. He'd make it up to her, explain himself.

"I've got to get back to the station," Nick said, leaving the alley. He turned to the uniform just pocketing his radio. "You two wait for the wagon and file your report."

"You got it," the cop answered.

Climbing into Lou's passenger seat, Nick shoved his hands through his drenched hair. "Make it a rush, will you? I've got some calls to make."

Maybe it was time to put in an APB on Rafe Collins, do a little squeezing, Nick thought, entering the precinct. Put the fear of God in Weston by arresting his number-one man who just might be persuaded to talk, to expose him and his tactics to the press.

There was one message in his box when he checked in. *Call Maggie. Important.*

He needed to go to his locker and change out of his clothes, soaking wet down to his underwear. But first things first. He dialed Maggie's house. She answered on the first ring. "Maggie, it's Nick. Something wrong?"

"You might say that." Maggie told him all of it, starting

with the article in the newspaper about the senator and his wife purchasing a house as part of their plans to adopt a young boy, how that news had frightened Tate. Then the phone call, all she'd overheard and all that Tate had told her Adam had said. She ended by saying that Tate had left for a walk just before it began raining.

"She's been gone for two hours, Nick. I know it's warm out, but she could still catch her death of cold getting soaking wet. I don't like this, not one bit."

Nick didn't like it, either. "She didn't mention heading somewhere specific, maybe stopping in to see someone?"

"No, just said she needed to think things through. I know she must have really upset Adam by hanging up on him that way." Nerves had Maggie sniffling. "Do you really think that awful man can get Josh by forcing Tate to sign some paper?"

"I can't imagine she'd sign, not for any amount of money." But what if he had Rafe kidnap her and hold her hostage until she signed. Powerful men had their ways, as did ruthless ones. "You say she left on foot? Is her car still there?"

"Yes, on foot. And her car's in my driveway."

"All right, Maggie. I'll find her. Don't worry."

"Oh, thank you, Nick. She didn't want me to phone you, but I just had to, you know."

"I know. You did the right thing. I'll check with you later." Nick hung up, his expression thoughtful.

Lou walked over, having changed into dry pants and shirt, his damp, sparse hair plastered to his head. "Well, I feel better."

"Lou, Tate's been out in this weather walking for hours. I need to go find her. Can you write up our report? I'll be back later to add my comments backing up your version."

"Sure, sure. Go find her."

Nick hurried off to his locker.

* * *

He was feeling enormously frustrated.

Nick had gone to Maggie's, checked with her to make sure Tate hadn't returned in the meantime, then driven the neighborhood streets, block by long block. He'd circled around the university campus area slowly, stopping to stare at the few stragglers out on such a wet day. No one looked remotely familiar.

Maggie had told him Tate had been wearing her work attire, black linen slacks and white blouse. Not even a jacket. He cruised a nearby shopping center, went in to a coffee shop, stopped by two fast-food places, thinking she might have gone in for a hot cup of coffee or simply to get out of the rain. No luck.

Next he'd called Brennan's, wondering if she might have caught a ride to work after all. But Dave Anderson said they hadn't seen or heard from her since her early-morning call saying she was taking a personal day. Beginning to get worried by the third hour, Nick called Maggie on his car phone, but she still hadn't heard, either. Fear had him phoning the precinct for reported accidents in the area but, thank goodness, there were none. As an afterthought, he called the closest hospital, and gratefully learned she wasn't there.

Stymied, he stopped the car and sat there, trying to figure out where Tate might have gone. Nick felt he knew her quite well. She was an extremely fair person and felt that it wasn't fair to tie him down to a woman with so many problems. That isn't at all how he felt, but he knew Tate did.

With no one else on earth had he ever felt such a close bond, almost as if he could see into her mind at times. Sitting in his car while the rain beat on the roof of his Taurus, he closed his eyes and tried to concentrate. Where would she have walked off to?

Long minutes later, he could come up with no viable answer. She wouldn't just walk away, leaving everyone behind and everything, including her purse, her keys. They hadn't parted on the best of terms earlier, but he knew she wouldn't deliberately worry Maggie, knowing how fragile her landlady was. Had she met with foul play? his policeman's mind wondered. Had that bastard Weston had her under surveillance and, after she'd hung up on him rejecting what he'd called his final offer, had he become furious and had her picked up by that burly aide?

Why hadn't he insisted she carry her gun with her at all times? Nick berated himself. He should have gotten her a cell phone, made sure she kept it with her. But, by leaving her purse and everything in it behind, he had the feeling she'd only intended to walk around, think things through, then go back to Maggie's. Only the skies had opened up and maybe she'd been forced to take shelter. Only where?

Again, he dialed Maggie and asked if Tate had any friends in the neighborhood, anyone she might have stopped to visit? Maggie said no. He hung up, feeling drained.

It was too soon to call in a missing persons report. A fine cop he was, couldn't find the one person who meant the world to him. Feeling anxious, dejected and disheartened, he headed home. He hadn't had a real meal in over twenty-four hours. Maybe if he made himself something to eat, he could think more clearly.

Nick turned onto the dirt road leading to his mobile home carefully, aware that rain made the path muddy and slippery. Cautiously he maneuvered the Taurus and was almost in the carport when he saw her. Instinctively braking, he noticed that she was sitting against the trailer wall on a rickety old folding chair he'd meant to throw out. Her legs drawn up close to her body, her arms wrapped around them, her head resting on her knees. When she saw his headlights, she looked up.

He shoved it in Park and stepped out, struggling between relief and fright. Acting on first impulse, he pulled her into his arms and held on. "Thank God you're all right," he whispered.

She didn't say a word, just wound her arms around him and lay her head on his chest, her teeth chattering. Her heart thumped erratically against his, revealing nerves. The roof of the lean-to carport was tin and the rain pounding on it sounded like little drummers playing off tune.

"Let's get you inside and dry you off," he said, leading her to his door, helping her in. She was shivering as he walked her to the small bathroom, turned on the shower and waited for the hot steam. She was already sliding off her cold, wet things. "Take your time," he told her as she stepped in. He could see the goose bumps on her skin. He drew the curtain and made sure there was a big clean towel for her before leaving the bathroom.

By the time he called Maggie to let her know Tate was with him and she was okay, he heard the shower turn off. Nick put on a pot of coffee, then went into the hallway and knocked on the bathroom door. "You okay?"

She opened the door, letting out the steam. She was wearing his blue terry-cloth robe that had been hanging on the back of the door, and she was towel-drying her hair. Her green eyes huge in her pale face, she nodded as she padded past him barefoot into the small kitchen and sat down at the table for two.

Nick poured them both coffee, thinking the last thing he needed was more caffeine, but he felt she should drink something hot and he didn't have any tea bags. He placed the mugs on the table and sat down opposite her. And waited.

Tate encircled the mug with both hands, her head down, staring into the hot brew. This wasn't going to be easy, but she knew she had to say it. Finally she looked up into those fathomless gray eyes watching her. "I owe you an apology."

Of all things he'd thought she might say, that hadn't been even on the long list. "Why…"

She held up a hand, stopping him. "Let me say this, get it all out, okay? It's kind of a long story." She drew in a deep breath for courage. "As I told you, my mother was gone by the time I was eight and my brother was six. Dad sat me down and told me I'd have to be the one to hold the family together while he worked. I was awfully young for that kind of responsibility, but there was no one else. I had no other choice, so I did as he asked."

Tate raised the mug and took a sip before continuing. "I learned to cook, to run the washer and dryer, to clean the house and even to iron. And I took care of Steve. Dad helped, but he worked long hours. Later, I found out that my mother had cleaned out their savings account so he had to start all over. Anyhow, my point is, I learned to be responsible and independent and ask for no help from anyone at an early age. I...I think that trait stayed with me to this day. I *hate* asking for help.

"For example, in high school, I was doing poorly in algebra and the teacher wanted to assign an all-A student to tutor me. I refused. Instead I stayed up late every night and often got up early. I studied and crammed and worked until I left that class with an A. And I did it without help."

She sighed, her eyes downcast. "Looking back, I know that I was foolishly stubborn, and for no particular reason except pride, I guess. I was proud that I could do so many things without help from anyone. My father praised me constantly and I ate it up. But it established a pattern inside me so that I have difficulty accepting help even when I badly need it."

Nick had already guessed some of this, but he let her tell it in her own way, wondering where she was going with it.

"When I was pregnant with Josh and Adam had nicely sashayed out of my life, I still had a year of college to finish. So I broke down for the first time and accepted help from Maggie and my two roommates. But even then, they offered.

I didn't ask. Too damn stubborn for my own good, although I probably would have asked in time, for my baby's sake.''

She set aside the mug and looked out the window. The skies were gray and gloomy, the rain still coming down. Tate wished it would end, that the sun would come out. She hurried on to finish.

"I was determined to get a job and support Josh and myself, asking help from no one. Maggie baby-sat him, but I paid her right from the start. Room and board, too. Sure, men asked me out, quite a few, but I had no trouble blowing them off. I was so certain they wanted only fun and games, not a woman with a child. Later, when Adam started harassing us, I still tried desperately to handle it alone. Both Molly and Laura offered to help, but I turned them down. Adam was my problem and I'd manage somehow. I was so sure I could do this alone.''

Turning her head, she looked at Nick. He hadn't said a word and even now, didn't look judgmental or impatient or angry. She'd walked for hours, ignoring the rain, trying to see where she'd gone wrong and how she might fix things. Finally she'd come to the conclusion that she'd been wrong to turn on him, to push him away. Perhaps he'd been a bit premature talking about marriage and the house, but his heart was in the right place. He cared about her and Josh and was unafraid to show it. In turn, she'd given him nothing but grief. She had to let him know how sorry she was and hope that he still wanted her.

"Then you came along." She allowed herself a small smile as she gazed at his wonderful face. "You were gentle and gentlemanly, a lethal combination in my book. For the very first time in my life, I fell in love." Tate saw his eyes grow warm as he placed a hand over hers.

"As you know, I wouldn't admit it, not even to myself. You offered help, but I turned you down repeatedly. See, to me, needing help meant I'd be weak and I needed to see myself as strong, so I could take care of Josh. I refused to believe, even after we made love so beautifully, that you cared for me, the woman. I'm not sure why, maybe because no other man had ever bothered to look beyond my face and body. You wouldn't even kiss me until I all but begged you to, and still I denied my feelings.''

''Yeah, you're a little stubborn,'' Nick said, his first comment.

''A lot stubborn. When you showed me your house this morning and drew a mental picture of how life with you could be for me and my son, I found myself wanting to move in that moment. But I told myself all that was a dream and not reality. Reality was that I had a son a madman was trying to take from me and it was up to me to stop him. You asked me to trust you and I said I did, but only a little. You see, from my viewpoint, nothing had changed, except for the worse. Josh was away from me, Rafe was stalking us and Adam called with what he said was his final offer.''

She told him about her phone conversation with Adam and his ultimatum, about being more truly frightened than she'd ever been in her life and about walking for hours trying to come up with a plan of action.

''So did you come up with a plan?''

Tate nodded. ''I found a twenty-dollar bill in my slacks pocket, a habit I have of always keeping some mad money readily available. I flagged down a cab and had him drive me here. I wasn't sure you'd be here, and when you weren't, I decided to wait for you.''

She was jumpy with nerves as she came to the end of her story, Nick thought. ''All right, I'm here. Now what?''

Tate licked her dry lips. ''Now is when I tell you that I'm sorry for acting so indifferent earlier to your wonderful plans. I assure you, it was an act. Now is also when I tell you again that I love you, and I've never said those words out loud to a man before, either. And now is when I swear that I trust you, not only to help me with Josh's father, but I trust you with my heart.'' She swallowed around a lump in her throat. ''If you still want me, that is.''

He took both her hands into his and smiled. ''Lady, you're exactly what I want. I told you before, I've always been certain I'd know the woman meant for me, and you're the one. I told my brother that night we stood watching you dance with Papa. She's the one, I said. And do you know what he said? Don't let her go.''

Nick rose, taking her up with him. ''I've been looking all over this city for you, ever since Maggie called to let me know you were out walking in a downpour. I only came home to get something to eat and I was going to go out again. Because I'm never going to let you go. What's that saying? You can run, but you can't hide. That's how I feel about you.''

Her arms in the too-large robe went around him as her hands curled over his shoulders. ''I don't want to run anymore. With you is where I want to be.'' Rising to her bare tiptoes, she pressed her mouth to his.

Like coming home, Tate thought as his lips, softer than she remembered, gently kissed her. He held her loosely, their bodies barely touching, as he gave to her through his kiss, letting her know she was loved. Deeply, surely, forever.

Tate eased back, her eyes fluttering open. ''Make love with me, Nick. Like the songs says, make the world go away.''

He needed no more encouragement as he picked her up and carried her into his bedroom. No man had ever carried her as if she weighed little more than a child, cradling her against his wide chest. She never would have guessed how wonderful it felt to give in, to let him be masterful.

The blinds were slanted, letting in a faint gray light, and now a soft summer rain pebbled the roof. Nick nuzzled her neck, thinking how good she tasted, how clean and fresh. He set her on her feet and stood looking down at her lovely face as his fingers threaded through her hair, gently massaging her scalp. He kept it up until she slowly relaxed, until she was almost purring. Her pulse was already racing, with anticipation, with arousal.

Then suddenly her eyes widened. "I'd better call Maggie. She must be worried sick."

"I called her while you were in the shower and told her you were with me." He bent to nibble her ear.

"That must have pleased her. You're her champion."

"The woman has taste. And speaking of taste..." He trailed tiny kisses along her throat, stopping at the spot where her pulse pounded, branding it with his tongue. *Mine,* he thought. *Forever mine.*

She needed him, wanted him, was impatient to have him. She who'd been celibate for years, who'd rarely even been slightly tempted, now felt wanton in her desire for this man. How quickly he'd changed her, she thought as her hands tugged his shirt upward. He straightened long enough to allow her to pull it off over his head and toss it aside. She buried her hands in the soft, curly hair of his chest, making a sound deep in her throat as her seeking fingers relearned him.

Nick stepped back and untied the belt of the robe she was wearing, certain there was nothing underneath. As the folds fell away, he drew in a stunned breath as his trembling hand rose to lightly skim her sensitive skin. "I wonder if I'll always feel so much when I see you like this. You're so beautiful, Tate." His voice was husky with desire reawakening.

"I want to be beautiful—for you."

He eased the robe from her shoulders, saw it pool on the floor, and let his eyes devour her as she lay back down on the bed they'd only left early that morning. He was sure he didn't deserve such beauty to be his alone. He would do everything in his power to guard it, cherish it.

Nick removed his clothes slowly, for there would be no fast loving this time. He wanted to give her the gift of his tenderness which wasn't always apparent in him. But she'd seen it and he meant for her to see it again and again. Her smoky-green eyes watched him as he shed his jeans and his briefs. He lowered to her, inhaling deeply of the scent she'd left on the bedcovers—honeysuckle, fragrant soap and warm woman.

His mouth touched hers, a mere brushing of lips, a mingling of breath. Then he let his tongue tangle with hers in a slow dance, eyes open and on each other, bodies moving closer together. He knew she was a passionate woman, yet she held herself in check and let him lead the way. He deepened the kiss and saw her eyes change to an indigo-green.

Tate was floating in a sensual delirium and her arms came around him, needing the contact. As his hands trailed down her skin, touching, teasing, she felt her bones melt. Her heart was already his and she knew her body would react this way only with him. Going limp in his arms, she let go and truly surrendered for the first time in her life.

Nick's heart was pounding so hard he was certain she must hear it. He'd experienced the passionate side of her, tasted desire on her soft skin, but to have her here with trust in her eyes, soft and pliant in his arms, aroused him greatly. She was a strong, caring, independent woman yet with him, she was able to show her vulnerable side. It was yet another gift for him to cherish.

Her skin hummed everywhere he touched, and he touched everywhere. He stroked almost reverently and for the first time, she felt a womanly pride in her body that could give him such pleasure. His mouth journeyed along her rib cage, stopping here and there to plant soft, moist kisses, worked its way down then slowly started back up, driving her mad. She was no longer able to lie still, but moved against him. Because he couldn't resist, he drove her up and reveled in her cry of protest when he switched his attention yet again to her breasts.

Now he was driven to show her more, to show her everything. With his hands streaking, with his teeth nipping, with his mouth and tongue tasting, he took her again and again, closer to the edge. Her breath trembled from between her parted lips as he brought an ache to places she'd scarcely known existed. Caught in a haze of wonder, Tate could only follow.

The velvety hair of his chest grazed her soft skin and caused an avalanche of sensation. Her shaky hands thrust into his hair and she held on as little bonfires of pleasure erupted. Her head spinning, she felt his strong arms quiver as he braced himself before bending to kiss her. Finally, fresh out of patience, Tate rolled to her back and took him inside her.

Now there was music inside her head and the chorus kept whispering his name. She breathed in his sharp masculine scent as all her senses came alive. Her breath trembled out as he moved within her.

Nick held himself in fierce control, moving slowly, wanting to make it last. He watched her eyes, the green darken with desire, and knew just when she was about to explode. His arms around her tightened in possession, in acknowledgment. She bolted as the final fire erupted through her. Then and only then did he allow himself to join her.

Had she fallen asleep or had she been so lost in the moment that she'd drifted out of herself? Tate didn't know which, knew only that her eyes opened slowly and she found herself lying across Nick who was languidly stroking her back. Her ear was pressed to his chest and she could hear the still thundering gallop of his heart. Their bodies were slick and damp with the loving, but she didn't mind. She found everything about their joining erotic.

Odd how a few weeks can change your life, she thought, still not moving. He'd come into her life such a short while ago, neatly moved himself into her heart and now, she couldn't imagine her days without him. Or her nights.

Despite how messed up her life was with problems, she was exactly where she wanted to be. He'd told her he'd take care of things, make everything right, and she believed him. She trusted him, and it felt good.

"I love you," he whispered into her hair.

Tate rose on her elbows braced on his chest and leaned forward to kiss him, long and thoroughly. "Mmm, and I love you, too. Despite everything, I feel so lucky to have found you."

Nick toyed with her hair, gazing into her lovely face. "A week ago, I didn't know you as well as now, the way your eyes turn emerald-green when you're aroused, the soft sounds you make low in the throat when I'm loving you. Now I know you better and I want you even more." He frowned, then it passed. "Is it all right if I say these things I feel, or are you going to back away from me again?"

She shook her head, her hair grazing her shoulders. "I'm not going anywhere and you can tell me anything you want."

"Even that I'd like to buy you a ring?" He hurried on. "Not a wedding ring yet, but a ring to seal the promise."

Tate held up her left hand. "Size five-and-a-half." She grinned foolishly, unable to stop smiling.

"Done," he said, then heard his stomach growling. "I think my stomach thinks my throat's been cut. Much as I love lying here with you naked in my arms, if I don't eat soon, I may start nibbling on you very seriously."

"We can't have that." She rolled from him, getting off the bed. "My clothes are sopping wet. I may have to borrow something to go home in." She picked up the robe, slipped it on.

They ate scrambled eggs and toast, trying to keep their minds off all their problems. But reality intruded and by the time they were doing the dishes, Nick was making plans.

"Do you know if Adam has a residence he keeps here, maybe an apartment or a house? If he represents Arizona, he has to have an Arizona address or it isn't legal."

"He uses his mother's address I believe. Why?"

That was the same information he'd learned earlier, but

he'd hoped Tate knew of a secret hideaway Adam had where they could catch him unaware. "Was he calling locally or long distance when you spoke with him?"

"I couldn't tell."

Nick put away the frying pan they'd used as Tate wiped down the counter. "Easy enough to find out. If it was local, then he has to be here. Maybe visiting his mother. I think it's time I paid him a little visit."

Tate's heart lurched. "Isn't that dangerous? I mean, accusing a United States senator..."

"Who said anything about accusing?" he said, hanging up the dish towel. "I just have a few questions for him. I'd ask them in such a way that he'd know we're on to him, just waiting for him to make a false move."

But she was skeptical. "I don't know. He doesn't intimidate easily."

"Neither do I." Nick glanced out the window, then at the clock. "Let's get you dressed and we'll go over to Maggie's."

She followed him into his room. "So let's see what funky little outfit you have for me to wear." She watched him study his clothes, picking through, trying to find something small. "You are spending tonight with us, aren't you?"

"You bet." He came up with a pair of drawstring gray sweatpants and a T-shirt. "Best I can do."

"They're fine." Quickly Tate got dressed while Nick gathered fresh clothes for the morning. "Do you want me to change the sheets?" she asked, gazing at the thoroughly disheveled bed.

"No," he answered, coming up behind her, kissing her neck. "Your scent is on them. I'm never going to wash them."

She turned within his arms. "You're crazy."

"Yeah, crazy in love."

* * *

Nick hung up the phone at his desk at the precinct. He'd been summoned by Internal Affairs to give his version of yesterday's shooting of Jorge Espinoza and had spent nearly an hour answering questions. They would give their final ruling in two days, but the lieutenant assured both Nick and his partner that there was no problem in the way the case was handled. After that, Nick had made a few calls.

The call Adam had made to Maggie's house yesterday had been local, traced to his mother's unlisted number. But when Nick had phoned that residence, a maid had answered and told him that Mrs. Weston was out of town and not expected back for several days.

Nick sat pondering what his next move should be. Maybe the mother was out of town, but Adam could still be there. He'd checked every source he had and no other address was listed for Adam Weston in or around Tucson. He apparently still used his mother's address when in town and to qualify for the senate seat he held.

The wily senator was harder to flush out than Nick had imagined.

No matter. Patience wins the race, he told himself. Meanwhile, he had other things to think about. He unlocked his top desk drawer and took out a small velvet box. Inside nestled a lovely emerald flanked by two small diamonds in a gold setting. As engagement rings went, Nick was certain there were many larger, more expensive. But this one suited Tate, he'd decided, the deep green color matching her eyes. He could hardly wait to watch her open it.

Nick tucked the box into his pocket and checked his watch. The day had literally dragged by, or so it seemed, probably because he had something important to do tonight. He was going to pick Tate up after work for a quiet dinner at a little French restaurant he saved for special occasions. And there, he was going to formally ask her to marry him.

He was aware that he was wearing a silly smile. He

couldn't help himself. He needed to make Tate his in some tangible way, to know she was promised to him. Tonight was the night.

Checking his watch, he frowned. Only four. Maybe he'd go to Brennan's and see if she could get off early. After all, she was in charge, right? What's one hour?

Signing out, Nick left, whistling.

But the happy mood vanished when he got to Brennan's and talked with Dave Anderson. "What do you mean, she rushed out of here an hour ago?"

"Just what I said," Dave managed to say, intimidated by Nick's cop persona. "She got this phone call. I was standing alongside her and she turned white as a sheet. She hung up and told me that her sitter had called and that Josh was hurt. Then she rushed out of here."

Nick frowned. But Josh was up north with Helen and Joe. Did the boy get hurt on the farm somehow? And why hadn't Tate called him when she heard the news? "Are you sure that's what she said?"

"Yes, positive." Dave looked nervous. "Is something wrong?"

"I don't know. So you say Maggie Davis called and told Tate that Josh was hurt. Apparently Tate left here to go home, then, right?"

"That would be my guess, but she didn't say."

"Okay, thanks." Nick hurried to his car, grabbed the phone and dialed Maggie's. After four rings, the answering machine picked up. He hung up, then tried again. Same result. Something was definitely not right. Starting his engine, Nick shifted and raced out of the lot, tires squealing.

Where in hell was Maggie this time?

Chapter 12

Nick swung the Taurus into Maggie's driveway, noticing that Tate's Buick convertible was parked in front. Odd since she always parked in the driveway, but she'd been upset and in a rush. Stopping to check out her car, he saw that her purse was on the passenger seat. She really had been rushing, he decided, grabbing the handle.

He hurried onto the porch and knocked, also ringing the doorbell. Pausing, he listened, but no one inside was coming. Where had Maggie gone? She hadn't driven herself. Had someone picked her up?

He tried the door and found it was not only unlocked, but the lock had been broken. His hand slid to his holster and he drew his gun, removed the safety and shoved the door in. Maggie was on the couch, her hands and feet tied, a gag in her mouth.

In shooting stance, Nick checked out the rooms before going over to untie her. He removed the gag and helped her sit up. "Are they gone?" he asked, glancing up the stairs.

Maggie rubbed her wrists. "There was only one, that dreadful man with the ponytail. He made me…oh, Lord, he made me call Tate at the bookstore and tell her that Josh was hurt, that she needed to come home right away. As soon as I got the words out, he hung up on her."

"Did she show up here? Her car's out front." He nodded toward Tate's purse where he'd dropped it entering. "Her bag's on the seat."

"I heard her car. You can't mistake that old rattletrap. But he'd already tied me up by then and I couldn't warn her. He was outside, waiting for her. The long black car was there, too. I'd seen it earlier. I just know he forced her go with him."

Nick viciously relegated his emotions to the back burner, to be dealt with later, trying to think like a cop, get the facts, act. "Did he call anyone from here or did you hear him talk with anyone outside?"

Distraught, Maggie shook her head. "No, he didn't make any other calls, just to Brennan's. I couldn't hear too well outside, but I don't think anyone else was there. When Tate arrived, I heard her voice, then his, kind of like they were arguing. Then two doors slammed and the car drove away."

Checking the door more closely, Nick saw that the dead bolt was undamaged. "You didn't have the dead bolt in place?"

Maggie's hands shook. "I…I must have forgotten. I'm so sorry. Where would he have taken Tate?"

"I don't know but I mean to find out." But first, he had to make sure Josh was all right. "Do you have the number for Tate's aunt and uncle up north? I'd like to check on Josh, just to be on the safe side."

"Tate wrote it down for me, but it's in code. In my address book, look under Ralph."

Nick pulled the desk drawer open, found the worn little book and looked under *R*. Sure enough, there was Ralph with a phone number. He quickly dialed, hoping this was one of the days up there that the phone was working.

After four rings, a woman's voice came on the line. "Hello, Helen? This is Nick Bennett in Tucson. How's everything up your way?" He didn't want to alarm the woman.

"Fine, fine. Josh is out with Joe in the calving barn. He loves to feed the abandoned newborns from a baby bottle."

"He's doing well, then?"

"Yes, indeed." She paused a moment. "Is Tate all right?"

"She's fine," he answered, praying he was right. "She'll phone later and talk with Josh. I've got to run now. Nice talking with you." Nick rung off. "Josh is okay," he told Maggie. He'd hoped as much, but he had to know for sure.

Nick went to Maggie to check her wrist where it had been tied around her cast and her ankles, saw there was no bruising. "Can I get you anything? Will you be all right if I leave?"

"Yes, yes, just go. Find her, please. Oh, I feel so terrible."

"Don't agonize, Maggie. A man like that, if he wanted in, he'd have found a way, even if the dead bolt had been in place." Holstering his gun, he walked to the door. "I'll call when I know something."

In his car, he sat still, trying to put all his police experience to work mentally. Trying to remove his feelings from the case and examine it objectively, professionally. Only yesterday, he hadn't been able to find Tate, though he'd been certain his mental connection with her would point the way. Only it hadn't.

So, putting mystical connections aside, he had to think logically this time. Yesterday, she'd been wandering around on her own. Today, she'd left involuntarily, he was certain. Oh, she might have gotten in Rafe Collins's car without a struggle if he told her he had Josh and would take her to him. But that wasn't voluntary in the usual sense.

He picked up his radio and spoke to dispatch, reporting a

long, black limo, possibly with government plates, the driver wanted for questioning. Next, he spoke with Arnie Fox, one of the other detectives since Lou was on forced leave, and asked him to run a list of all black limousines with either Arizona plates and/or government plates as to ownership, registration, etcetera, and to get back to him. Arnie said he'd do it ASAP.

Still thinking hard, Nick started out driving aimlessly, trying to review in his mind everything Tate had told him about Adam and his henchman. Where would they take her? he asked himself. If their intention was to force her to sign that paper Adam had mentioned giving him custody, they'd have to take her somewhere private and remote. Because Tate wasn't going to meekly give in and they knew that.

A restaurant would be too public. Maybe a motel room? Nah, too chancy. Not his mother's most likely because, even if Mrs. Weston was away, there were neighbors and the housekeeper who'd answered the phone. Adam couldn't risk being seen in a compromising situation where he might be recognized.

Nick found himself on the outskirts of town. Maybe Adam had Tate in the back seat of that limo while Rafe drove around, much as he was doing. She'd mentioned that Adam was a smooth talker so perhaps he thought he could persuade her. The day pigs fly, Nick thought.

Think! he commanded himself. He had her somewhere and Nick was her only hope of rescue right now.

Tate was scared to death. Seated in the back of the limo with Adam glowering at her, she watched him from under lowered lashes.

She'd made him furious by ripping up the paper he'd thrust at her to sign. That much she knew. He'd backhanded her when she'd done that and her right cheek stung like the devil. She couldn't help wondering what else he'd do, how far he'd go to get his way. Naturally he'd whipped another copy of the form from his briefcase, but she had no intention of signing that one, either.

Her ace in the hole was that Adam didn't know where Josh was. She'd die before she'd tell him.

"You could just disappear, you know," Adam said, his deep voice, so often praised by the media as smooth and trustworthy, sounding churlish under pressure. "Then, with you out of the way, I could move in, prove Josh is my blood and everyone would say what a shame it is that his mother had died."

"Go on, invent little scenarios, as many as you like. None of it's going to happen. Oh, sure, you could hurt me, but you could also be caught and lose your precious standing in the senate and that marvelous house and your trophy wife. What would Mummsy say after how hard she's worked to put you where you are?"

"Shut up!"

Not a bad idea, Tate thought. Goading a desperate man with the upper hand wasn't terribly wise. But she couldn't listen to his rantings without reacting.

When she'd gotten the call from Maggie at Brennan's, her heart had literally stopped for a second. How would Maggie know Josh was hurt when he was miles away? Helen must have called Maggie, looking for her, she decided. Had there been an accident on the ranch? But before she could think to ask, Maggie had hung up. That's when Tate had first begun to suspect something more was wrong. Maggie would never just leave her hanging, not knowing how she felt about her son.

Like a crazed person, she'd driven home and all her fears had been realized. Rafe was there, asking her to get into the limo and just talk with Adam. When she'd smelled a rat and refused, turning to escape into the house and call Nick, Rafe had grabbed her and shoved her into the back seat. In moments, he'd slammed the door shut and driven off.

Adam had just sat there, with that oily smile that seemed to win over the masses and now turned her stomach, greeting her like an old friend. "Tate. How nice of you to join us." She'd wanted to spit in his eye.

Leaning forward, Adam tapped on the glass between the front seat and back, and waited for it to slide open. "Rafe, we're moving to Plan B."

"Right, boss." Checking his rearview mirrors, Rafe executed a U-turn and the big car glided in the opposite direction.

Through the tinted windows, Tate watched the sun lowering in the sky. It would be twilight soon. Things always seemed worse as the day darkened. Earlier, she'd taken a chance and tried to open her door, but all the locks were controlled from the driver's seat.

Where were they taking her and what was Plan B? How could she get away from them? There had to be a way. She'd have to be alert and watch for an opening. She was not going to let Adam have Josh no matter what it cost her.

Closing her eyes, she pictured Nick, trying desperately to send him a mind message. *Come find me, please. I need you.*

It wasn't long before she recognized the area they were driving through. Suddenly she knew where she was going, and her heart leaped to her throat. *Oh, no!* Tate thought. *Not again.*

Adam was very intimidating, Tate had told Nick. And she was afraid of him, of the power that enabled him to constantly have his way. She was also afraid of Rafe who'd once beaten her, almost killed Laura and put Maggie in the hospital as well. So she'd be frightened and nervous, Nick knew. And angry with herself that she'd fallen for the ploy, because by now she had to know that Josh was okay since he wasn't with them.

Stopping at the side of the road, Nick watched the heavy rush hour traffic whiz by him. Not a limo in sight. Why hadn't Arnie called back with a list of limos yet? He was the slowest man on the force. Damn it, this waiting, this not knowing, was driving him nuts. Every minute counted and here he was, stuck.

Think like Adam, Nick instructed himself. Okay, he wanted Tate's cooperation, so that she'd sign the papers. But Nick knew Tate would never sign. So Adam had to resort to intimidation. To work on her fear. What was Tate so afraid of that she might cooperate, something Adam knew about her?

Mount Lemmon.

Would the arrogant senator risk being seen, though it was a cloudy day and moving toward twilight? Of course he would, Nick thought, easing onto the highway again. That was where Adam had had Rafe dangle her over the precipice once before, so he knew how terrified she was of heights. She'd even dreamed that Adam had held Josh out over the edge, taunting her.

Nick wasn't positive, but it was as good a lead as he had. The road leading up the mountain wasn't far. He gunned the engine, not putting his flashing red light on just yet, but he would if he had to. Praying he'd be on time, Nick swerved around an SUV, crossing the double yellow line, taking chances. Time was of the essence.

By the time he arrived at the base of Mount Lemmon, it was already dusk and growing darker. The shops and restaurants were closed, the parking spaces available. Not at all the bustling place they'd visited several weeks ago in the afternoon sunshine.

Passing the trail leading up, the one he and Tate had walked with Josh that day, Nick drove slowly, his eyes searching. Finally he found what he was looking for: the black limo. He pulled in next to it, got out and peered through the shadowy windows. No one inside. Checking the rear of the vehicle, he saw the government plates. That was all he needed to know. He was on the right track.

Walking briskly, he hurried back to the trail and started up. He met two stragglers coming down, but after ten minutes of climbing, he couldn't see anyone else. The sky was darkening and a half moon could be seen playing hide and seek with a high ridge as he followed the winding path.

The bastard was smart, Nick thought, he had to give him that. He'd waited until nearly dark, when the tourist area would be deserted, abandoned by sightseers and shopkeepers alike. He'd be free to frighten Tate into doing his bidding without being recognized.

Not if he could help it.

Every little while, Nick stopped to listen, but he heard no voices, no sounds except the gentle splash of the stream bisecting the two sections and the occasional night bird. He kept going, taking his weapon in hand now. He could sense he was getting closer to the spot Tate had pointed out to him, though he'd seen it only once.

Nick wasn't sure how much longer he'd climbed when he heard the first cry, the one that sent a cold chill up his spine. Stopping in his tracks, he crouched down, narrowing his gaze as he looked around. Then he heard it again, coming from just around the next bend. Stealthily he crept along.

As he peered around the tall rock formation, he heard a man shout. Three people were on the narrow trail just ahead and around from where he hunkered down to watch. A tall man wearing gray pants and a white shirt, his blond hair shifting in a light breeze, was standing with his back pressed to the wall of rock. That was probably Senator Adam Weston and he didn't seem too fond of heights, either. The stocky man dressed in black with a long ponytail, undoubtedly Rafe Collins, had ahold of the woman's arm bent around her back.

Even at this distance, Nick couldn't miss that red hair even though he couldn't see Tate's face.

"Shut up!" Adam snarled at Tate. He glanced around looking worried.

Tate prayed that a hiker or two would be coming down the trail and spot them. There still could be people on these trails despite the hour. Adam had taken a chance, bringing her up here, hoping to frighten her into signing. But she had no intention of cooperating. However, Rafe could be cruel, she remembered. If only Nick would somehow figure out where she was and find her.

"I don't think anyone else is up here by now, boss," Rafe said, gazing up farther along the path. "We're clear."

Nick was amazed at how well the sound of their voices traveled in the canyon.

"All right," Adam said, his voice hard. "Tate, I'm through fooling around. This has taken way too much of my time. I ask you one last time, will you sign these papers?" He held the contract out to her.

"The day hell freezes over," Tate said calmly, her arm going numb under the big jerk's steely grip. She shifted sideways, hoping he'd loosen his hand for just a moment, long enough for her to break free and make a run for it.

"Fine, you leave me no choice." Adam didn't sound resigned, just angry.

From the corner of her eye, Tate caught a slight movement, then saw moonlight reflecting off something metallic in someone's hand. Shifting her gaze back to Adam so he wouldn't notice, she felt her heart soar. It was Nick. Had to be him. How on earth had he found her? She hadn't really believed mental telepathy would work, but he was here and she wouldn't question how.

Time. They needed time, Tate thought.

"Rafe, pick her up and hold her over that ledge," Adam ordered. "Then we'll see how willing she is to reconsider."

"Wait!" Tate cried out. She had to buy some time. "Let's talk this over, Adam. Maybe if you give me visitation rights, I'll sign Josh over to you."

Adam's blue eyes narrowed suspiciously. "You're hardly in a position to bargain. No, I want you out of the picture entirely. That way, he'll forget you and become ours. It ruins a kid, going back and forth, confusing him. I only want the best for Josh. Don't you see that?"

Peripherally she saw Nick move a little closer. She had to go in another direction with Adam. "You mentioned money. How much money?"

"That was before you put me through all this hell. Now, I plan to take what's mine and there's not a damn thing you can do about it. You're not getting one red cent."

Despite her position, she felt a rush of anger. Angry that he'd think she'd give Josh up for money and furious that he was so arrogant to think that his son was like a thing, to be bargained over. "Have you thought about the fact that after I sign and you take Josh, I can still go to the authorities and prove he's mine? DNA testing works both ways, you know."

It was obvious that Adam was seething that she would dare challenge him as he pushed away from the rock and stepped closer to her, his handsome face turning ugly. "You just try that and Rafe here will see that you disappear without a trace."

Just then, Nick took another step and a rock slipped down the gulley, sounding loud in the sudden silence.

Adam, sensing danger, grabbed Tate and positioned her in front of himself as Rafe spun around and drew his gun. "Who's there?" Adam asked. When he saw the detective who'd been hanging around Tate's place stand up, he tightened his grip on her.

Keeping his eyes on Bennett, Adam spoke to Rafe. "Get him."

But Rafe's shot pinged off the rock Nick ducked behind.

Not one to watch passively, Tate began squirming, fighting Adam, punching his sides with her fists, fairly certain he didn't have a weapon. Now that Nick was here, she felt bolder, more confident.

"Hold still, damn it!" Adam told her, looking furious that things had gotten so out of hand.

"Let her go, Weston," Nick shouted, his voice coming from behind a closer rock formation now.

Noticing the detective was gaining on them, Rafe raised his arm, taking aim. But just then, Nick got off a shot, hitting Rafe in one knee. With a scream, the man went down, his gun flying out of his hand and skittering down the canyon.

Nick, too, had guessed that Adam wasn't carrying a weapon. Men like him rarely got their hands dirty, relying on their underlings to take care of their messes, so that if caught, his hands would be clean. Only not this time.

Walking toward them, Nick kept his gun on Adam, relying on Tate to somehow get free of him so he could get off a shot. "Let her go, Weston. It's over."

But Adam couldn't give up easily, Nick knew. He couldn't afford to lose everything because of this one misstep, which made him dangerous. "I'm a United States senator," he shouted. "You can't hurt me." But the air of bravado sounded thin.

"We'll just see about that," Nick answered. His eyes met Tate's and she seemed to understand his silent message because suddenly she went as limp as a rag doll, deadweight in Adam's grip, nearly knocking him off his feet.

Swearing ripely, Adam dropped her and started up the path, scrambling to get away.

Nick remembered from his research that Adam had been an athlete in college and had obviously kept in shape. He undoubtedly thought he could make it, get back to the limo and get out of there. Being a senator gave him a false sense of power in this situation. Huffing, Adam broke into a run.

Tate scooted away from the dangerous edge of the cliff as Nick followed after Adam.

Then Adam made another mistake. He took the time to glance over his shoulder to see how closely the detective was following him, and misjudged his next step. In a whirl of loose stones, he fell over the edge, saved from dropping all the way down by grabbing a scraggly branch jutting out from a rock crevice. Dangling there, his feet unable to find purchase, he stared up at Nick. "Help me," he begged. "Hurry."

Nick dropped to his stomach on the narrow path and crawled closer to the edge, leaning over to assess the situation. He wasn't sure Adam could reach his hand even if he stretched as far down as he could. After all he'd put Tate and her friends through, the man probably didn't deserve saving. He'd ordered Rafe to kill Nick just moments ago.

But Nick was a cop, sworn to do the right thing. Besides, no matter how terrible Adam Weston was, he was still Josh's father. Nick knew he'd never be able to look the boy in the eye if he'd deliberately let his father die. He had to try to save him.

Nick glanced up at Tate, who'd come up alongside him, and handed her his gun. "Here, hold this on Rafe in case he tries something."

Reluctantly she took the gun, but saw that Rafe was lying pretty much where he'd fallen, still moaning in pain.

"Hurry up. This limb won't hold forever," Adam wailed.

Nick tested a fat tree root by the edge and thought it would hold. He circled one arm around it, then stretched his other arm down, fingers spread. "Grab hold and I'll try to pull you up." The man had to weigh two hundred pounds to his one-eighty.

Adam struggled to reach Nick's hand, coming up short. His expensive shoes scraped against the rocks, trying to get some leverage. Then the branch slipped a notch and Adam cried out.

"Try again," Nick told him. "Try harder. It's your life."

Grunting, swearing, sweating, Adam stretched, ripping his silk shirt on sharp rocks. Finally he touched Nick's fingertips.

"A little more," Nick urged.

Desperation had Adam making a near superhuman effort and finally, Nick grasped his hand.

"Okay, you're going to have to help me here," Nick said. "Try to find some footholds for your feet, because I can't support your weight with one arm unless you help." Nick noticed that for once Adam had set aside his arrogance and was following Nick's directions.

It took some time but, inch by inch, Nick managed to pull Adam up over the ledge. "Keep the gun on him, Tate," Nick said as Adam eased himself onto solid ground. There he lay, pulling in great gulps of air.

Nick scrambled to his feet and went over to him. Without a word, he took handcuffs from his back pocket, flipped the big man over and cuffed him, all the while reciting his Miranda rights. He didn't want any screw-ups, wanted to do this by the book, because he knew Adam would call in his high-priced lawyers at his first opportunity.

"I'm arresting you for the attempted murder of Tate Monroe, along with several other charges that will be explained to you later," he told Adam. "Do you understand your rights as I've said them?" When Adam didn't respond, Nick grabbed his shoulder, the one that had been nearly dislocated on the way up. "Do you understand?"

"Yes," Adam snarled.

Nick checked his watch, then took a small notebook and pen from his pocket, jotting down the time. "You're my witness, Tate. I read him his rights and he said he understood them."

"Yes," she murmured, still unable to believe the events of the last couple of hours.

Nick took the gun from Tate, glanced over to make sure Rafe was still incapacitated, then took her in his arms. "It's over. It's finally over."

"Your arm must be killing you," she said, holding him.

"Small price to pay." He let her go and dug out his keys. "My car's parked up the street from where the path begins. I need you to radio in for a patrol car while I guard these guys. My code number's 682. Just press the button and the dispatcher will answer. Tell her the story and give her our location. Explain that I have a suspect in custody and we'll need an ambulance, too." He touched her lovely face. "Can you remember all that?" He hoped she wasn't in shock, though she looked okay.

"Yes, but one question. How'd you know where to find me?"

He smiled at her and the smile took the weariness from his face. "When you love someone, you can almost crawl into their mind at times. But logically, I could think of no other place he'd take you where he knew you'd be frightened enough to sign. Or so he thought."

"Thank you," she whispered, kissing him, then giving Rafe wide berth, she started down the path.

The moon helped, but it was still pretty dark, Tate thought as she slowed her steps. The path was quite narrow in spots. After all that had happened up there, she didn't want to fall and ruin everything.

It was past nine by the time the patrol car arrived, took down Nick's story and arrested the senator. The EMS wagon drove off with Rafe still moaning, leaving Tate and Nick at the foot of the mountain, strolling to his car.

"I wonder how long before the media gets wind of this,"

Nick mused out loud. "I think Adam can kiss his career plans goodbye."

"Did you hear him just now yelling for his lawyer, reminding everyone he was a senator? Do you think some hot-shot attorney can get him off?"

"We're going to see to it that that doesn't happen. I was a witness to him threatening you if you didn't sign the papers. I heard every word clear as day. He may be a senator, but a cop's word goes pretty far in court, too. Then there's Maggie's testimony about Rafe—he didn't bother to wear a ski mask this last time. We've got the note, the phone recording. And maybe, if we're lucky, we can persuade Rafe to give up his boss."

She looked at him, puzzled. "You think Rafe will turn against the hand that's been feeding him?"

"To save his own skin and get a lighter sentence? You betcha." He opened the door for her, then got behind the wheel, rubbing the sore muscles of his right arm. "That guy weighs a ton."

"What will happen to Adam now? Jail?"

Nick shrugged as he started the car. "Hard to say. Depends on his lawyer and how he pleads. Prison is very likely. Attempted murder is a serious charge. He'll be kicked out of the senate and, with a felony conviction on his record, there go his chances for further political office. Maybe his important connection with his father-in-law will end once the venerable old senator discovers what his son-in-law's been up to. And maybe even his little wife will take a hike. Couldn't happen to a nicer guy."

Tate leaned her head back and sighed. "I can't believe it's finally over and we can live without fear. I can go get Josh and..."

"*We* can go get Josh, tomorrow."

She smiled. "Right. For now, let's just go home. I could curl up in bed for a week."

Nick grinned as he turned onto the highway. "That can be arranged."

It was close to midnight, but Tate didn't feel tired. She felt invigorated after they'd made love on Nick's rumpled bed in his mobile home. It had been a long day, but for the first time in years, she felt safe.

They'd driven to Maggie's and told her the whole story, finishing with the best news of all, that the threats and stalking had come to an end. They'd called up north and talked with Helen, informing her as well, and saying they'd drive up to get Josh tomorrow. Then, knowing they could leave Maggie alone without fear, they'd decided to spend the night at Nick's place.

Lying on his side watching her, Nick wondered what she was thinking. "Penny for your thoughts."

Tate turned toward him, smiling. "Do you remember that first evening when you took Josh and me to Giovanni's?"

"Sure. You were scared of me and I was intrigued with you."

"You were? Well, anyhow, do you remember that after tasting the pizza, you said it was almost better than...and you paused and said, better than most pizzas?"

"Yeah, I remember." He was smiling.

"Uh-huh. What you'd almost said was better than sex, right?"

"You guessed it." He snuggled closer, nuzzling her. "Only it wasn't, was it? No pizza's better than this. But that was before I'd made love with you."

She smiled, admiring his quick come-back. "Fast on your feet, aren't you?"

"Fast?" He pulled her to him, his hands swooping down her body, still heated from their lovemaking. "You want fast?"

"No, I kind of like slow better. Long, lazy and slow."

"I'll keep that in mind." He kissed her playfully. "Oh, wait. I have something for you." Turning, he picked up his jeans that he'd dropped on the floor in his haste to get to bed, and searched in his pocket. Finding the little velvet box, he rolled back to her and held it out. "Do you have any idea what this might be?"

What woman wouldn't recognize a jeweler's box? Tate thought, taking it from him. Even though she'd suspected this moment was coming, she hadn't known when. "I have a pretty good idea." With fingers trembling, Tate opened the lid. "Oh," she murmured. "It's beautiful."

"I was wondering if you'd wear it for a while."

She raised a brow in surprise. "Like, how long?"

"Oh, fifty or sixty years." He took the ring out, slipped it on the third finger of her left hand. The emerald had a fire of its own in the soft lamplight, and the two diamonds, only slightly smaller, winked and glowed.

Admiring it, Tate held her hand out. "What happens then, after fifty or sixty years?" she asked.

Nick aligned their bodies so they were barely touching yet beginning to come alive again, his eyes on hers. "Then we renegotiate," he replied before kissing her.

* * * * *

Celebrate
Silhouette's 20th Anniversary

with *New York Times* bestselling author

LINDA HOWARD

and the long-awaited story of
CHANCE MACKENZIE

in

A GAME OF CHANCE

IM #1021
On sale in August 2000

Hot on the trail of a suspected terrorist, covert intelligence officer Chance Mackenzie found, seduced and subtly convinced the man's daughter, Sunny Miller, to lead her father out of hiding. The plan worked, but then Sunny discovered the truth behind Chance's so-called affections. Now the agent who *always* got his man had to figure out a way to get his woman!

Available at your favorite retail outlet.

Silhouette®
Where love comes alive™

Visit Silhouette at www.eHarlequin.com   SIMCHANCE

Look Who's Celebrating Our 20ᵗʰ Anniversary:

Celebrate **20** YEARS

"In 1980, Silhouette gave a home to my first book and became my family. Happy 20ᵗʰ Anniversary! And may we celebrate twenty more."

—*New York Times* bestselling author
Nora Roberts

"Twenty years of Silhouette! I can hardly believe it. Looking back on it, I find that my life and my books for Silhouette were inextricably intertwined.... Every Silhouette I wrote was a piece of my life. So, thank you, Silhouette, and may you have many more anniversaries."

—International bestselling author
Candace Camp

"Twenty years publishing fiction by women, for women, and about women is something to celebrate! I am honored to be a part of Silhouette's proud tradition— one that I have no doubt will continue being cherished by women the world over for a long, long time to come."

—International bestselling author
Maggie Shayne

INTIMATE MOMENTS®
Silhouette®

If you enjoyed what you just read,
then we've got an offer you can't resist!

Take 2 bestselling love stories FREE!
Plus get a FREE surprise gift!

**Don't miss
an exciting opportunity
to save on the purchase of
Harlequin and Silhouette books!**

Buy any two Harlequin or
Silhouette books and save
$10.00 off future Harlequin
and Silhouette purchases

OR

buy any three
Harlequin or Silhouette books
and save **$20.00 off** future
Harlequin and Silhouette purchases.

**Watch for details
coming in October 2000!**

PHQ400

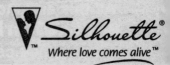

COMING NEXT MONTH